Jim Wrenn

To INA
with all best wishes!
Bill C

A Novel by William Guerrant

To Rose Scruggs and her children

.

In time a man disappears
from his lifelong fields, from
the streams he has walked beside,
from the woods where he sat and waited.
Thinking of this, he seems to
miss himself in those places
as if always he has been there,
watching for himself to return.
But first he must disappear,
and this he foresees with hope,
with thanks. Let others come.

Wendell Berry
Sabbaths: 2007, VII

*****

"'Tis well said," replied Candide, "but we must
cultivate our gardens."

JAMES WRENN

James Wrenn, age 86, passed away yesterday, September 27, 1996, at his home in Maple Grove. The son of Henry and Caroline Adams Wrenn, he was predeceased by his wife, Julia Robertson Wrenn, and by his son, Billy. Mr. Wrenn was a farmer, who spent his entire life on his family's farm.

He is survived by his sister, Pearl Wrenn Humston, eight nieces and nephews, 29 grandnieces and grandnephews, and numerous additional nieces and nephews of the succeeding generations.

Graveside services will be conducted at 1 p.m. on Sunday, September 29, 1996, at the Wrenn Family Cemetery located on Clouded Hills Road in Maple Grove, with the Rev. Joseph B. Wainwright officiating.

1910

Pearl entered the room in her usual style—the way a storm enters when the door blows open. Barefoot, wearing her housecoat, waving a cigarette around in one hand and a crumpled newspaper in the other, her presence silenced them instantly.

Despite standing barely more than five feet tall, Pearl commanded attention easily. She appeared to be exactly the same width from her shoulders to her knees, and she was crowned with a bizarrely sculpted pile of hair, colored an arresting shade of red that appeared nowhere else in nature, other than atop the one inch gray roots that sprang from her head. Her face bore the wrinkles that are earned by 82 years of life, but she wore them defiantly—her proof that she'd been kicking ass for a very long time.

After a few uncomfortable seconds, Dottie spoke up. "You need to get dressed, Mama. It's about time for us to leave for the cemetery."

Pearl ignored her.

"Who done this?" she demanded, waving the paper while scanning the blank faces staring back at her. "Who told them this?"

Someone asked cautiously, "What do you mean, Aunt Pearl?"

"This obituary! It's wrong!"

Sarah's husband Johnny stepped forward. Having been the principal author, he felt obliged to come to its defense.

"What's the matter with it, Aunt Pearl?" he asked with an uneasy smile.

"It's wrong! That's what's the matter with it! His name won't 'James.' His name was Jim!"

"Well, Aunt Pearl, 'Jim' is just a nickname for 'James,'" Johnny answered, feeling relieved that he hadn't miscounted the tribe.

Pearl raised her voice. "His name was Jim! Our mama named him Jim! Like in the Bible!"

"Now Aunt Pearl," Johnny answered with a chuckle, "I'm no Bible expert, but I'm pretty sure there ain't no Jim's in the Bible. There is a James though."

"His name won't James! It was Jim!" Pearl shouted. No one dared to speak.

"Y'all don't know nothing!" Pearl huffed, as she threw the paper down on the table and marched out of the room.

"Oh, boy," someone muttered, triggering a few sighs and nervous giggles.

Bobby rose from a chair in the back and walked slowly toward the door. Eighteen years old, he was the youngest person in the room. He was also the only person there who was in mourning.

"Aunt Pearl is right," he said softly as he exited. "His name was Jim."

The words they heard were "Pearl" and "Jim." The words he spoke were "Purl" and "Gem."

It was the first time the boy had eaten his fill at supper since before his Daddy died. His mother had made his favorite foods—chicken and dumplings and a chocolate pie, laboring over the stove despite being so weak she could barely stand.

His little sister was sleeping soundly as his mother shoveled coal generously into the stove. Normally she let the fire die down after they ate. On very cold nights, like this one, they went to bed early, relying on blankets to keep them warm, rather than coal, which cost money. But tonight she twisted open the drafts, feeding oxygen to the fire and letting it roar, sending its radiating warmth into the room. This is better than Christmas, the boy thought, as he watched his mother empty the last of the coal from the bin into the stove.

"Pull a chair over here, son," his mother said. "Let's sit by the stove and talk a spell."

The boy dragged a chair from the table, positioned it next to his mother's, and hopped up onto it.

"You're a smart boy. You got a good life ahead of you. I don't know what you're going to do, but I'm already proud of you."

The boy wiggled in the chair, holding his feet out toward the stove to let his toes capture the heat.

His mother coughed hoarsely into her handkerchief.

"Somebody's coming here tomorrow to git y'all."

Startled, the boy looked up, directly into his mother's tired eyes.

"To git us? What do you mean, Mama?"

"Y'all gonna go live with somebody else for a while," she answered, as a tear slid silently down her face.

Confused and frightened, the boy felt his own eyes swelling with water.

"Where are we going, Mama? Who we gonna live with?"

"The one the good Lord sends," the woman answered confidently.

It didn't feel like Christmas any more. The boy's head swam, his stomach knotted.

"I'm mighty sorry for it, son. I surely wish I could do better."

She coughed roughly, reddening the handkerchief.

Gazing into the vents at the glowing coals, her eyes seemed focused on something more distant. She sighed deeply.

"I'm gonna tell it all to you."

The boy listened, and she talked deep into the night.

Part One

"It's true, Lillie Mae. Money in your pocket every week. And your own house too."

Fuller Snead was 17, gangly and clumsy, as boys that age often are. Tall and skinny, the legs of his unhemmed pants ended six inches above his dirty bare feet. Sandy blonde bangs fell across his eyes, requiring him to push them away every few seconds in order to see the person before him. His pointed chin wore a coat of wispy fuzziness that held the promise of a beard, but with the assurance that it would come slowly, and reluctantly. Fuller's family had the distinction of being so poor that they were regarded as pitiful even by their impoverished neighbors. Folks said Fuller's daddy was too lazy to work, and too stupid to make whiskey that was fit to drink. Though they were correct in those assessments of Leander Snead, all would freely acknowledge Brother Leander's gift—when the Holy Ghost got ahold of him he could put to shame all the other preachers at the Lord Jehovah Gospel Bible Church.

Lillie dragged her foot across the path, drawing a line in the sand with her toe. Behind her, from within the church, she could hear shouting, hands clapping, feet stomping. Brother Leander had the Holy Ghost.

"You been saying you was running off to that mill for as long as I can remember. If it's all you say it is, why ain't you done gone yet?"

Fuller pushed out his chest, fists clenched.

"I'm fixing to go, Lillie Mae. I am. I'm fixing to go."

She knew she needed to go back inside. It was expected that folks would sometimes leave the clapboard building during the day-long services, in order to go to the bushes or to the outhouse, or for the men to smoke a cigarette or take a drink. But a young'un who left too often or stayed out too long would get a whipping. Lillie Mae was 14, and too old to still be getting whippings. But she got them anyway.

"Time to go back in, Fuller. Don't you want to hear your Daddy prophesize?" Lillie asked teasingly.

Fuller stamped his foot, pushed the hair out of his eyes and answered, "I mean it, Lillie Mae. I'm going."

~~~

This time of year, in the heart of summer, the sky was still light when the last hymn was sung and the last prophecy spoken, even though the sun had long since ducked behind a mountain. The families that lived north of the church climbed into Ernest Epperson's big wagon, and his team pulled them all homeward. The families were deposited at points on the road near to the paths leading into the hollers and up the hillsides where they lived, just as they had been gathered up early that morning.

A familiar sadness settled over Lillie Mae Duggins as the wagon bounced along the rutted road. She cherished Sundays, just as she dreaded Mondays. On Sundays she felt safe. Lillie Mae had no particular affinity for church; given a choice she'd much rather be in her garden than sitting on a bench listening to men hollering about the righteous anger of God. But church was her sanctuary; the Lord's Day, her refuge. On Sundays her father was usually sober. And on the days when he was too drunk to go to church, he stayed home. Either way, she knew that for most of that one day each week, there was little danger of the violent explosions that darkened her life on the other six.

Lillie had learned to distinguish the categories of drinking men—happy drunks were men made jolly by whiskey, sad drunks were men who whiskey made gloomy, sleepy drunks were men who passed out quickly, frisky drunks were men who whiskey emboldened inappropriately, bumbling drunks were the men who stumbled, staggered and slurred. But Jubal Early Duggins, Lillie's father, was in the category reserved for the worst of them all—mean drunks.

When sober, Jube was merely sullen. But when drunk, as he was whenever there was whiskey to be had, Jube roared with violence and anger. He made the whiskey that he used to set himself afire in a still by the creek below their house. Had there been any other men around when Jube was drunk, he would have fought them. But he drank his whiskey alone, and so when the beast within him came to life and commanded him to fury, it was his wife and children who became his victims.

Gurtie Duggins endured her husband's abuse, and by her example she taught her children to do the same. She allowed no criticism, no complaints— secure in the belief that wives are to submit to their husbands, children are to obey their father, and that in this world there must be tribulation. So if one of the children suggested that a beating had been excessive or unjust, the payment would be a second whipping, this one from their mother. But over the years, Gurtie had also learned to read the clouds in Jube's eyes and she had acquired the ability to anticipate his explosions. With a keenly developed sense of when danger was near, she knew the precise moment to divert him with some provocation, so that his blows would fall on her, rather than on her children. So Lillie and her brothers took their whelps, cuts, and bruises, but more often they watched in terror as their mother was slapped, punched, or kicked, unaware (until years later) that she had been enfolding them under her wings like a mother hen.

Mr. Epperson stopped his team to let them out at a curve in the road near to the ford. The Duggins family—Lillie Mae, her parents, and her two younger brothers—climbed down from the wagon. "Much obliged, Ernest," her father grunted as they disappeared single file into the woods, on the trail that would lead them home, to a single room enclosed by mud-chinked chestnut logs, hand-hewn, notched, and stacked a generation earlier.

A hoot owl called out in the distance.

~~~

Lillie Mae was beating dough when her father pushed the door open and stepped into the cabin. She knew instantly that he was drunk, and that his blood was up. A chill ran up her spine and she began her familiar silent mantra, praying urgently: "Please don't let him be mean. Please don't let him be mean."

She was the first person Jube saw when he came into the room, so he aimed his anger at her.

"Girl, you left the damn barn door open and now the cow is in the garden."

Lillie hadn't been in the barn that day. The accusation was false, but she knew it didn't matter. Had the cow not been in the garden, he would have discovered some other justification for his rage, and had she not been at the table, he would have found someone else to bear it.

Gurtie had been washing clothes on the other side of the room when her husband entered. Understanding immediately what the situation required of her, she stood up, letting the washboard slide down into the tub as she edged toward her daughter.

"Jube, are you sure it wasn't you that left that door open? Didn't you go out there after we milked?"

The spark touched the powder.

Jube wheeled quickly around, his fist crashing into Gurtie's face, sending her tumbling backwards, tripping over the wash tub and falling to the floor.

Most of the time this kind of victory was sufficient to satisfy Jube's demons. Usually he struck fiercely, then walked away. But today his fire burned too hot to be put out by one punch. He dropped to his knees and wrapped his hands around Gurtie's throat, determined to choke the life out of her.

Terrified, Lillie began to scream through her sobs.

"Please stop it, Paw! Please don't hurt her! Paw! Please stop! Please stop!"

Lillie's brothers were just returning from cutting hay when they heard her alarm. The oldest rushed into the house first. He saw Lillie standing with her hands over her ears, screaming frantically. Across the room he saw their father, bent over their mother, wringing her neck while shaking her head.

Screaming, "Stop it, Paw!" the boy rushed forward and grabbed his father's arm, trying to break the grip on his mother's throat. Surprised by the interference, Jube released the woman, sat up, and took a wild swing at the boy's face, grazing his chin and sending him staggering backwards. Although unhurt by the punch, the boy bent over, grimacing in pain, the sudden movement having jarred the ribs cracked a few days earlier when his father had kicked him in the side after knocking him down.

Looking up he saw that the crazed drunken man had returned to choking his wife, banging her head against the floor as he did. The screams and wails of his sister filling the cabin, a movement at the door caught the boy's attention. Glancing over, he saw his younger brother standing in the doorway, terror on his face. And there, over the door, the boy saw and recognized the solution.

Already tall at age 13, he didn't need a stool to reach the shotgun that hung above the door, always loaded and ready for any fox or bear that might invade the chicken coop. As his younger brother watched in wide-eyed horror, the boy took down the gun, cocked it, and stepped toward his father. Blinded by his drunken fury, Jube never even noticed the boy advancing, nor did he feel the barrel when it pressed against the pit of his right arm.

The boy squeezed the trigger, painting the cabin wall with his father.

For a few seconds, which passed like hours, they were all frozen in place as the blast rang and echoed in their ears. Gurtie moved first, scrambling to her feet, whispering as she glanced frantically around the room, "Oh, Lord Jesus. Oh, Lord Jesus."

Looking at her son, holding the still-smoking gun, she screamed, "What did you do?!" Turning to her husband, who was emptying onto the cabin floor, she fell to her knees.

"Jube! Jube!"

She looked up again at the boy, still holding the gun. "Run and fetch the doctor! Hurry!" She turned next to her daughter, who was standing open-mouthed and wide-eyed, "Get me some clean rags, Lillie Mae. Hurry up!"

No one moved. Gurtie's pleading eyes darted to each of them. "Hurry up!" she repeated as she turned back to her husband's limp body. "Jube! Oh, Jube!"

The older boy calmly re-hung the gun. Looking at his still-frozen brother, he said simply, "C'mon." Lillie watched as they turned and walked out the door.

~~~

While her mother continued to tug and press on Jube's body, muttering incoherently while imagining that she could somehow hold him together until the doctor arrived, the fog began to clear in Lillie's mind. She ran out the door to find her brothers leading the mule from the barn.

The older boy looked at her and said quickly, "He'd a kilt her, Lillie Mae. And he'd a kilt us all when he got around to it." After a pause he added, "You can tell the sheriff I done it and I ain't sorry for it."

"Where are y'all going?" Lillie asked, her voice trembling.

"We ain't staying here no more. She's as crazy as him," the boy answered.

"Where are y'all going to?" she repeated, urgently.

"We're just going. Bye, Lillie Mae," the older boy replied, turning and walking down the road, leading the mule. Lillie glanced quickly to the younger boy, his frightened eyes looking into hers for a moment before turning hurriedly away as he scrambled toward his brother.

Things here have ended, she realized. I should go too, she thought.

Dazed, Lillie walked back into the cabin and climbed the steep stairs to the loft bedroom she shared with her brothers. She stuffed her few possessions into a flour sack and she put on her only pair of shoes. She didn't know where the boys had gone, but she knew they hadn't gone for a doctor, and she knew they weren't coming back.

After climbing back down, Lillie stood at the door and took a long look around the single room that had always been her home, tears streaming down her face.

She looked at her mother, who was now sitting on the floor, swaying back and forth, cradling Jube's head in her lap.

"Goodbye, Maw," she said, her heart stabbed by the pain of the words, words her mother didn't hear.

Lillie slept in the woods that night.

~~~

As always, Lillie woke before dawn. She picked blackberries for breakfast, then washed her face in the creek, feeling strangely serene. It was like those bright summer mornings after a stormy night, when the birds are singing and there are limbs on the fence. Maybe I dreamed it all, she thought. Maybe it wasn't real.

Standing in the road, she faced east, watching the sky turning orange in anticipation of the sun's arrival. She had always loved the orange and yellow glow of the moments just before sunrise—a temporary beauty, colors precious because they pass so quickly. In spite of everything, Lillie felt a warm assurance. Everything is going to be all right, she thought.

Something had compelled her to leave, to run. But in the calm of the awakening day she knew the truth—she had nowhere to go but back home. Maybe things will be better now, she thought.

She heard the horse before she saw it. It was approaching from the north at a steady pace—walking, not trotting. Likely the sheriff, she thought. Lillie considered going back into the woods to hide, but she quickly changed her mind. Whatever's meant to be, will be, she thought. And she waited for the horse to come over the hill.

Fifty yards away, it crested the hill and came toward her—a large chestnut gelding, saddled and at least 16 hands tall. It was a horse she had never seen before, and sitting astride it, to her surprise, was Fuller Snead. He was beaming.

"Good morning, Lillie Mae. Ain't it a fine morning?"

"Morning, Fuller," she answered, taking another hard look at the horse. "Where'd you get that horse?"

Fuller drew himself up tall in the saddle.

"Never mind where I got him. I got him now. And I got me eight dollars too. I'm a'going to Danville, Lillie Mae. And I ain't never gonna set foot in these sorry hills again."

"What about your folks, Fuller?"

"Ain't nobody gonna miss me. I'm going to Danville, like I said."

Lillie felt her chest tighten.

"You been saying it a long time, Fuller. And now you're really going."

Fuller suddenly swung his left leg across the horse and dismounted, landing nimbly before Lillie. He had nothing to lose. Holding the reins in his left hand, he reached out with the other and took Lillie by her hand.

"Come on and go with me, Lillie Mae. Let's get married. I know I ain't much of a catch, but I can work as hard as any man and I'll do right by you. We can make us some good money in Danville. They got picture shows and motor cars. We can have us a good life there."

Swelled with emotion, Lillie began to weep.

Expecting to be rejected, and believing he had offended her, Fuller said, "I'm sorry, Lillie Mae. I didn't mean no harm," as he turned to remount.

"Oh, Fuller. I'm the one who's sorry. I'm sorry about so much." She paused, then continued, "Yes, I'll marry you. And I'll go to Danville with you."

"Woo-hoo!!" Fuller shouted, throwing his hands into the air and startling the horse, its head jerking up sharply, nearly yanking the reins from his hands.

"Whoa boy. Whoa there." He settled the horse, then turned back to Lillie, drawing her to him, hugging her so tightly she could barely breath.

"This is the very best day ever!" he exclaimed. "We are going to have us a life, Lillie Mae. A good life!"

At that moment, Fuller felt sure he could rope the moon. He relaxed his grip on Lillie, who was still sobbing.

"I reckon we ought to go see your folks then. Can we go right now?" Fuller asked anxiously.

"We ain't got to do that, Fuller. I'm grown enough. Let's just go."

"But don't you need to get anything Lillie Mae? Don't you want to say goodbye?"

"I got what I need, Fuller. If we're going, let's just go on and go. Right now."

Fuller drew her to him again, planting an awkward, but sincere, kiss upon her face. He boosted her up onto the saddle and then swung up behind her. He gave the horse a little kick in the side, and they rode away.

~~~

Lillie kept her hair braided and beneath a bonnet. When she let it down to brush it, it fell to her waist.

Her eyes were the same dark brown as her hair, and she had the rounded chubby cheeks of a child. The rest of her, however, had outgrown her girlish face. Although Lillie kept the curves of her hips and breasts modestly hidden beneath high-necked loose-fitting dresses, they were betrayed when she stretched, or when she bent over, or when the sun shone through the fabric to reveal the outline of her blooming body. Or when she bounced along a dusty road, sharing a horseback perch with a boy flooded with desire.

As night fell, Fuller led the horse into the woods and tied it to a tree.

According to Fuller, an irrevocable commitment to marriage was sufficiently binding on the promisors to make morally permissible the immediate enjoyment of all matrimonial privileges. Although she was somewhat dubious of his reasoning, and doubtful of his objectivity, Lillie Mae was willing to commence partaking of the benefits of wedded life, and so she therefore pronounced Fuller's argument valid. Thereafter, and with great enthusiasm, they proceeded to enjoy all the advantages of blissful marriage, as frequently as possible.

They spent the first night of their journey on a pallet, in a grove of white oaks.

~ ~ ~

It was late in the morning before they resumed the trip. They might not have traveled at all that day, had they not realized that the victuals Fuller had packed were nearly all gone.

"We'll make Hillsville by nighttime," Fuller said. "We'll get a room there."

Lillie nodded, satisfied to trust Fuller with the details.

"I reckon since we're going where nobody knows us, and seeing as how we're starting over and all, we might ought to use different names."

"Why?" Lillie asked, puzzled.

"Why not, Lillie Mae? We ain't got to answer to nobody. We can name ourselves whatever we like." After a pause, he added, "And just in case somebody might come looking for us, we'd be making it harder to be found."

Lillie wondered again about Fuller's horse and his eight dollars, but she pushed the worry quickly from her mind. She was in a dream now and she would admit no thought that might awaken her.

"We just got married," Fuller continued. "We done come down from Bluefield and we're riding to Norfolk, where I got me a job waiting with an uncle at the shipyard there."

"What, Fuller? You ain't never been to Bluefield and you ain't got no uncle in Norfolk."

"It's a story, Lillie Mae. I'm just making up a story." Hearing no objection, he added, "I'm Samuel Scruggs and you're my wife Rose."

"Rose? Oh for goodness sakes, Fuller. What on earth has gotten into you?"

"Just go along with it a while, Lillie Mae," Fuller replied, a hint of pleading in his tone. "Just until I can get us to Danville and we're set up good. I just don't want nothing messing it up till then."

Lillie Mae thought about it for a few moments, then shook her head and said, "I ain't gonna tell lies, Fuller."

"It ain't a lie to tell folks something that ain't none of their business in the first place. Besides that, we

ain't gotta say nothing unless'n we're asked di
Then I'll do the talking."

Fuller's logic was curious and his motives unclear.
But Lillie could sense his growing frustration, and she
still felt a comforting assurance that everything was
going to be all right. She resolved to trust him.

So, on the road to Hillsville, Virginia, on September
8, 1909, Fuller Snead and Lillie Mae Duggins became
Samuel and Rose Scruggs, newlyweds from Bluefield.

~ ~ ~

When they got to Danville, three days later, Fuller
sold the horse. Lillie never learned where or how he
got it.

The Dan River flows east from the Blue Ridge
mountains, weaving lazily along the border of Virginia
and North Carolina, carrying toward the ocean the
water of the hundreds of streams that empty into it.
The city of Danville rests on the south bank of the
river, just a few miles north of the state border.
Originally best known as a tobacco market, with the
arrival of the cotton mills the town's population had
doubled over the previous twenty years. By 1909
nearly 20,000 people were living there, many of them
mill employees.

Fuller and Lillie both took jobs at the mill, renting a
company house a half mile from the factory, which
sat on the banks of the river. Their name changes,
which Fuller had assured Lillie were only temporary,
became *de facto* permanent. The mill identified them as

Mr. and Mrs. Samuel Scruggs, and therefore so did the rest of their new community. And the wedding ceremony, which Fuller had said would happen when they got to Danville, never occurred.

Lillie was satisfied that she and Fuller were married "in the eyes of the Lord," so she didn't worry much about the absence of any official ceremony. But she laughed off Fuller's insistence that she call him Samuel, and she wouldn't answer to Rose at home. Although she chose her battles carefully, there were some fields Lillie would not concede.

"At the mill you can call yourself William Howard Taft, for all I care. But here at home you are Fuller Snead."

She added, with emphasis, "And I am Lillie Mae Snead. Your wife."

To his credit, Fuller knew when to admit defeat. He gave up his attempt to enforce the aliases at home.

Lillie worked as a spinner, and Fuller's job was in the weave room. For both of them, their jobs meant standing for ten hours a day, six days a week, in deafening noise, breathing cotton dust, and racing to keep pace with the machines. They were now full-fledged employees of the Riverside and Dan River Cotton Mills. To the world outside the mill villages, however, they were just two more hillbilly lint-heads.

For their first four weeks on the job, the so-called "learning period," they were unpaid. After that, Lillie's pay was $4.50 per week—75 cents per day. Fuller's job was "piece work"—his earnings depended upon how much fabric his looms produced—and he usually made about $1.50 per day—$9 per week. Every workday began at 7 a.m. and ended at 6 p.m., with a one-hour dinner break at noon. Each Saturday, after the final shift of the week, employees received their pay for the week. From the salaries, the mill deducted their rent as well as any charges for food or coal they had purchased during the week. If they had seen a doctor, his fee was deducted from their pay as well. The mill economy was entirely self-contained.

Because they were cheaper to employ, two thirds of the mill workers were women. Children were cheaper still, so a full quarter of the workers were between 10 and 16 years old. Children younger than 10 weren't paid, but their mothers were allowed and encouraged to bring them to work, to help with their jobs, thus speeding production. Consequently, there were usually as many children on the mill floor as there were adults.

Most of their fellow employees were economic refugees from subsistence farms in the mountains of western Virginia and North Carolina, and from hardscrabble farms of the Piedmont. Textile mills recruited their workers among such folks, advertising that a family working in the mill ("public work," the flyers called it) would earn five times as much as they ever earned on their farms.

While not as lucrative as the promotional flyers had promised, it was true that most of the mill workers, like Lillie and Fuller, had a regular income for the first time in their lives, giving them a little money to spend and a home to live in. Some mill workers, glad to be free of the struggles of subsistence farming, regarded the trade an advantageous transaction. For many others, however, the thrill of regular wages was soon dulled by the grinding monotony of the job, and they came to see the value of things previously unappreciated—things such as sunlight, fresh air, and homegrown food.

Fuller seemed to find their new life satisfactory, and he settled into it quickly. But it weighed hard on Lillie. The roar of the machines kept her ears ringing, even during the twelve hours a day when she was not on the factory floor. She rarely saw the sun and she rarely breathed good air. She began to long for the quiet beauty of the mountains.

Within a month of starting the job, Lillie began to suspect that homesickness was not the only thing growing inside her. Once she was no longer in doubt, with a shaking voice she broke the news to Fuller, as they walked home from work on a chilly December night. To soothe his wife's fears, Fuller concealed his own anxiety, pretending to be pleased. Later, after Fuller had fallen into the deep sleep of a factory worker, Lillie stepped outside into the cold night air. Through wrinkles in the smoke she caught glimpses of stars, twinkling reminders of the night sky she had long loved. She prayed silently for favor, choosing to believe that everything was going to be all right.

Pregnant women were not uncommon among the mill workers. So Lillie labored on, even as she swelled with the promise of a child.

~ ~ ~

The Riverside and Dan River Mills were not a single factory, but rather seven distinct textile mills lining the Dan River as it wound its way through Danville. Separate companies until they merged just before Lillie and Fuller arrived, the Dan River Mills were located on the western edge of town, while the mills of the old Riverside Corporation were in the heart of the city, within sight of Main Street. Most of the employees in the Dan River facilities lived in the mill village known as Schoolfield, named for one of the mill's founders. Lying just outside the city limits, Schoolfield had, in addition to hundreds of identical four-room houses where the mill workers lived, a movie theater, a bowling alley, a hospital, dormitories for unmarried female mill workers, a meeting hall, a nursey, a kindergarten, and even its own police and fire departments, all of which were entirely owned by the mill. Because they worked in the old Riverside facility, however, Lillie and Fuller did not live in Schoolfield, but rather in a three-room mill-owned house in the part of Danville known as "Mechanicsville," just across from "Mill Number One," their workplace in what was now called the "Riverside Division." Just as in Schoolfield, a mill whistle sounded at 6 a.m. to wake any sleeping workers, and again at 6 p.m., to announce the end of their workday. And just as in Schoolfield, the medical needs of the mill workers were met by company-paid physicians, nurses, and midwives, whose fees were deducted from the employees' pay.

~~~

It was around 3 a.m. when Lillie's water broke. Even as she faced with dread the day that lay before her, she was thankful that she hadn't gone into labor on the spinning room floor.

Lillie was scared, but for Fuller's benefit she put on a brave face. Fuller was also afraid, but he didn't try to conceal it. Feeling a powerful urge to be helpful, but having utterly no idea what to do, he bungled around the house, rearranging things pointlessly and peppering Lillie with questions and nonsensical advice. While his concern warmed her heart, she felt relieved when he finally left for work, a little earlier than usual, leaving himself time to stop at the main floor office and request the assistance of the company midwife.

The midwife arrived about an hour after sunrise, Lillie having already descended into hard and painful labor. A heavy woman wearing a billowing dress with a bright red scarf draped across her substantial shoulders, her cheerfulness contrasted sharply with Lillie's misery.

"Well, shugga, you picked a fine day to have a baby," she chirped as she entered the bedroom where Lillie lay gritting her teeth in pain. "Now don't you worry 'bout a thing, shugga. We gonna have us a pretty baby today, with no trouble a'tall." Lillie forced an awkward smile, but could not bring herself to share in the woman's confidence.

The midwife's reputation had preceded her. The young mothers who were Lillie's co-workers sang the praises of the woman known to them only as "Aunt Dora." Unmarried and childless, Dora Woods had helped deliver thousands of babies in her thirty-plus years of midwifery, a profession she genuinely loved and enjoyed. Skilled at comforting and coaching the women she assisted, Aunt Dora had also successfully navigated numerous natal emergencies among the mill women, and she was uniformly admired. Although reassured by all that she'd heard, the woman's presence was nevertheless unsettling to Lillie, in large part, perhaps, because she had never before been in the company of a black person. The mill workers, like Lillie's neighbors in the mountains, were all white. But her unease with Aunt Dora soon passed, partly because of the woman's soothing manners, and partly because the pain of her contractions soon trivialized all other concerns.

Fuller rushed home from the mill at noon, during his dinner break. Lillie was in labor and seemed to him to be in great pain. Yet Aunt Dora was humming happily, exuding confidence, her eyes sparkling like the dangling earrings that framed her smiling face.

"Everything is just fine here, Mr. Scruggs. This baby don't want to be borned just yet, but it won't be much longer. You can on back to work now. There ain't a thing in the world to be worried about."

Fuller kissed Lillie on the forehead, and squeezed her hand. "I'll be home as soon as I can," he said. She answered with a nervous smile.

Aunt Dora had brought along a young boy, whose job would be to go fetch the doctor should that become necessary. The boy waited for the order, playing in another room until needed. "It's best to try to make it without the doctor," Aunt Dora advised. "No point in spending all that money if you don't have to." "Besides," she added, "he'll just want to knock you out and that ain't the best way to bring in a baby if'n you ask me."

As the day passed into afternoon and Lillie's increasingly painful contractions had still not generated a baby, Aunt Dora became concerned. "Go and git the doctor," she hollered out the door. The boy answered quickly "Yes'm," and they heard the door slam behind him.

"I hate to see you having such a hard time ma'am. Seeing how this is your first young'un, I think it's best to bring the doctor on over," Aunt Dora said as she mopped Lillie's forehead. Lillie murmured her approval of the plan. She didn't like the idea of admitting an unknown man into the room, doctor or not. But she was anxious for the chloroform at any cost.

More hours passed, Lillie's suffering continued, and the doctor hadn't come. The boy had returned long ago with a report: "I left word that we needed the doctor here. They say he having a hard time with another white woman but that he'll be over here just as soon as he can." Lillie groaned with the news. If Aunt Dora was bothered, she didn't show it. She continued to nurse and coach her patient, humming a hymn and wearing a smile.

The baby arrived just before the doctor. After over 12 hours of stubborn reluctance, he was born in a rush—a red-faced boy with a patch of black hair and a piercing voice. By the time the doctor arrived, Aunt Dora had cleaned the baby, pronouncing him to be "a fine pretty boy," and he was nursing hungrily, while Lillie sipped a mug of soup that Aunt Dora had prepared for her. Confirming that all was well, the doctor only stayed a few moments.

Lillie and Fuller had never discussed what their child would be named. Lillie took that as authority to choose the name herself, and she had resolved to name him after her brother.

In due course, Aunt Dora asked her, "What y'all naming this little boy?"

Looking down at the child, while her mind roamed into a bittersweet past, Lillie answered, "His name is Gemariah."

Aunt Dora cocked an eyebrow. "Jimmy what?"

"It's my brother's name. It comes from the Bible," Lillie answered with a tired, gentle smile.

"I know the Bible right good, ma'am, but I can't recall where that name is at," Aunt Dora answered.

Lillie's eyed clouded with tears and she pulled the baby tightly to her chest as she recalled the exact words her mother had told her when she asked about her brother Gem's name. "The words of the Lord came to Jeremiah, and Baruch wrote them all on the roll of a book. Jeremiah said, 'I am shut up. I cannot go into the house of the Lord.' So Baruch read the words of Jeremiah in the house of the Lord, in the chamber of Gemariah."

"Oh, shugga!" Aunt Dora exclaimed suddenly. "I do know where that is!" She dug a tattered book from the bag she had dropped in the corner of the room, thumbing quickly into the heart of it. "Here it is! The 36th chapter of the book of Isaiah! And the king tore the pages outta that book and burned them up. Well, shut my mouth. Gemariah. It's a mighty fine name for a boy."

With a dreamy look, her mind still wandering among the shadows of her past, Lillie continued, "I wonder if my maw just liked the name Gem." She sighed. "She named my brother Gem and she gave him Ariah as a second name. That will be my boy's name too."

"Well bless your heart, shugga. This boy gonna make your mama proud, and your brother too."

The words drew tears from Lillie's eyes.

~~~

Aunt Dora was gathering her things, preparing to leave, when she noticed the Bible on the table next to Lillie's bed.

"You want me to write your boy's name down in your Bible shugga?" In a day when it wasn't common,

Aunt Dora's literacy was a source of pride. "I write real good," she added with a smile.

"I'd thank you kindly," Lillie replied.

Lillie had purchased the Bible on a Sunday afternoon a few weeks earlier, from a persistent young door-to-door salesman, who had persuaded her that no home was complete without its very own family Bible. Had Fuller been home at the time, the transaction would not have occurred. "Seventy-five cents!" he exclaimed, upon being told what she paid for it. In Fuller's home the Bible had been an arsenal, from which Leander extracted the weapons he used to attack all the things he didn't like, including Fuller. "That's a big waste of hard-earned money, Lillie Mae."

Lillie held her ground. "We ought to have a family Bible, Fuller. All families has them. I ain't bought hardly nothing for me since we started working here, and I used my own money."

Fuller let it pass, choosing not to bring up the fact that neither he nor Lillie knew how to read.

Now, weeks later, the Bible was about to begin fulfilling its intended purpose. From her bag Aunt Dora produced a pencil and the small knife she had slipped beneath Lillie's mattress soon after her arrival. She quickly trimmed the pencil, then opened the book to the blank pages that separated the old and new testaments—the pages where, for generations, American families had recorded their additions and subtractions.

"Mercy, shugga! You ain't wrote y'all's names in here yet," Aunt Dora exclaimed as she began to write. "What day was y'all married?"

Suddenly all the mist cleared from Lillie's mind and she snapped alert.

"Never mind, Aunt Dora," she said quickly. "Don't you bother with that. We can do it later."

"Well we might as well do it now, shugga. I done already wrote y'all's names down. I just need to know what day y'all got married."

Lillie's heart fluttered, then sagged. She knew that Aunt Dora must have written the names of the people she was sent to help—Samuel and Rose Scruggs. Lillie imagined that having those names written in the Bible gave them permanence, and she felt the pain of loss.

"Don't you remember what day it was, shugga?"

Lillie felt trapped. She said the first word that popped into her mind: "Tuesday."

"Tuesday!" Aunt Dora replied with a laugh. "I mean what day of the year was it?"

"It was... It was…," Lillie paused, never having willingly told a lie in her life. She crossed her fingers and continued, "It was September…the tenth." The words came with difficulty. She choked back tears.

Aunt Dora smiled approvingly as she carefully recorded the date of the joyful and blessed union of Mr. and Mrs. Scruggs. And she took particular pride in making the first entry under "Births":

Gem Ariah Scruggs, born June 25, 1910

~~~

Fuller arrived home just as Aunt Dora was leaving.

"Y'all got a pretty boy," she said proudly as he burst in the door. "You can go on in now. Everything is just fine, just like I said it would be."

Fuller felt relief flood over him when he saw Lillie's weak smile, the baby asleep beside her. He fell to his knees at the side of the bed and kissed her joyously. "Are you all right, Lillie Mae?" he asked, looking straight into her eyes.

"I'm tired, but I reckon I'm all right, Fuller." She paused then continued, "I named him Gem. I hope that's all right by you."

Fuller had known Gem Duggins, so he knew immediately who she had named him for.

"It's a good name, Lillie Mae. It's a good name."

Later that evening, just before turning in for the night, Fuller brought up the subject he had carefully avoided for nearly ten months.

"Lillie Mae, I feel right bad about taking you away from your people the way I did. I know you must miss 'em awful bad. I'm gonna think on how I can get you back up there to see them."

"Don't worry about that, Fuller. I'm all right. This is a good day."

"But I am gonna do it, Lillie Mae. I'll figure something out."

~~~

Three days later Lillie was back on the job, depositing Gem in the mill nursery and resuming her place in the spinning room.

All the spinners in the mill were female, and most were young girls. Being 15 and (seemingly) married, Lillie was among the most senior of the workers. About half of them were under 14 years old.

As the thread was spun onto hundreds of spools, a spinner's job was to move up and down between two rows of large spinning machines that faced each other, repairing any breaks in the cotton thread, a practice they called "putting up ends." When they spotted a broken end, the workers would grab the loose end and insert it into the rollers on the machines, which would twist it into the thread to keep the spool running. The job required nimble fingers (which is why young girls were favored), sharp eyes, and constant movement. It was believed that outside air caused the thread to break more often, so there was no air circulation. The windows were kept tightly shut during all seasons, so that the spinning room was usually hot and humid, but sometimes icy cold in the winter.

The spinners stuffed cotton into their ears to muffle the banging roar of the machines and they worked barefoot, as the spinning room floor was always slick with cotton oil. Nearly all of the girls dipped snuff while working, a practice management encouraged because the powdered tobacco was a stimulant and was believed to quiet the workers' nerves. So the girls chewed sweet gum twigs into soft brushes (which they called "toothbrushes"), dipped them into the cans of snuff they carried in their apron pockets, then rubbed the tobacco onto the teeth and gums under their lower lips. They chewed the twig between dips, spitting the tobacco juice into spittoons, or often directly onto the floor.

And it was into this work life that Lillie settled—day after 10-hour day, week after six-day week, year after long-year.

~~~

About six months after Gem was born, Lillie recognized one of the doffers as Acie Tucker, a boy she'd known back home. Acie was about ten years old, the typical age for doffers—young boys whose job was to remove and replace the bobbins of thread on the spinning machines once they were full. She caught his eye, and Acie's quick smile showed that he remembered her. During the noontime dinner break, after she'd nursed Gem, Lillie sought him out.

Acie was excited to see her. He explained that he had only recently started work and was "terrible homesick." Still, he announced with pride that he was making 40 cents a day and sending the money home to his mother. "Ma says it's a mighty big help."

It was with some trepidation that Lillie finally asked the question that was pressing on her heart, "What news do you have for me, Acie? I ain't heard a thing from home since the day I left."

The boy's smile vanished and his eyes fell to the floor.

"It's all right, Acie. I ain't scared to hear it," Lillie assured him.

"Well, everybody figured you must have run off with Fuller, and his Ma and Pa done disowned him," Acie began. Her brothers had disappeared, he told her, and that no one knows what happened to them. "Folks figured that either Gem or Amos must have shot Mr. Jube when he was fightin' drunk. Couldn't nobody ever get the story from Miz Gurtie. She just won't right in the head after that." He hesitated, then continued. "I'm sorry, Lillie Mae, but she passed last year."

Acie paused respectfully, but seeing no immediate reaction from Lillie he continued, "After Miz Gurtie passed, Mr. Perry from over in town come and took y'all's place 'cause he said Mr. Jube owed him money." The boy paused again. "I'm mighty sorry to be bringing you all this bad news, Lillie Mae."

Lillie let it all pass over her like a wave, sensing the closing of a distant door.

She sat quietly for a few moments, then, as she noticed the other spinners beginning to move back toward the machines, she looked into Acie's nervous face. "I'm real glad to see you again, Acie, and I 'preciate you telling me about home. Me and Fuller done started us a whole new life here. He done took the name Samuel Scruggs, and I'm Rose now. Please don't tell nobody no different, Acie, and we'd be much obliged."

The boy looked confused, but he nodded in agreement.

"Reckon it's time for us to get back to work now," Lillie said, as she painted her gum with snuff.

~ ~ ~

Lillie usually rose by 4 o'clock, long before the 6 a.m. whistle sounded, in order to prepare breakfast and attend to house work before leaving for the mill. First she would start a fire in the stove, fanning the sleeping coals to life, igniting kindling that would in turn ignite the larger chunks of coal she'd add as the fire grew. She would then churn the 25-cent gallon of sweet milk, which a nearby farmer left on their doorstep every morning. She would skim off the butter into a butter dish, pour some of the buttermilk into her bread bowl, and pour the rest into a wide-mouthed jar. She would then add flour and lard to the bread bowl, kneading it all into dough that she would pinch into biscuits. Most mornings their breakfast was buttered biscuits, molasses (which they called "syrup"), and buttermilk. After they'd eaten, Lillie would wash the dishes in a pot she'd filled with water from the community well-pump the previous evening. Most days, she'd dampen the fire and set a pot of pinto beans on the stove to cook during the day.

Some days they wrapped buttered biscuits or wedges of cornbread in handkerchiefs and took their dinner with them to the mill. But because they lived close by, they would normally come home for dinner—usually buttered biscuits, beans, and (when their finances permitted it) fat back. They ate supper when they got home from work—whatever was left over from dinner. Lillie tried to make Sunday dinners special. Sometimes she would fry a chicken, but more often she'd make fat back gravy and bake a pie. Nearly all their food was purchased from the company-owned store, usually with what they called "jap flaps" or "mill money"—coupons that would be given to workers at the end of each day as a sort of advance, the value of which would be deducted from the pay they'd receive every Saturday evening.

Every Sunday morning Lillie and Gem walked two blocks to the Forrest Memorial Methodist Episcopal Church South. In a city known for its imposing churches, this one was modest by comparison, built from the bricks of a tobacco prizery that once stood across the street. But to Lillie it was a grand place. Stained glass, mahogany pews, liturgy, a choir, a robed pastor—all were new to her. Most fascinating and disconcerting of all was the organ. No musical instruments had been permitted in the Gospel Bible Church—the "one true church," as the "elders" had often reminded them. And while the twenty minute Methodist sermons could sometimes be stern and dour, she greatly preferred them to the shouting tirades of the team of hard-shell preachers who took turns berating the congregation during the all-day affairs she grew up attending.

Although the church was not owned by the mill, most of the congregants were mill workers, so Lillie did not feel conspicuous or ashamed in her homemade clothes. Gem seemed to especially enjoy the music, and when he was old enough he held his own hymnal, singing along as if he could read it.

Lillie accepted her lot, but she hated the monotony and the ugliness of the spinning room and she sorely missed life on the farm. In time, she created a little kitchen garden behind their house. Later, she bought a couple of hens and fashioned a makeshift coop for them.

Fuller tolerated these things, but didn't encourage them and did little to help. When Lillie suggested that they buy a pig, he drew the line. "Ain't we working hard enough already, Lillie Mae? We ain't got time to raise a hog, and we ain't got the money for it neither."

So she satisfied herself with her potatoes, tomatoes, and string beans, squeezing her gardening into the precious light hours of summertime that preceded and followed their shifts in the mill—all as she continued to keep house and tend to the needs of the family.

In January of 1913, Lillie discovered that her domestic responsibilities were soon to increase further. She was going to have another baby.

~~~

In time, changes would come, bringing better working conditions and higher wages. But in the early years of the 20th century, the mill workers occupied the lowest rung of Danville's social ladder—lower even than negroes (in the vernacular of that day), among whom there was a middle and professional class. Mill workers, by comparison, were uniformly poor and uneducated. Pale-skinned and malnourished, commonly referred to as "lintheads," they were recognizable on sight—the dregs of society.

Long accustomed to being at the bottom of the social pecking order, any stigma attached to his linthead status was of little consequence to Fuller. He had improved his condition, and he knew it. Having never taken any pleasure in farming, mill work suited him. Instead of trying to beat a corn crop out of poor, rocky, hillside soils, now he drew steady, reliable pay. Routine hunger, once his constant companion, was now a thing of the past. His meals were simple, but he no longer had to worry about whether they would occur. Fuller took pride in being the head of his household, with a home of his own. Now he spent his nights with a wife and son he adored, rather than living in a cold, one-room, dirt-floor cabin where he felt unwanted and unloved. He enjoyed being a father and a husband. Unlike Lillie, Fuller found his job satisfying. While Lillie increasingly despaired, Fuller was content.

And he did his job well. Fuller tended the giant looms, fifteen at a time, that turned cotton thread into cloth. It was a difficult, physically demanding job. The "weave room" was kept hot and humid, in the belief that doing so reduced thread breakage. The stagnant air was clouded with cotton dust and the roar of the machines was deafening. The looms were driven by thick belts hanging from the high ceilings above them, powered by water turbines on the river below. A weavers' job was to set up the machines, by putting in their beams and harnesses and by manually setting the initial threads into place. Once operating, the large metal arms of the looms pushed steel shuttles, twice a second, through the "drawn in" wooden frames, weaving the thread together while the workers carefully watched for, and repaired, any breaks in the thread. Paid according to how much cloth their looms produced, weavers who were quick in setting up the looms and repairing broken thread could produce more cloth, and therefore make more money, than those who were slower. Fuller was a fast learner and a hard worker. He took pride in his workmanship, and in being one of the highest producing weavers in the mill.

~~~

Lillie's labor pains began late in the night of August 3, 1913. Once again she was spared the indignity of going into labor on the spinning room floor, but this time there had been no risk of that—she had been unable to work for the last two months of her pregnancy. Lillie had been strong and healthy during the entire time she was carrying Gem, with no morning sickness and no loss of vigor. But this time was very different. Every morning she woke with nausea and every night she had trouble sleeping. Her legs ached so badly that, despite determined effort, she was unable to stay on her feet long enough to do her job in the spinning room. For a couple of months her sympathetic supervisor assigned her to lighter clean-up duties. When, in the fifth month of her pregnancy, she became too weak even for that work, she took to her bed, rising only to answer nature's calls and to prepare meager meals for Fuller and Gem. After such a dreadful pregnancy, she was fearfully apprehensive about the impending delivery, but anxious to have it over with.

Once again Aunt Dora was at her side and, as before, her cheerful optimism and confident competence helped settle Lillie's strained nerves. But whereas she had labored long and hard to deliver Gem, this time the baby came quickly and almost effortlessly, as if to compensate for the debilitating pregnancy.

"A pretty baby girl!" Aunt Dora exclaimed, raising her voice to be heard over the child's piercing squeals.

Fuller burst into the room as soon as he heard the baby's cry, trailed by a curious Gem. Beaming with pride and overjoyed to see Lillie well (and the horrid pregnancy ended), he kissed his wife and hugged a giggling Aunt Dora.

Once again Lillie took the initiative on choosing a name, Fuller having expressed no opinion on the matter. "I want to name her Clara Pearl," she said, as the screaming baby sought her breast.

"Fine by me, Lillie Mae," Fuller answered quickly. "Clara Pearl it is!"

"We'll call her Pearl," Lillie said, the child gnawing on a nipple.

~~~

Lillie regained her strength quickly and three weeks later she was back on the spinning room floor, now with two children in the mill nursery.

Troubled by the fact that the new baby's birth had not yet been properly recorded in their Bible, but knowing that neither she nor Fuller was capable of doing it, Lillie decided to seek help at the mill. After Pearl's quick and relatively uneventful birth, Aunt Dora had not offered to be their biblical scrivener, as she had after Gem's delivery. She had just wished them all good night and hurried away once the baby was cleaned. Inside the mill, where illiteracy was the norm, there was no shame in asking for help with such things. So, during a dinner break Lillie approached Bertie Bovry, one of her co-workers, a girl who she knew had completed three grades of school before coming to work at the mill.

"Bertie, would you mind writing my Clara Pearl's name down for me, so I can copy it into our Bible?" Lillie asked her timidly, handing her a nubby pencil and a scrap of paper.

"Why sure I will Miz Rose! I'd be pleased to do that," the girl chirped in response, happy to demonstrate her skills.

She wrote out the name and date Lillie gave her, and returned the paper and pencil with a glowing smile.

Later that night, Lillie very carefully copied into the Bible the words the girl had written, the same words she would later trace and hand over to satisfy the new state law requiring birth certificates:

Clara Purl Scruggs, born Aug. 3, 1913

~~~

In time, it became clear that Purl's relatively easy entry into the world was out of character, merely a brief interruption of the trouble-making that she began in Lillie's womb and that she ardently resumed once she had drawn her first breaths. The baby seemed impossible to please and was awake crying most of every night, leaving Lillie exhausted and drained and making her job more difficult than ever.

Back home in the mountains, the folks would use moonshine whiskey to settle a restless baby, dipping a finger in it and rubbing it on the child's gums and tongue. Now that she had a town job though, Lillie didn't have to rely on such crude country remedies. On the advice of one of the other spinners, she went to the company store and exchanged some of her mill money for a bottle of "Mrs. Winslow's Soothing Syrup," a popular and heavily-advertised cure for fussy babies. To her relief, the syrup did indeed soothe Purl, allowing Lillie the first good night's sleep she'd had in months. The syrup's success was unsurprising, considering that its principal ingredients were morphine sulphate and powdered opium. Of course, Lillie didn't know that—ingredients weren't listed on medicines in those days and the words would have been meaningless to her even if they had been. But she could see that it worked, so when the first bottle was near empty, she bought another one.

Before the second bottle was empty, however, the baby seemed to become immune to it. Mrs. Winslow's potion just wasn't powerful enough to subdue Purl, who recommenced her seemingly interminable squallings. As Gem would put it many years later, "Purl came into the world raising hell and she never let up her whole life."

~~~

Fuller was well-liked by his co-workers. He was kind to the new workers and respectful of the old ones. When someone needed help, he gave it without grumbling. He enjoyed a good joke, but never at someone else's expense. He was one of those natural leaders who earned respect without seeking it. The supervisors liked him too—because he was a good worker whose illiteracy made him ineligible for promotion, so that he posed no threat to them.

While the strains of life as a mill-working mother were rapidly aging Lillie, Fuller looked little different than the day he and Lillie left home. Thanks to Lillie, his clothes now fit him better. Once a week (to please Lillie) he shaved his still-boyish face. Even as Lillie faded, Fuller flourished, despite it all.

~~~

Much was happening in the spring of 1917 that would someday fill the pages of history books—Woodrow Wilson was beginning his second term in office, the country was lurching toward entry in the European Great War, the women's suffrage movement was gaining steam, as was the national prohibition movement. But in the lives of Lillie and Fuller, a/k/a Rose and Samuel, those events were of little consequence. They churned along, cogs in an enormous textile machine, living simply and doing their best. Fuller toiled and Lillie span.

Being six, Gem was now old enough to help his mother in the spinning room, so he spent most days by her side, helping her piece up broken ends. Purl, meanwhile, carried the "terrible two's" into her third year, tormenting the nursery workers until the end of the day, when that burden fell back on Lillie.

~~~

One morning in March, Wilburn Elliott and John Hall showed up in the weave room at mill number one to begin their learning period, having traveled to Danville from some place in North Carolina that Fuller had never heard of, bringing along Appalachian twangs and a friendly irreverence that he found agreeable. Fuller struck up a friendship with them almost immediately.

In time Fuller learned that the men were sharing a house in Mechanicsville with several other mill workers/former mountaineers, not far from where he and Lillie lived. Although he found that he enjoyed their company, Fuller declined their frequent invitations to come over after work and "take a drink." He wasn't a teetotaler, but whiskey held no great charms for him. Given the choice of going out drinking after supper, or going to bed, he preferred the latter.

About a month after the new fellows arrived, however, he decided one night to visit them. "Going to go see Wilburn and John," he told Lillie, who was busy washing clothes and trying to pacify Purl. "All right," she replied absentmindedly as he left.

Having grown accustomed to the tidy house Lillie kept, Fuller was at first taken aback by the place—a dirty chaotic four-room mess, crowded with men. Always boisterous, his new friends were even louder than normal when they greeted him rowdily, the smell of strong whiskey on their breath.

"Hot damn, Sam'l! Come on in and have a slug!" John exclaimed, pulling him into one of the back rooms.

There Fuller discovered what seemed to be a makeshift saloon. A thin bushy-faced man, unknown to him, stood behind a plank stretched across a stack of blocks, pouring whiskey from a jug into a cup. "Five cents for a cup, 75 cents for a jug," he said.

Alcohol was illegal in Virginia in 1917, having been outlawed the year before, three years before nationwide prohibition would take effect. But the ban had little immediate effect among those accustomed to making their own, and who in any event felt no obligation to obey laws with which they disagreed.

Wilburn stepped forward. "Lemme buy you a drink, Sam," he said, handing the man a nickel while taking the cup and passing it to Fuller.

"Much obliged," Fuller said as he lifted the cup to his lips and took a sip.

They stared at him a second, then began roaring with laughter.

"Why you being so tender with that thing, Sam?" Wilburn asked between laughs. "Throw it on back!"

"I'm a slow drinker, boys," Fuller answered, having never found teasing about his light drinking embarrassing.

"Any damn slower, Sam'l, and you won't be drinking at all!" John laughed.

"I never could hold my whiskey, fellas," Fuller said with a smile.

Wilburn laughed loudly again and answered, "Well hellfire, Sam! When did that ever stop a man from drinking?"

Fuller just smiled, shrugged his shoulders and took another sip.

John pushed him toward an open door. "Well come on, Sam'l. If you're gonna drink yer likker like you're at a church picnic, you might as well play some cards."

Fuller had grown up in a time and place where gambling was strictly forbidden. Plenty of times he'd heard preachers decry card-playing—"the devil's game" they called it, often with whiskey on their breath. The practice was so universally condemned in his community that even now, in his 25th year, he'd never even seen a deck of cards. So naturally he found the sight before him fascinating. Six men were sitting around a table holding cards, sometimes throwing one down, sometimes picking one up. The language they were speaking meant nothing to him— he wondered if it was some sort of Satanic code. Most amazing to him was the pile of coins in the center of the table. "Three jacks," one of the men said as he dropped his cards on the table and raked the pile of money toward him. Fuller had never seen anything like it, and he was entranced.

"Deal us in, boys!" Wilburn shouted as he and John pulled stools to the table. Turning to Fuller he asked, "You in, Sam?"

"I don't know how to play, Wilburn. Never played before," Fuller replied calmly.

"Damned if you ain't something, Sam. Well rev'rin, you can just watch me a while and I'll learn you how," Wilburn answered between guffaws.

Fuller was a fast learner. After watching a few hands he was ready to play and he took a seat at the table.

He found it all thrilling—the anticipation of the next card, the mystery of his opponents' hidden hands, the strategy, the wagering, the bluffing, and, most of all, the risk. It was a rush like he'd never felt before. When he won his first hand, Fuller felt as alive and invigorated as he'd ever felt in his life.

Walking home two hours later, he was carrying ten cents more in his pocket than he'd left home with. He had a bounce in his step, unaware that he was approaching a cliff.

~ ~ ~

Perhaps all men have some deep flaw—some potentially fatal weakness, some dangerous vulnerability, a propensity to some addiction. Some may be fortunate enough to never have their soft spots tested. Others may experience temptation, but successfully resist it their entire lives. But for many, a spear will thrust deeply through their armor's chink. For some it is greed, for some whiskey, for others the wives of their neighbors. And for some, it is gambling.

At home that night, Fuller dreamed of kings, queens, jokers, and jackpots. Straights and flushes clouded his brain at work the next day. He worked anxiously, counting the hours till he could be back at the table. After rushing through his supper, he hurried away, leaving Lillie puzzled at his curious behavior.

The glue that had held their lives together was beginning to dissolve.

Night after night he went back. Soon it wasn't fun anymore, yet back he went. Most nights he lost money—not a lot, but any is a lot when you have very little. Angry at himself, he began to snap and snarl at Lillie and the children. Insufficient sleep affected his job performance. His production fell and so did his pay. By now Lillie worried that he might be seeing another girl. When she gently suggested one evening that he stay home after supper and not go visit his friends, he stormed out, slamming the door behind him. She cried herself to sleep. The next morning Fuller sheepishly apologized.

Fuller still sipped his liquor, but now he began to sip more of it, finding that it settled his nerves. But it also emboldened him.

He'd been gambling steadily for over a month when, on a muggy night in early May, Fuller sensed that his luck was changing. He'd drawn a dream hand—four aces—and the pot was rich. Motioning for another drink, hoping it would slow his racing heart, he resolved to gather his winnings and leave. When a buck-toothed boy sitting across from him laid down a straight flush with a shout, and reached for the pile of coins that Fuller had already mentally claimed, he felt as if he was being kicked in the head by a mule. Someone handed him his drink. He chugged it down and called for another, noticing John and Wilburn exchange a quick glance.

Now he was angry, and what little judgment that he could muster at the card table was being washed away by alcohol. Determined to win back his money, Fuller wagered heavier. And he drank more. With each losing hand he became more reckless, and more drunk.

When the game finally closed down, Fuller's money was gone, along with the use of his legs. John and Wilburn helped him home, depositing him at his front door. Staggering inside, he tripped over Lillie's churn, fell into the table and then onto the floor, awakening them all. As he lay there, with the room spinning around him, Fuller saw their faces all looking into his—Lillie sobbing, Gem horrified, Purl screaming. He turned away in shame. Then he vomited.

~~~

Lillie got no sleep that night. After dragging Fuller to bed she began cleaning up the mess, while pleading with her confused and frightened son. "Your Daddy is sick, but he's going to be all right. Just go on to bed, Gem." Gem reluctantly returned to bed, but not to sleep. He could hear his mother crying as she mopped the floor. Purl howled till morning.

A few hours later, just before dawn, a haggard Fuller emerged as Lillie was preparing breakfast. As Gem tracked him with a frightened stare, Fuller walked over to Lillie, looked into her swollen red eyes and promised, "I ain't never going back there again, Lillie Mae. I'm mighty sorry. I'm going to make this up to you." Fighting back her anger, she melted and wrapped him in a hug. "I'm scared, Fuller," she whispered through sobs. "I'm scared."

"Everything's going to be all right, Lillie Mae," he answered, battling back tears of his own.

~~~

Fuller walked to work that morning, under a thick dark cloud of shame and guilt.

For almost seven years, ever since Gem was born, he had been squirreling away whatever money he could spare—a dime here, a nickel there. When he had enough, his plan was to give Lillie Mae a surprise—the chance to go home and see her family. He'd managed to accumulate over $20 and was near his goal. He had often imagined how good it was going to feel to give that money to Lillie, to tell her she didn't have to go to work for a whole month, and that she should take the children and go back home for a while. He imagined how overjoyed she would be. Whenever he was feeling blue he'd think about that happy day and it would cheer him up.

But it was all gone now. He'd pissed it all away playing cards.

As he had been doing nearly every day for nearly eight years now, Fuller set his looms. He did his job as always, but his mind wasn't in it. The fifteen monsters he tended were banging together, sending shock waves through his pounding hungover head, taunting him. Already severely dehydrated, the cotton dust he was breathing made it worse by the hour. Most of all he was deeply ashamed, replaying in his mind every stupid and humiliating moment of the night before—the dumb wagers, the loss of control, the horrified eyes of his wife and children as he lay sprawled in his own puke. The money. Lillie's trip home. All gone because he was a fool.

A weaver is on the move constantly. There is no allowance for a savage headache, or for the desperate thirst of a hangover, or for a desire to rest. Keep moving, or the line stops. Keep moving, or lose your job. Move, move, move. Move while thinking about the money lost, the regretted wagers, the stupid decision to play while drunk. I'm a fool becomes I'm a failure becomes distraction becomes carelessness, and Fuller's shirt becomes tangled in the loom and then it is his arm, rather than a sheet of cotton, that is being woven.

~ ~ ~

During a stoppage caused by a thread break, and with his mind elsewhere, Fuller had reached underneath the cloth, inadvertently pushing the gripper handle forward, restarting the machine while his arm was between the shuttle dagger and the frame. Fortunately, the machine shut off, but not before driving the shuttle into him a half dozen times, dislocating his shoulder and tearing deep painful cuts into his arm. The company doctor stitched him up with catgut and sent him home, estimating a six-week recovery period.

Lillie had made it through her day, but it had felt like torture after her sleepless and worried night. She had been praying fervently all day that their lives would return to normal now. When she got home, she discovered that those prayers had not been answered.

Now Fuller added a painful and debilitating injury to his shame. He tried to downplay the severity of it, but it was impossible to conceal. "What are we going to do, Fuller?" Lillie asked him, fear in her voice.

"It's going to be all right Lillie. I'll have to lay out a week to let it heal some, but then I'll go back. We'll be able to make it." Fuller put on a good front, while burning with the guilt of having squandered their savings—savings that would have carried them through this.

Lillie usually spent about $6 per week on food, from their combined pay of about $14. But Fuller made twice as much as her. Lillie's pay alone was only $4.50 per week. She did the frightening math in her head. After their $1 per week rent, she would have only $3.50 left to buy their food. They would manage, but it would be tight. She would make cornbread with water. There would be no milk or butter this week. She was sorry that it was too early to have anything in the garden. But we'll make it, she thought.

~ ~ ~

Sadly, Lillie's calculations were in error. When she went to get some "mill money" the next day after work, she was told she didn't have any available. "But I ain't taken none this week. I got my whole pay to use," she protested. The clerk's response stabbed her like a knife, "You have a $7 charge for the doctor who tended to your husband. That doesn't leave you with anything available for a slip."

So there was no money for food that week. Worse, because her pay wasn't enough to cover the doctor and the rent, she would begin next week with a debt of $3.50. Adding the rent to that meant that her entire pay for the following week was already spent too. So there would be no money for food that week either, unless Fuller was back at work.

Lillie explained the situation to Fuller, with desperation in her voice. She had some flour left and could make hoe cakes with it, and enough beans for a couple of meager meals, but after that they'd have no money and nothing to eat for two weeks. "This is all my fault Lillie Mae. But I'm going to fix it," he replied.

The next day he showed up at work as usual, sweating through his clothes as his arm throbbed with pain. "You ain't in no shape to work, with your arm all tore up like that!" his supervisor told him. "Go back home and get well. Your job will be waiting for you." As a dejected Fuller walked away, the supervisor added, "Be careful with that arm, Samuel. If you don't let it heal proper, you'll never be fit to work."

Fuller spent the day in bed, in intense pain, convinced that no pain had ever been more deserved. "I'm a damned fool," he repeated silently for hours.

The strain was obvious on Lillie's face when she returned home that evening. Fuller described his rebuff, which she had expected. "Some of the girls got some washing and mending I can do," Lillie told him. "I'll make enough from that to buy some more beans when these run out." And Fuller felt his burden of guilt grow heavier.

~ ~ ~

The next morning Fuller intercepted some of his co-workers as they were marching to work, John and Wilburn among them. Masking his pain and feigning cheerfulness he spoke to them, "Boys, I can't stand laying around the house all day doing nothin'. It's about to drive me crazy. Y'all got any work needs doing during the day, just let me know and I'll help you with it."

There were few grunts from the crowd as it shuffled along, but no one answered him directly. After a few awkward moments Wilburn spoke up, "How's your arm feeling, Sam?"

"Well it hurt right smart at first, but now it ain't too bad. It's healing real good. I 'spect it'll be back to normal in day or so."

Wilburn, looking dubious, stepped closer to Fuller and said quietly, "If'n you need a little money to carry you through, Sam, we can let you have some."

Fuller replied sharply and quickly, "I ain't asking for no handout, Wilburn. Just looking for something to do during the day and thought y'all might could use a little help with something, that's all."

"All right Sam, but you just let us know," Wilburn replied as the men filed through the mill gate, leaving Fuller behind.

~~~

Every evening, after a full day at the mill and all of her normal housekeeping work, Lillie worked late into the night mending and washing the clothes of other mill girls—girls who passed the work to her as a way to help her out without shaming her. With the money she earned, she was able to keep them all fed—barely. Both she and Fuller felt their hearts breaking when the children said they were hungry, as Gem did occasionally and Purl did regularly. "These are trials," Lillie told him, "and they'll make us stronger." He was not comforted.

Fuller walked around Mechanicsville every day, looking for temporary work. But what could he do with only one arm, his left arm at that? One warehouseman answered his request for work with, "I'll pay you 25 cents to unload that wagon for me," pointing to a wagon weighed down with bales of twine. But despite his best efforts, and a powerful desire to succeed, Fuller couldn't do it. All he managed to accomplish was to tear out some of his stitches, before walking away defeated.

He showed up at the mill every Monday morning after his injury. Week after week he was sent home and told he would not be allowed to resume work until his arm was healed.

One morning, during Fuller's fourth week of convalescence, Lillie discovered a gallon of milk and some groceries on their doorstep. Knowing that Fuller would be hurt if he knew the truth, she pretended to have bought them.

Fortunately, she had planted her tomatoes and string beans before the accident, and now her little garden was coming to life. Lillie had never been happier to see it. Because she had no time for it, she put Gem in charge of tending the young plants. He took his new responsibilities very seriously and it seemed to Lillie that he had a green thumb. He kept the plants watered and weeded, he mashed the beetles and worms, and with a watering mouth, he dreamed anxiously of thick tomato slices and pots full of string beans.

~~~

Near the end of May they rented the children's bedroom to two new weave-room workers for 50 cents per week, and Gem and Purl began sleeping on a pallet in their parents' room. Renting the room pained Fuller, who had taken pride in having a house of his own, but he knew it had to be done. He assured Lillie that the change was only temporary. "Just for a couple of months, Lillie Mae. By then everything will be all right and we can have the whole house again."

The renters were brothers from somewhere in the hills, who rarely spoke or made eye contact with their housemates. Fuller told Lillie their name was Haskins, but they introduced themselves only as Tick and Tom. Wearing shaggy hair, ill-fitting overalls, and battered brogans, Lillie guessed they were about 15 and 16 years old, and she soon realized that the money they contributed to the house food budget was insufficient to satisfy their appetites. Nevertheless, their presence brought some financial relief, and for that she was glad. Unfortunately, their presence also brought the pungent consequences of their disinterest in personal hygiene, and for that she was not glad.

~~~

In June Fuller was finally cleared to return to work. Having been thoroughly chastised by his fall, he was determined to get his family's lives back to normal. The roar of the looms was music to his ears.

The workday had hardly begun when the supervisor shut down production and gathered the workers for an announcement. "We're doing draft registration out front today. Every man over 21 will be required to register. Because you're working here, you're all exempt—you won't be conscripted. But the law requires you all to register anyway. We're to take you out a few at a time so we can keep the lines running."

On the very day Fuller was injured, the United States had declared war on Germany and its allies. A few of the single men in Mechanicsville had volunteered immediately, but the vast majority just continued life as usual. Although generally aware of the war, it was of no great concern to Fuller, who was of course preoccupied with his family's survival.

Because President Wilson's call for volunteers had produced far fewer men than the war would require, the shortfall would have to be met by conscription. Fuller had learned about the draft while waiting for his arm to heal. Only single men and unemployed married men dependent upon the income of their wives would be taken, he'd been told (feeling a pang of shame). Later he learned that all the millworkers were exempt, now that the mill was producing uniforms and blankets for the army. Nevertheless, every man between 21 and 31 years old was required to register.

The registrar had set up a table in front of the mill entrance and was sitting behind it as the men formed a small queue in front of him. Standing beside him was the doctor who had the responsibility of noting any registrant who was obviously physically unfit. Everyone drafted would be subject to a more thorough physical examination if they made it past this one, which was only intended to weed out the most egregious cases.

When Fuller made it to the front of the line he dutifully registered as Samuel Scruggs, and was marked as "Class IV exempted due to extreme hardship: Married registrants with dependent spouse and/or dependent children with insufficient family income if drafted," and secondarily temporarily Class III exempted as "registrants employed in agricultural labor or industrial enterprises essential to the war effort." When the registrant dismissed him and Fuller turned away, the doctor called after him, "Mr. Scruggs, how long have you had that cough?"

~~~

It had been a while. Fuller couldn't remember exactly when the cough had arrived, but it had worsened while he was recuperating from his injury.

Lillie noticed it too of course, and it was like a black cloud that hung over their precarious existence. They could not afford for Fuller to miss work and they could not afford a doctor. So they both chose to pretend there was nothing unusual or serious about the cough. It would pass. It had to.

But it didn't pass. After Fuller returned to the weave room the coughing fits were more frequent and more severe. Whatever was causing them was probably made worse by breathing stagnant air polluted with cotton dust ten hours every day.

He was having trouble keeping his looms going. His injured arm was weaker, but his weakness wasn't limited to the arm. Fuller simply was not the man he had been, however much he wanted to believe he was. And now it was the others who were having to step in to help him. He put on a good show, laughing and saying things like, "Thanks boys, I'll be back to full speed soon and then I'll go back to doing my job and your'n too." But after a couple of weeks it was clear to all that he was getting worse, not better. Production was falling and the supervisor began to spend a lot of time watching Fuller's looms.

Fuller soldiered on, working with all the strength his failing body could muster. But it wasn't good enough. At the end of a stiflingly hot day in mid-July, his supervisor intercepted him as Fuller was leaving after closing down the looms. "I'm sorry to tell you this, Samuel, but you're being dismissed. You can finish out this week, but that's it."

"That ain't right, Mr. Webb. You know I'm one of the best workers in this mill," Fuller answered, masking his alarm.

"You have been, Samuel, and I'm letting you finish this week. But you know as well as me that you aren't able to do this job anymore. You need to take some time off and get well. When you get your strength back, I'll take you back on."

Swallowing his pride, Fuller spoke candidly, "Mr. Webb, the truth is that we can't make it without me working. I'll do better. But I just can't lose my job right now."

The supervisor had genuinely come to like Fuller, so it was with difficulty that he said, "I'm keeping you on till the end of the week, Samuel, but that's it." He paused, then added, "I'm sorry about it."

Fuller knew there was no point arguing. His stomach was tied in knots and his mind was racing as he walked home, wheezing.

~~~

Fuller never had a medical diagnosis of his condition. Tuberculosis, commonly called "consumption," was common among the urban poor in those days. And respiratory diseases of all sorts were common among mill workers, both because of the working conditions and because of the generally unsanitary conditions of the mill villages. Maybe he had consumption, maybe it was something else. It really didn't matter to them. What mattered was that he no longer had his job.

Lillie took the news as well as she could. Fuller was dejected and she wanted to spare him any more pain. "We'll get by, Fuller. Just like before. You probably went back to work too soon. This time you stay out till your body is healed."

"All right, Lillie Mae. We'll do the best we can. When I get my strength back, we'll have a good life again."

Two weeks later, Lillie was preparing breakfast and the mid-summer sun was already shining brightly when the mill whistle sounded at six. It was a beautiful morning, but Fuller never woke to see it. Having been careful not to disturb him when she rose, when Lillie went to tell him breakfast was ready she found him cold and still.

~~~

The brothers Haskins passed the news to their supervisor that morning, believing it was the right thing to do. The supervisor, likewise believing it was the right thing to do, notified the company doctor. And the company doctor, believing it was the right thing to do, proceeded at once to the Scruggs residence, where he confirmed the unfortunate demise of Mr. Scruggs and proceeded to make arrangements for the burial. The costs of the doctor, the coffin, and the burial were all charged against Lillie's pay.

~~~

Lillie's grief was intense and profound. She'd know Fuller all her life, and loved him for half of it. For the past eight years he had been the center of her world. She could not imagine life without him and she ached in every fiber of her body. Perhaps, unknowingly, she was grieving all that she'd lost.

The children suffered too. Gem withdrew, spending time with his tomato plants and crying silently. Four-year old Purl understood less, of course, but there was pain and loss in her eyes as well.

It took two days for Lillie to compose herself sufficiently to return to work. As much as she hated and dreaded it, she knew she had no choice.

Tick and Tom voluntarily increased their share of the rent and food budget. "It's only fittin'," Tick had said.

In the weeks that followed, the house was quiet, cloaked in sadness.

~~~

Most of Lillie's spirit had left with Fuller. She went through the motions of life, but her heart was very badly broken and her grief weighed heavily on her. At night she dreamed of Fuller—smiling from atop that big horse, proudly holding his babies, the excitement of his first payday, his passion and his boyish grin. Some mornings she awoke with the dreams so real and fresh in her head that she imagined him still alive.

Then the reality would settle on her, and she would be even sadder than before as she trudged off to another long day in the spinning room.

Gem begged her to let him start working as a doffer. Even though he was only seven, and most of the doffers were at least nine, he knew there were some who were his age. "I'll just tell 'em I'm twelve," he pleaded. But Lillie resisted and Gem relented.

Winter arrived early that year, and it would be the coldest one on record. By then she had an unshakable cough, which she recognized all too well. Only 22 years old, she felt and looked three times older.

Lillie understood what her cough and her increasing weakness meant. Whereas until the very end Fuller had gone to sleep each night with the hope that he'd be recovered and back to normal in the morning, she was resigned to a different fate.

~~~

The Haskins brothers lied about their ages and joined the army. It was mid-December when they told Lillie. "Rather take our chances with the Huns than keep breathing that foul mill air every day," one of them said. "But we're gonna get some other fellas to take our place here, ma'am," the other quickly added.

Lillie thanked them with a kind smile, but said she'd just as soon not have any boarders for now. She was at a loss as to what to do. She had no home to retreat to and two children depending on her. But she couldn't bear the thought of strangers moving into the house just then. She convinced herself that some path forward was going to open.

~~~

Lillie drew her pay on Saturday, four days before Christmas. She had been expecting to be fired for the past couple of weeks. She was growing weaker and her coughing, which often produced blood, was getting worse. But to her relief, nothing was said and she was paid as usual. Sending Gem and Purl on home ahead of her, she stopped at the company store and bought the groceries she could afford, along with a toy soldier and a small doll.

Monday was Christmas Eve and Lillie knew she didn't have the strength for a 10-hour shift at the mill. She sent Gem to tell them she was sick, but that she expected to be back at work on Wednesday.

On Christmas morning Lillie allowed the children to sleep in, waking them with the smell of baking cookies. Gem was thrilled with his new toy, the sadness of the last few months temporarily suspended. Lillie mustered the strength to walk to church, and what Gem experienced there that morning took his young breath away. The sanctuary gleamed with white, replacing the purples of Advent, and the organ filled the space with celebratory music. Proudly holding his mother's hand as they walked home, he looked into her face and saw plainly that she was happy. It was a day the boy would never forget.

The next morning it was snowing and bitterly cold as Lillie and the children slogged their way to the mill. There had been snow on the ground for over 20 consecutive days now—the longest stretch anyone could remember. She knew she would be miserable in the spinning room that day, but until the way forward opened (as she was still expecting it would) she knew she had no choice but to continue on.

A new girl was already being trained at her station when Lillie walked onto the spinning room floor. Her supervisor approached. "I'm real sorry, Rose, but you've been discharged," he said, seeming to be sincerely troubled by it. She just nodded in response, as a tear fell softly down her cheek. A final door had closed.

~~~

Isaac Bell did not feel like doing paperwork. His office was cold and the morning sun was shining outside, reflecting brightly on newly-fallen snow. Rising from his desk he walked to the door, took his coat off the peg beside it and called out to the clerk, "I'm going out. What have you got?"

Looking up at his chief, the clerk answered, "It's quiet today. Just some eviction notices for Mechanicsville."

"I'll take them. I need the exercise and the air," Bell said, taking the papers the clerk handed him.

The job responsibilities of chief of police did not include serving eviction notices, but Bell hated feeling chained to his desk. It wasn't unusual for him to walk a beat, respond to calls, even serve papers. He told his staff that it was important for him to stay connected with day to day police work. True, but that wasn't his main motivation. Mostly he just needed to get out from behind his desk sometimes.

Mechanicsville was only a few blocks away. He knew the area well. Several times a year he'd break up a card game, or an unlicensed tavern, or a brothel. And several times a month there were former mill-workers to evict.

When the tenant is the landlord's employee, the landlord doesn't have to worry about whether the rent will be paid. The mill took its rent right off the top on every payday. But once the tenant was no longer employed by the mill, there was no pay from which to take the rent. And besides, the mill houses were for mill workers only. So when a worker was fired, they were also evicted, as quickly as possible.

Bell didn't care for serving eviction notices, but it was part of the job and he'd done it many times. Usually the former workers had already abandoned the place by the time the eviction notice came. Only rarely was it necessary physically to evict anyone.

On this bright frigid Monday morning, the last day of 1917, he had three notices to serve. The first two houses were abandoned. He tacked the notices to their doors, and entered the date and time in his journal. The final notice was for a house on Floyd Street. It was on his way back, so he saved it for last.

Gem answered the knock on the door, then stood wide-eyed in alarm at the sight of the policeman. Bell was not an insensitive man, but he'd long ago learned to suppress any compassion for the evicted mill-workers. Nine times out of ten, he reminded himself, there's a lazy drunkard to blame. "Good morning, young man. Is Mrs. Scruggs here?"

Gem eventually managed, "Yes, sir," but remained frozen.

"Will you please tell her I need to speak to her." His words were not meant to be taken as a question.

Gem hesitated, then answered, "She's out in the johnny house right now, sir. She's feeling real poorly this morning."

Bell, his eyes narrowing, stared at the child. It wouldn't be the first time he'd been given the run-around by a little mill rat, he thought.

"How old are you?" he asked Gem.

"I'm 7, sir," Gem answered directly.

That looks about right, Bell thought. Glancing about the house he could see that it was well-kept. He could also see plainly that its inhabitants were poor. Gem was barefoot, despite the cold. His clothes were layered—clean but shabby. In the corner a little girl was playing with a headless doll, murmuring something. A pot of beans was boiling on the stove.

The law required that he leave the papers with a resident at least 12 years old, unless the house had been abandoned, in which case he could tack them to the door. Leaving the paperwork with the boy wasn't an option.

"Well then, I reckon I'll just have to wait on her," Bell said, with a slight smile intended to lighten the mood. After a few moments of awkward silence he spoke again to Gem, "Where is y'all's father?"

"Our Daddy died in September," Gem answered quickly. "He worked in the weave room until he got sick. He was the best weaver in the mill."

Bell cleared his throat. "Mighty sorry to hear that." Just then he noticed that a woman had entered the room, so quietly that he hadn't heard her.

"What can I do for you, sir?" she asked him.

Lillie had long since lost the chubby red cheeks she'd ridden into Danville with eight years ago. Now her face was taut, pale, and gaunt, her cheeks sunken. Her large brown eyes still reflected expressively, like deep pools of water, but they were the only evidence of the girlish beauty she'd once had. A once-white floor-length dress hung on her thin wiry frame, her hair hidden under a bonnet. She stood not much taller than her son. Bell towered over her.

"Mrs. Scruggs?" he asked.

She sighed and nodded.

"I am here to serve you with a Writ of Eviction." Repeating words he'd spoken many times over the years, Bell handed her the papers.

"I'm afraid you'll have to explain that to me, sir," she replied as she accepted them from him.

"It means you are being ejected for nonpayment of rent. You are required to vacate these premises within 48 hours. Failure to do so will result in removal by force." Bell was using his "official" voice, but trying hard not to sound like a bully, uncomfortably aware of Gem's stare.

"All right," Lillie answered softly, looking at the floor while wringing the papers in her hands, fighting back tears.

"Good day then, ma'am," Bell said firmly with a slight bow, turning to the door and preparing to put on his cap.

"Sir, may I speak to you for minute?" Lillie's voice was a bit louder now, but cracking.

"Well ma'am, I have other duties that require…"

Lillie interrupted him. "Just for a minute, sir. It's real important." Bell looked uncertain. "It's police business, sir," she added, getting his attention.

She had Gem's full attention too, and he was greatly disappointed when his mother told him to take his sister into the other room so she could talk privately with the policeman. He ached to stay, but knew not to protest. Only the thought that it would hurt his mother's feelings kept him from listening through the door, though he wanted to very badly.

Lillie knew she had to make her case quickly. It was the most painful thing she'd ever experienced in her life.

"I've done the best I could for these children. My boy is smart and well-behaved. He's a good worker. My daughter is spirited, but she's young. I've done all I can for them sir, but I can't do it no more. My husband is gone and I'm afraid I'm not far behind him." She swallowed back a deep lump rising in her throat and fought a powerful urge to cry. "We ain't got nowhere to go, and nobody to go to."

Lillie looked into Bell's eyes and could see that he was puzzled.

"It hurts my heart to think of what's going to happen to my children, sir. I've prayed with all my heart that they would be able to go to school and live a decent life. What I'm asking, sir, is if you would please find some nice kind folks who would…" She hesitated, her eyes filling with tears. "…who would adopt them and take care of them." Heartbroken and ashamed, she couldn't hold it back any longer. She dropped her chin to her chest and sobbed softly, whispering, "Fuller, I am so, so, sorry."

Bell found himself unexpectedly moved, his tough reserve shaken. Shuffling his feet, he stammered, "Well ma'am, uh, it's not our policy, uh, I mean, our jurisdiction, uh…"

Lillie didn't move. She had drained herself of all she could say. She would not, could not, plead any more. Her head was still bowed, and she was still crying softly, whispering "I am so sorry," when Bell changed course, finding his firm voice again.

"Yes ma'am, I will see what I can do. I can't make any promises, but I will make some inquiries on their behalf," Bell said as he turned to leave. "Don't worry about this writ just yet. Y'all can stay here a little longer. I'll come back soon."

Lillie didn't look up but he heard her say quietly as he went out the door, "Thank you, sir."

~~~

Bell walked briskly back toward his office, drinking in the cold morning air and asking himself over and over, "What the devil have you gotten yourself into Isaac?"

Entering the station, he banged the snow off his boots, hung his hat and coat on their peg and dropped the service affidavits on the clerk's desk.

"Where's the other one?" the clerk asked.

"Pardon me?" Bell responded, turning to face him.

"The other writ, sir. There were three of them."

"Right. The Scruggs writ was defective. Material inconsistency," Bell said as he turned away from the clerk's inquisitive look. "Tell them they'll have to have it reissued."

Bell dropped into the chair behind his desk and began to busy himself with a stack of papers, before calling out to the clerk, "Court is closed tomorrow so no point returning it today. Send it to them on Wednesday."

"Yes, sir," the clerk replied, unanswered questions ringing in his tone of voice.

~~~

Bell spent most of the day regretting his agreement to help the woman. He replayed the scene in his mind repeatedly, imagining all the proper ways to respond to her request, growing increasingly irritated and increasingly irritable.

By afternoon he'd arrived at a solution. He'd go back there, explain that he had neither the time nor the ability to find a home for the children, and propose instead that she discuss the situation with the director of the orphanage, offering to make the necessary introduction. It seemed to him the proper and professional way to both extricate himself from the situation, and to assure that it was dealt with via appropriate channels.

Feeling a sense of relief, he turned his attention to preparing for the evening. New Year's Eve always brought bedevilment to town, and it would be his job to keep the peace. Mrs. Scruggs and her children would have to wait.

~~~

Bell slept in the next day. The department had added a few residents to the drunk tank overnight, but it had been relatively quiet, in part because of the sub-zero temperature. Weather that cold imposes a natural limit to how rowdy a man can be. Still, he'd been up late and so had earned a morning off, he reasoned.

Despite his best efforts to push them out of his mind, he awoke thinking of the mill family. It was the little boy that kept coming to his mind now—the tenderness he had shown toward his mother, the pride he seemed to take in his father's memory. "A damn shame," Bell muttered, as he dressed for work.

Tomorrow, he resolved, he'd go back out there and direct them to the proper authorities.

~~~

"We just got the new Scruggs writ. You want me to send one of the boys out to serve it?"

Normally something this routine would not need the Chief's attention. But the Clerk sensed that Bell had taken an unusual interest in this one, so he thought it best to ask.

"What? Oh, right. Never mind that. I'll serve it. I'm going that way anyway. Just leave it there for me," Bell answered without looking up, sorry to have been reminded of Mrs. Scruggs. Might as well get it over with, he thought, as he rose from his desk.

Stepping out into the cutting, icy wind, Bell stuffed the papers into his pocket and fastened the top buttons of his coat. The gray afternoon sky threatened to add more snow to the dirty piles that already lined the streets and sidewalks, awaiting a long overdue thaw. Before him, directly across the street, he watched as several men shuffled up the steps and into the building that housed the presses of the *Danville Times-News*. And then it dawned on him. "Of course," he thought. "Of course."

~~~

"Well howdy, Chief!"

On seeing Bell enter the room, George Carter sprang to his feet and extended his hand. Bell shook it firmly.

"What brings you to my humble abode? Got a story for me?" There was a mischievousness in his tone, as usual.

"As a matter of fact, George, I do," Bell answered, taking a seat.

Clean-shaven, neatly groomed, and smartly dressed, George Carter imagined himself a victim. He should have been living in New York or Philadelphia, among his intellectual equals, but instead he was stuck in his backwater hometown. He should have been writing for a newspaper whose prestige was worthy of his talents, but instead he was a reporter for the *Danville Times-News*, whose publisher was his uncle. The only satisfaction George found in his job was that it presented him with occasions to mock and ridicule the rubes and bumpkins with whom he was unjustly imprisoned. When Bell entered, George had just put the finishing touches on a story about a robbery attempt by a transient negro, foiled by a local Greek restauranteur. "Our dusky visitor was subdued promptly by the intrepid Hellenic hash-slinger," he had written, delighted at the opportunity to insult both parties in a single sentence.

Bell was well aware of his son-in-law's character flaws. George Carter had been a whiny pretentious boy, before evolving into an arrogant dandy of a man. But his daughter had been smitten by the boy, who had promised her a high-fashion big-city life somewhere. She had not seen, as Bell had, that the boy was at his core a coward, lacking the self-confidence and pluck that it would take to move to a distant city and work his way up the ladder somewhere. He knew George would stay in Danville, take a job with his uncle's paper, and earn a reliable income for his family. Both his daughter and George, Bell believed, would eventually settle down and lose their highfalutin notions.

"George, there's a young widow out in Mechanicsville that needs to find somebody to adopt her children. It's a tough situation. I told her I'd try to help."

George leaned forward, intrigued, while Bell told him the story.

"That's rich, Chief," George said with a smile when Bell had finished. "Oh yeah, that's rich. I can't get it in tomorrow's paper, but I'll run it on Thursday."

"All right, George. Thanks," Bell said, rising. Stepping through the door he looked back, "You and Betsy are coming over for dinner on Sunday, right?"

"Yessiree. We'll be there," George answered as he resumed his scribbling.

As he exited the building, Bell turned toward home and supper, with the writ still in his pocket.

~~~

"We got an inquiry from the mill about the Scruggs writ," the clerk announced as Bell was preparing to leave his office the next afternoon.

"Yeah, it slipped my mind yesterday. I still have it. I'm taking it out there now," he answered.

His plan was to tell the woman about the story, offer to send over someone from the orphanage, and to serve the writ. At that point he would have done his duty, as he saw it. But first he wanted to confirm that George had written the story.

"Got it right here Chief! Planning to set it on the front-page tomorrow," George said cheerfully, answering Bell's inquiry.

"May I see it," Bell said, not intending it to be taken as a question.

"Sure," George answered. Although some reporters composed their text directly on the Linotype machine, George preferred to write his out by hand first. He handed Bell his hand-written story.

A scowl grew across Bell's face as he read. "This is outrageous George." He looked directly into his son-in-law's puzzled face. "This is outrageous."

"Uh, why do you say that, Chief?"

Bell looked down and began reading aloud, "Having been discharged by her employer, the children have become a burden to Mrs. Scruggs, and she would now prefer that someone else assume the financial obligations attendant to feeding and educating them." Lifting his eyes for a moment Bell studied George's face, sternly, then resumed reading, "The opportunity to increase their households in such an uncomplicated fashion will surely be attractive to many of our city's finest families. But for those not fortunate enough to procure these youngsters, take heart. No doubt an ample quantity of such children will soon become available once the news of this transaction becomes known among the mill-workers."

Bell's hand became a fist, crumpling the paper. "Didn't you listen to a goddamn thing I said, George?"

Unprepared for Bell's anger, George was temporarily staggered. Despite the temptation, he sensed that this was no time for wit.

"Well sir, yes. Of course I did. I aimed to capture all the essential facts there. And I made the story a little more interesting."

"Interesting?" Bell's voice was hot. "What you mean is 'amusing,' in some cold-hearted way. This woman is heart-broken and you've taken that as an invitation to insult her."

George stayed silent. His father-in-law had never before raised his voice at him.

Bell continued, more composed now. "Perhaps I didn't make myself clear enough. I want this story to portray Mrs. Scruggs and her predicament sympathetically. It's not my place to tell you how to do your job any more than it is yours to tell me how to do mine. But in this case our duties overlap and I must insist that the tenor of this story match the seriousness with which the Department takes it. I will take responsibility for vouching for this woman's motives. In fact, I insist that you say so directly in your story. That should relieve you of any concerns you may have."

"I understand," George answered, suppressing his desire to fight. He would not have allowed himself to be intimidated by a cop, even the Chief of Police. But he would not do battle with his father-in-law. So he surrendered the field. "We're ready to go to print now. I'll revise the story and we'll run it on Friday."

"All right, George," Bell said calmly as he stood to leave. "I'll come see it this time tomorrow."

Turning as he reached the doorway, Bell looked back and said, "This is just business, George. I hope you took no offense."

George nodded.

~ ~ ~

"Perfect. It's exactly right," Bell said as he returned the handwritten story to George. He had come over, as promised, to review the story before it went to print. "Are you sure this will be in tomorrow's paper?"

"It will. Front page," George answered crisply.

"All right. Thanks, George. Well done."

Bell had not returned to the Scruggs house since his initial visit four days earlier. He now knew he couldn't put it off any longer.

Once again it was Gem who opened the door. Looking past the boy, Bell saw his mother, stepping away from the stove while wiping her hands on her apron. She seemed to have aged over those few days.

"Good afternoon, sir," she said, managing a weak, weary smile. "It's good to see you."

"I need to speak privately with you, ma'am," Bell replied, noting how Gem's face fell when he did. "Police business," he quickly added.

"Gem, take your sister and…," Lillie began.

"Yes, ma'am," Gem interrupted, his voice dripping with disappointment as he took Purl's hand and led her into the back room.

Bell spoke quietly, but directly. "The matter we discussed regarding your children will be the subject of an article in tomorrow morning's paper. I am hopeful that it will produce the results you desire."

"I thank you kindly, sir. It does my heart good to know that," Lillie replied softly, before coughing.

"I regard it my duty to add, ma'am, that we cannot be certain of any success. You might therefore wish to consider contacting…," he proceeded with his carefully planned words, until Lillie stopped him.

"Sir, I have a calm assurance on my heart that the Lord will take care of this. I am much obliged for your help."

Bell hesitated, then decided not to risk upsetting the woman's "calm assurance."

"All right, ma'am. There is a second matter I must address. I am now formally serving you with this Writ of Eviction. As I mentioned on Monday, you must vacate these premises within…"

Again Lillie broke in. "I understand you, sir, and I thank you for your patience."

"Allow me to add, ma'am, as a personal matter, that I wish the very best to you and your children," Bell added, awkwardly.

"Thank you, sir." Lillie looked up, her shining brown eyes seeming out of place on her pallid, tired face. "It is well with my soul."

~ ~ ~

"Gem," Lillie called, as soon as the policeman was gone.

"Yes, ma'am," Gem answered, rushing into the room. "What was the police business?" he asked anxiously.

"Oh, 'tweren't nothing much." She handed the boy a knife. "Bring me that last hen, Gem. We're gonna have chicken and dumplin's for supper tonight," she said, setting the hungry child's face alight.

While Lillie prepared the chicken, she sent Gem to the store with her final few coins, to get the mixings for a pie. The boy's heart was singing as he bounded out of the store, so that he didn't hear the woman at the counter, who had intended to be heard: "How foolish to waste money on chocolate syrup, as poor as they is."

~ ~ ~

Bell left home after supper that night—to attend to some paperwork, he told his wife. Snow had been falling steadily since afternoon, and the sidewalks and roads were slick and treacherous. Walking slowly and carefully along the muffled icy streets, he marveled, as he had often before, at how quiet the city becomes during snowfall. He thought back over the years he had spent walking a beat here—of all the time he had invested in this place that had always been his home, of all the changes that had occurred. If every man has a calling, he thought, then this is mine. He could count many mistakes in his life, but he took satisfaction in believing that he had always done his duty to the best of his ability.

It was long past midnight as he approached the loading dock behind the Times-News Building. Young black men were catching bundles of papers being tossed to them off the dock, stacking them in wagons to which mules, snorting and braying in the frigid snowy air, were hitched, waiting. Reaching into one of the wagons, Bell pulled out a newspaper. Holding it out under a lantern he saw what he was looking for, and he stuffed the paper into this coat.

By the time he reached Floyd Street, the snow had stopped falling and the sky was clearing. The half-moon shone brightly, despite the smoke from a thousand chimneys, reflecting its light off the newly fallen snow. The Hunter, the celestial giant he had admired since boyhood, was setting in the west. It will be a pretty day, he thought.

Bell stepped up to the door of the house and carefully slid the paper beneath it. From inside, he could have sworn he heard the woman's voice, speaking quietly.

Part Two

Henry Wrenn wanted to go home. He was not one of those tobacco farmers who spent all year looking forward to spending a night in Danville after the crop was sold. Even as a young man, he had felt no desire for the saloons, or for the enterprising women anxious to exchange intimacy for cash. Certainly now, in his 76th year, such things held no charm for him. But by the time he'd settled up after yesterday's sale, it was snowing and it was too late to try for home. So, reluctantly, he'd taken a room at a hotel on Main Street, paying extra to have the bed to himself, even though he was a very frugal man.

Finishing his breakfast in the hotel dining room the next morning, Henry checked his watch. It was almost five. It would be dawn soon and he was eager to leave. He spoke to the attendant, "Have someone bring my horse and wagon around, please." Knowing it would take a few minutes, he sat back down and nodded to the girl who poured more coffee into his cup.

From across the room Henry heard a man laughing, calling out loudly, "Hey Freida, you want any more chaps? 'Cause here's a woman who's giving hers away."

Henry noticed the couple for the first time. Well-dressed and middle-aged, they were having breakfast at a table across the room. The man was laughing, peering over the top of a newspaper at the woman.

"What? Let me see that," the woman answered, taking the paper from the man. After a few moments she spoke again, "Well, my word! Isn't it dreadful! Those poor souls. I shall see that this is addressed by the BDL."

The man chuckled, took the paper back and replied, "Oh, I'm sure you will my dear. I'm sure you will."

Henry noticed someone stirring by his side and he turned to face him. It was a young boy. "I done brought yo' wagon up for you, suh," the boy said.

"Thank you," Henry answered, standing and handing the boy a nickel. As he was leaving, he dropped a coin into a dish on the counter and took a newspaper.

~~~

Henry could see that the hitching had been correctly done, and the horse appeared to be rested and fed. He produced one of the hotel's sugar lumps from his pocket, and the horse took it from his open palm. Henry patted him on the side of his massive neck, whispering, "Good boy." An enormous Clydesdale, the horse had been with Henry every day for over 20 years, as had his sire and grandsire before him.

Climbing onto the wagon seat, Henry said "Let's go home, Buck," as he shook the reins. There were a few inches of fresh snow on the road and the air was frigid. But Henry was unconcerned. Buck liked the cold, and he could pull a wagon through a lot worse than this. As the horse pulled away, Henry smiled at the familiar sound of wheels creaking and hooves crunching snow.

The bridge at the north end of Main Street would take him across the river and toward Maple Grove— home. But instead of crossing over, Henry turned the horse left, along the road that ran parallel to the river. It had been a while since he'd been to Mechanicsville, but he knew the area well, having sold tobacco to a plug factory there for many years before it closed.

After about a quarter mile he turned left again, and presently drew up before a small house on Floyd Street. Taking the newspaper from under the seat, Henry looked again at the story, squinting to see it in the dim light of early morning.

BOY AND GIRL TO ADOPT

Mother, Weary of Hopeless Struggle
of Providing for Them, Wishes
to Find Them Homes.

Who wants a seven-year-old boy, or
a four-year-old girl?

Mrs. Rose Scruggs, a widow living
at 604 Floyd street, has such a boy
and such a girl, whom she is willing
to have some one legally adopt who
can better provide for their comfort
than she has been able to do.

The mother is not an unnatural one
but is rather moved by considerations
of the welfare of her children primar-
ily and only incidentally of her own.
She has found it hard struggle under
existing costs of living to provide
shelter and sustenance for her two
little ones, and has now reached a
point where she considers that it
would be best for them if she could
insure the comfort, welfare and educational opportunities to which children are entitled.

Chief of Police Bell is responsible
for the statement that this is the attitude of Mrs. Scruggs with respect
to the two children. Any person de-
siring to adopt either of the children
legally and open the door of opportunity to these young lives and rescue
them from penury may communicate
with the mother directly or through
the police department.

Henry had found the story moving. So, with the proceeds of his crop in his pocket, he had decided to stop by the house on his way home, to offer the woman some financial assistance.

He hesitated at the door, wondering if it might be too early. Then, just as he raised his hand to knock, the door suddenly swung open, surprising him. Standing before him in the doorway was a young boy, who was staring intently into Henry's face as if he was searching it for something. After a moment, Henry spoke, "Good morning, young man. I wonder if I might have a word with your mother."

The boy stepped backward, with a gesture that invited Henry in, all while continuing his intense, discomforting stare. Henry removed his hat and stepped inside.

Henry Wrenn was a large man, broad-shouldered and nearly six feet tall. His hair, like his bushy mustache, was mostly gray, but streaked with black reminders of younger days. He was dressed for town, but his large and calloused hands revealed him to be a farmer or mechanic. He was imposing, but not nearly as fascinating as the boy's gaping stare would suggest.

Henry heard a child fussing in another room, but from a quick glance around he could see that he and the boy were the only people in this one. "Is your mother home?" Henry asked.

The question broke the spell Henry seemed to have cast on the boy. He saw the wonder in the boy's eyes turn quickly to something else—something more like fear or painful bewilderment. "Yes, sir," the boy said, dropping his eyes toward the floor.

"Would you please ask her if I might speak to her a moment?"

The boy seemed confused and troubled. He opened his mouth as if to speak, but then stopped and looked away. Something's not right here, Henry realized.

"Where is your mother, son?" Henry asked, trying to soothe the boy's nerves.

The boy pointed at a doorway. "She's in yonder."

Henry looked at the doorway, then back at the boy. "Do you want me to go in there?" he asked, sensing that was what the boy wanted. The boy nodded his head rapidly, his eyes pleading.

Henry stepped into the doorway and peered into the room beyond it. He saw a woman lying on a cot, wearing an apron and a work dress. "Ma'am?" he said softly. When there was no response Henry stepped closer, reaching out to touch a cold, lifeless arm, confirming what he had suspected. He stepped quickly back into the front room, where the boy was still standing.

Henry bent down so he could look the boy directly in his eyes. Speaking as calmly as he could, he asked, "Son, have you checked on your mother lately?"

The boy's quivering lip and moist eyes gave him his answer. With a cracking voice, the boy asked, "Sir, are you the one the good Lord sent?"

The question startled Henry. "I beg your pardon," he responded reflexively.

"Mama said the good Lord would send someone to git us today. Are you the one he sent?"

"Well, um, I, uh…" Henry had no idea what to say, so he changed the subject.

"Have you children had any breakfast?"

"No, sir," the boy replied. "There ain't no food left." After a pause he added, "And there ain't no coal neither."

For the first time since entering, Henry realized that there was no fire in the house. It was as cold inside as outside—freezing cold.

"Do you all have any people around here?" Henry asked, thinking surely they must have some kin that would take them in.

"There ain't nobody but us, sir." The boy answered as he quickly brushed a tear off his cheek. After a pause, "Me and my sister."

Great God, Henry thought. He closed his eyes tightly and squeezed his temple between the thumb and forefinger of his massive left hand, trying to calculate the options in his mind. When he opened his eyes, the boy was still standing there, tears streaming down his face, his shoulders shaking. Henry sighed deeply.

"Are you ready to go?" Henry asked, looking into the boy's eyes and being answered with a nod. "Let's go then."

The mill whistle screamed as they were crossing over the river.

~~~

Caroline Wrenn had been expecting her husband's return all morning and she smiled when she heard Buck's familiar clomping steps. Turning away from the stove and glancing out the window, she was astonished to see her Henry sitting in the center of the wagon seat, holding the reins, flanked by two small children.

Henry stopped the wagon beneath a towering red oak, in front of a simple two-story white house with a large front porch that held a swing on one end, and two rockers on the other. They had made good time, traveling the 15 miles from Danville to Maple Grove in about four hours. As he stepped down from the wagon, a ruddy round-faced woman emerged from the door, wiping her hands on her apron.

"Well howdy!" she said cheerfully. "Have you brought us company, Mr. Wrenn?"

Although he was only seven years her senior, Caroline had never called her husband anything other than "Mr. Wrenn." Henry began protesting the formality as soon as they were married, in the winter of 1866. He had gone to Tennessee in search of mules and, at the home of a distant cousin, had found not only mules, but a pretty 18-year-old widow as well. After a brief courtship, they were married and Henry returned to his family's farm in Virginia with desperately-needed mules, and with a bride who still called him mister. Eventually, after a few decades of failure, he finally gave up asking her to call him Henry.

"I have indeed," he answered, opening his arms for a hug. Once hugged, he released his wife and turned toward the wagon, where the children were still sitting, the girl fidgeting and the boy frozen and wide-eyed.

"I have brought two hungry children, to go along with one hungry old man."

Caroline walked to the wagon, with a welcoming smile.

"Please come on down, children," she motioned to them. "We'll be having dinner directly and there's plenty for us all."

The children climbed down from the wagon and stood before her, the boy holding a little homemade satchel.

Smiling, she took one hand from each of them and said pleasantly, "Please tell me your names."

The boy answered, "I'm Gem. This is my sister Purl."

The words he spoke were "Gem" and "Purl." The words she heard were "Jim" and "Pearl."

~ ~ ~

Caroline was burning with curiosity. Once the children were sufficiently occupied by their meal, she motioned for Henry to join her on the porch. There, he told her everything.

"For goodness sakes, Mr. Wrenn! You can't just drive off with someone else's children like that!"

"Well, Caroline, I couldn't just leave them there."

"But it's against the law to take children that way! You could probably be arrested. I imagine it's a very serious crime to do that sort of thing."

Henry stroked his mustache and looked off into the distance for a few moments, before looking back into his wife's face.

"Yes, Caroline, I see what you mean. I reckon I could just take them back."

"Take them back?!" she quickly replied, her face flushing. "Take them back?! You will do nothing of the sort, Mr. Wrenn. I will not consent to it! Return these precious hungry children to a cold empty house with no food and no mother to care for them?? Pshaw!"

Henry cleared his throat, but there was a gleam in his eyes. "Well then, what ought we do?"

"We're going to take care of them," she said, turning to go back inside. "At least for a while."

The food she had placed on the table was their normal midday fare, but for Jim, accustomed to a sparse and meager diet, it was an amazing feast. Every meal at the Wrenn farm, as he would come to learn, included fresh milk, freshly-baked bread, one or two choices of meat, and a variety of vegetables, all from their gardens or cellars, as well as a cake or pie, something that had always been a rare treat for the children.

"Is everything all right?" Caroline asked as she stepped back in, with Henry following her.

"It's real good. Thank you, ma'am," Jim answered.

She smiled and nodded. "Now Jim, you didn't tell me your last name. What might it be?"

She was surprised to see distress sweep swiftly over the boy's face.

Thinking quickly through the long story his mother had shared with him the night before, it dawned on Jim suddenly and frighteningly that he wasn't sure how to answer her question. What was his last name? Should he say "Scruggs"? Should he say "Snead"?

After a few seconds, tears beginning to fill his eyes, Jim answered painfully, "I don't know, ma'am."

"Oh, bless your heart!" Caroline burst out, beginning to cry as she hugged the boy. "Bless your precious heart!"

Henry watched, his heart swelling, and laughter in his eyes.

~ ~ ~

That night, after putting the children to bed on a pallet she'd made for them, Henry and Caroline sat in rockers by the stove, Caroline knitting, pondering the extraordinary day.

"What are we going to tell people, Mr. Wrenn?"

"What people?" he asked, without looking at her.

"The neighbors. The people at church," she replied, not looking up from her knitting.

93

"Don't tell them anything," Henry answered gruffly, then adding, with a chuckle, "It will give the old hens something to gossip about."

"Be serious, Mr. Wrenn. We have to tell them something."

Henry thought quietly for a moment, then spoke. "Then tell them they're my cousins. Orphans. We've taken them in."

"Your cousins! We are not going to weave lies." Caroline shook her head defiantly.

Henry thought for a few moments, then answered, "It's not a lie Caroline. The way I see it, they are my cousins. Yours too. We're all kin if you go back to Adam and Eve. I grant you they are likely very distant cousins, but they are my cousins nonetheless."

Henry seemed pleased to have solved the problem, and satisfied with his reasoning. Caroline did not seem so impressed.

"Oh, pshaw!" Still shaking her head, Caroline said, "Your cousins. My word, Mr. Wrenn." She sat silently a while, then continued, "Everyone around here knows your people. You do not have any orphaned cousins." She stopped knitting, as if deep in thought.

After a few moments, the knitting resumed and Caroline spoke, still without looking up. "But I don't have any people around here. We will say the children are orphans. *My* cousins."

~~~

From the pallet in the next room, Jim could hear them talking, but he couldn't make out what they were saying.

He wasn't trying to hear—he was trying not to be heard.

The night before, sitting before their stove, his mother had told him the story of her life, and therefore the story of his. "It's a lot to put on a little boy," she had told him, "but these are things I want you to know."

She had also spoken with a calm assurance about the kind person who she knew in her heart was coming the next day to take him and Purl away, although she didn't know exactly who it would be. She had given him careful instructions on how to behave in the new life she expected for him. "This is real important, Gem. I want you to listen to me and to do all that I say."

She had made him promise, but that hadn't been necessary. He was prepared to obey his mother in whatever she told him to do.

"When you're at the new place, you can't be sad." Lillie had looked directly into his terrified eyes, emphasizing the point. "You can't be sad, Gem. It will hurt their feelings if you are sad."

So now, in the new place, he muffled his sobs in the dark, crushed by the absence of his mother. It was as if his heart was being torn from his chest. He wanted to wail and scream, but he saw her pleading face, her voice still clear in his mind, "You can't be sad, Gem." He longed desperately for her hug.

He felt as if a great weight was crushing down on him. It was a weight no little boy should ever have to feel.

That night, and every night for weeks afterwards, he cried himself to sleep.

~~~

Born Caroline Adams, she had been Caroline Crawley on that January day when she saw her father riding up the road toward their farm with a tall dark-haired stranger riding beside him. She had acquired her new surname 21 months earlier, when she had married her childhood sweetheart while he was home on leave. Two days after the ceremony Luke Crawley rode off to rejoin his regiment, and less than two months after that he was dead, killed in the shadow of a Virginia mountain.

Henry had been immediately smitten by the young widow. With the encouragement of her parents, he proposed marriage. Two weeks later, they left Adams Spring, Tennessee for Maple Grove, Virginia, husband and wife.

The next year brought a painful miscarriage, and Caroline was never with child again.

Now, over 50 years after that disappointment, and following a fitful night of prayer, doubt and, ultimately, resolution, she was determined to keep and raise the young orphans who had so improbably appeared in her life. But she remained troubled by the possibility that Henry had committed a crime in taking them.

Well before sunrise, as she was preparing breakfast and after Henry had left to do his morning chores, the boy emerged from the room where he and his sister had slept. Afraid of embarrassing him, Caroline pretended not to notice his puffy red eyes.

"Well good morning, Jim," she said, as cheerfully as she could. "I see that you're dressed already. I hope the pallet was comfortable."

"Yes, ma'am. Thank you," he sheepishly replied.

After a few efforts to sustain pointless dialog ("I hope you were warm enough." "It's going to be another cold one." "Breakfast will be ready soon." Etc.), she decided to get right to the important business, before Henry returned.

Caroline sat down in a chair at the table and pulled the boy close, so she could look him directly in the eyes.

"Jim, we are most grateful that you and Pearl have come here. We are very deeply sorry for your loss. We are going to do our best for you. Do you understand?"

His heart stabbed with pain, the boy fought back tears and nodded.

"I'm very sorry to ask you to do this, Jim, but it is important that you say nothing to anyone else about your life before you came here. We are going to tell people that you and your sister are orphans, which is of course true. But for your sake we are going to let them think you came here from far away. You don't have to answer any questions about your past, Jim. That way you will not lie. It is past now. Do you understand? Is that all right with you, Jim?" Her eyes were growing moist and her hands beginning to shake as she finished.

The idea that he wouldn't have to talk about the events that even now were breaking his heart was a great relief to the boy. Yes, he thought. That is definitely all right. And besides, his mother had told him that when he got to his new home he should be obedient and unquestioning. He nodded his agreement.

"Oh, thank goodness," Caroline said tearfully, wrapping her arms around the boy.

Then, after a moment, she pulled back, a concerned look spreading across her face. She looked again into the boy's eyes, "What about your sister, Jim? Is she old enough to understand? What does she remember?"

"It's all right, ma'am," he answered confidently. "She's too young."

~~~

As it turned out, Caroline didn't need to worry about her husband being charged with any crime.

About eight hours after Henry Wrenn's wagon had rolled across the bridge leaving town, Frieda Bray appeared before the Scruggs residence on Floyd Street, at the head of a delegation of the Benevolent Daughters of the Lord, on a mission of mercy.

"Here we are, ladies!" Frieda announced to the women, as they emerged from their carriages. After shaking the wrinkles from her skirt, she addressed them, "Let us first offer a prayer of thanksgiving, before we proceed with our Christian duty."

Frieda had, of course, notified the press, so that the news of the compassion and selflessness of she and her friends could be duly published for the public benefit. After confirming that the reporter was close enough to hear, she bowed her head and began, speaking as loudly as she thought proper for a lady of her station.

"Our blessed and merciful Father in heaven, we give thanks for the opportunity to come once again to the assistance of the poor and unfortunate souls you have placed among us. On this glorious day, we give thanks for the many generous acts of kindness and mercy you have entrusted to the Benevolent Daughters of the Lord. Amen."

"Amen," the gathered ladies responded in unison.

For George Carter, it was a glorious day indeed. He couldn't remember a story he enjoyed writing more than the one he penned that evening.

An impressive assembly of the Benevolent Daughters of the Lord gathered yesterday afternoon on Floyd Street, home (until recently) of the despairing mother referenced in our story of the 4th inst., with the purpose of delivering solace and relief to the unfortunate woman, and with the further intent to facilitate her children's immediate enrollment into the Danville Orphanage. Led in their most admirable philanthropic endeavor by the esteemed Mrs. W. T. Bray, one of the most generous benefactors of the many necessitous paupers of our fair city, the said Benevolent Daughters, whose generosity and munificence are exceeded only by their piety and Christian humility, were sadly disappointed to discover that the objects of their intended charity were no longer in need of it, the children in issue having evidently relocated and their mother having shuffled off this mortal coil.

As there are invariably among this class of persons a multitudinous body of physical relations, it is uncertain into which particular bosom the young lambs have now been gathered. Whoever among their kin took the children, they were thoughtful enough to leave behind the mother's body, thus presenting the most Benevolent Daughters with the unanticipated opportunity of seeing to the proper Christian disposal of same, an obligation they dutifully undertook, despite having been denied their principal objective.

From across the street, Isaac Bell watched the proceedings briefly, then moved toward a knot of ragged boys who he had seen watching from a distance. From one of them he learned that Gem and his sister had left at daybreak, with a well-dressed old man driving a farmer's wagon being pulled by a big red horse. Bell allowed himself a slight smile as he walked back toward the station, satisfied that he had done his duty.

~~~

Henry Wrenn was kin to most of the people in Maple Grove. His great-great grandfather Peter Wrenn had moved to the county while the Revolution was underway, when the place was still a dangerous unsettled frontier. Along the banks of a wide fast-flowing creek, Peter carved out a farm, built a grist mill, planted roots and sunk them deep. He spread his seed across the land. The farm on which Henry was born and raised—the same farm he now owned and tended 77 years later—was a 150-acre slice of Peter's original holdings.

In a time and place where large families were the norm, Henry had only one sibling—a twin brother named Asa. In April 1861, amid the fervor that followed Virginia's secession, Henry and Asa enlisted in the infantry company one of his uncles was raising, a motley aggregation of enthusiastic and naïve farm boys who called themselves the "Maple Grove Riflemen" (despite the fact that few of them had ever fired a rifle). Five months later Henry returned to Maple Grove bearing Asa's body, which had been drained of life by dysentery in a Richmond field hospital. Although the enthusiasm was gone, the sense of duty remained, so with his brother duly buried in the family cemetery, Henry was preparing to return to his regiment, despite the pleas of his grief-stricken mother, when a letter arrived from Captain Wrenn, advising that, for now, the Commonwealth did not require the services of Private Wrenn. Henry and his father tended the farm as the war ground on, until in October 1864 the Commonwealth decided that Private Wrenn's services were required after all, directing him to join the few surviving Maple Grove Riflemen, shivering and starving in the trenches around Petersburg. In the closing scenes of the war, Henry served honorably and he managed to stay alive. His mother's prayers were answered when she saw him in early April 1865, walking down the road toward home, ragged, skinny and exhausted, carrying a bouquet of dogwood blossoms.

It was a season of privation and profound change. The family that had shared the farm with them for generations was now gone, liberated by the war and in pursuit of happiness elsewhere. Henry and his parents planted a small crop of tobacco that year, but concentrated their efforts on making sure they grew and preserved enough food to get them through the winter. Like most of the families around them, their efforts were made more difficult by the fact that the war had made scarce two of farming's most precious necessities—strong men and draft animals. In search of the latter, Henry traveled to Tennessee that January.

His journey took him to a farm near Chattanooga, home of descendants of one of his maternal great grand-uncles—and therefore his distant cousins. He married one of them and brought her home with him, along with a half dozen mules purchased with money his mother had wisely squirreled away when the storm clouds of war had gathered, and a big Clydesdale stallion named Buck, a wedding gift from his bride's parents.

They sold four of the mules to neighbors, on credit. With the two that remained, and with Buck, Henry broke the land that spring.

For a few years, they rented part of the farm to a sharecropper. Later, Henry hired hands in the summer. But neither suited him. In 1874 he told his elderly father, "A man can't work land right without loving it. And a man can't love land without owning it." Do what you think best, the old man had replied. So, beginning in 1875, Henry made the unconventional decision to reduce significantly the amount of tobacco they grew, and to take on nothing that he and Caroline couldn't do themselves. From that point on they raised small crops, and those crops provided them with all they needed.

In time Henry's parents joined his brother in the family cemetery. And there were no additions to compensate for the subtractions. He and Caroline had come to realize eventually that something about their failed first pregnancy had eliminated the possibility of any others. This was a source of great disappointment to both of them, but they left it unspoken, out of concern for the feelings of the other.

For over 40 years Henry and Caroline lived alone, raising their crops and tending their animals. They lived comfortably, but simply, kept healthy and vigorous by good food and hard work. They rarely left the farm, other than to attend church, two miles away. Contented, they grew old, deeply and profoundly attached to each other, to their home, and to the land.

But there was a great untapped potential in both of them—a potential that could only be realized as parents. And now, into the twilight of their lives two children had unexpectedly fallen. And Henry, like Caroline, resolved to make the best of it.

With a full heart, he took young Jim under his wing, determined to teach him all he knew.

~ ~ ~

And so the boy Jim shadowed the man Henry Wrenn every day, at first out of obedience to his mother, but soon because he came to love and enjoy farm work. A quick and eager learner, he soaked up everything Henry could teach him. And the old man had the accumulated wisdom of generations to pass on.

That winter they cut and stacked wood, they built a new curing barn, they tended to the livestock, they kept the cow milked and the smoke house smoking. Henry taught Jim to hitch and harness the horse and mules. He watched with pride as the boy's capacity for carrying pails of milk and buckets of well water grew daily, as he began to fill out the sturdy new work clothes Caroline had made for him.

When spring approached, they prepared a plant bed and seeded the tobacco. When the earth thawed and dried, Henry taught Jim to plow and prepare a vegetable garden and, later, a tobacco field. When the sow farrowed, he taught Jim how to cut the little boars. They built and repaired fences, they hauled and forked hay.

Henry taught the boy how to make and sharpen tools, and he took him along on his occasional trips to the depot store, where he bought guano, coffee, sugar, and hundred pound sacks of dried pinto beans.

In early summer Buck drew a plow through the red soil, creating the beds and shaping the rows into which they dropped chunks of seed potatoes, beans, and seedlings—tomatoes and tobacco. In the sweltering heat of long summer days they chopped weeds, squished bugs, hauled buckets of water to thirsty plants, and watched as their crops grew rapidly, affirming the value of their labor.

When the tobacco began to ripen and yellow, Henry and Jim "pulled" it—they broke off the ripe leaves and laid them in a "slide," a sled that Buck pulled to the barn, where Caroline strung the leaves together and hung them on tobacco sticks, which Henry, in turn, hung in barns to cure. When the barns were full, Henry fired them, and he and Jim slept outside under sheds on the warm summer nights, keeping the fires tended and burning.

From the gardens, they harvested vegetables and from the orchard, fruit. They cut and shocked the corn and hay. By late fall the gardens were winding down and the cellar was full. Henry taught Jim how to extract honey from their beehives and, once it was cold, how to slaughter a hog and a steer. He taught him the stars and the moon signs—what meant it was time to plant, what meant it was time to harvest, what meant it was time to kill a hog, what meant the fish were biting, and what meant they weren't.

Henry took Jim with him when he carried their corn to the mill for grinding. When the air grew cold and wet for winter, they worked in the packing barn, stripping the cured tobacco and bundling it for market.

On Sundays, they rested. And on those days Henry told the boy the stories of 150 years and beyond—the stories that came with the farm, of the lives that finished in the graveyard behind their house.

"Take care of this place," Henry told him often, "and it will take care of you. Love it, and it will love you back."

Jim fell asleep every night with the satisfying exhaustion that comes from a good day's work. He still dreamed of his parents—his Daddy's laugh, his mother's sad smile. Sometimes he woke from dreams so real that it took a few minutes for him to remember that he wasn't in their house in town, that he wasn't going with his mother to the spinning room that day. But gradually, as the year wore on, the intensity of his dreams started to fade. Some nights his dreams didn't take him back to Mechanicsville at all. The grip those days held on his heart was loosening.

~~~

Henry usually plowed with a single horse, rather than a team, at first out of necessity and later because he had come to prefer it that way. Over time he grew so attached to Buck, a docile giant, that he quit using mules, which he found to be consistently stubborn and temperamental.

Soon after he had returned from Tennessee with the original Buck, Henry worked out an arrangement with a nearby farmer who kept Clydesdales on his place, trading annual stud service from Buck for a broken and trained replacement every 20 years or so.

When the original Buck retired, about ten years after he had arrived, Henry named his replacement Buck as well. The current Buck was the third of that name to work the Wrenn farm, and the summer of 1918 would be his last. That fall Buck number four arrived on the farm, beginning what would be a fine and productive career of his own.

~ ~ ~

Although elementary school education had been compulsory in Virginia since 1908, in the rural farming communities the law wasn't enforced. Some children went to school, but most didn't.

Henry and Caroline intended to send Jim to school, but when September arrived they decided to wait another year. Their motives were mixed. Because Henry enjoyed the boy's company, and because he still had a lot to teach him, he suggested the delay. Caroline readily assented, out of her concern that Jim's heart might still be too tender for the things she imagined the other children would say to him.

She no longer worried about their little community. Despite their unsatisfied curiosity, the neighbors had stopped asking questions. In obedience to both his biological and his foster mother, when the other children asked him about his past, Jim said nothing. Soon, like their parents, they too stopped asking.

When it came time to register for Sunday school that fall, it was the first time since the children's arrival that Caroline had been required to state their last names. Without hesitation, she wrote "Wrenn." Sometime earlier she had begun to refer to them as "our children," rather than as "the children." None of this was lost on Jim. He was Jim Wrenn now, and that was fine by him.

~~~

On November 11, 1918, an armistice was signed in France, ending what was then known as "the Great War." It had been the deadliest conflict in human history, taking the lives of over 17 million people. But the toll of the war was to be much greater than that. It was also responsible for the emergence of the deadliest pandemic in world history, a pandemic that would claim far more lives than the war itself.

America mobilized upon entering the war in 1917, gathering into its army millions of young men from farms, towns, and cities across the country. Their training camps became ideal vectors for the spread of disease. In March 1918, in Ft. Riley, Kansas, the Spanish Influenza took its first victim. Within a year, it would reach every country on the globe, killing as many as 100 million people—five percent of the world's population.

The epidemic struck southside Virginia in October 1918. On October 8, as the first deaths began to occur, the City of Danville ordered all schools, churches, and theaters closed, and the surrounding counties followed suit. A few days later, with the death toll still rising, the order was extended to all businesses and public gathering places. Temporary hospitals were established. The pall of death hung over the area, as it hung over the world.

By early November the worst seemed to be over. Schools and businesses, including the tobacco markets, reopened. The losses had been heavy, but the people began to return to life as normal.

~~~

Maple Grove had been spared. The school had closed, along with the churches. No one went to town. And with the tobacco markets closed, there was little reason to go. When the markets re-opened in November, and word spread that the crisis had passed, the folks of Maple Grove breathed a collective sigh of relief.

On a cool Monday morning in the last week of November, a few days before Thanksgiving, Henry drove the tobacco crop to Danville, with Jim by his side. As they approached the city he began to wonder if that had been a good idea. As they descended the long hill from North Danville to the river, the mill came into view and Henry could sense Jim stiffening and steeling his nerves. It was the first time either of them had been to Danville since the day they met on that cold January morning almost eleven months earlier. Henry wanted to say something soothing to Jim, but as he struggled to find the right words he realized that the best thing he could do in this moment was stay quiet. As Buck pulled the wagon over the bridge, which crossed into the city like a valley between the massive factories that flanked it along the riverfront, Henry glanced over at Jim and saw that he was sitting bolt upright, staring straight ahead, refusing even to acknowledge the factory as they passed by it. Such a terrible burden for a child to carry, Henry thought, while Jim was silently repeating the words his mother had emphasized—don't be sad.

Once they were over the river and out of sight of the mill, the tension in the wagon lessened. But there was still a sense of unease about the town.

The flags and banners decorating Main Street were evidence of the end of the war, the victory announced two weeks earlier. But the mood of the city wasn't celebratory. The shock of the deadly flu epidemic had not yet worn off.

It was not entirely somber though, especially at the tobacco warehouses. The sudden popularity of cigarettes, and the demand that followed the government's decision to issue them to the soldiers, had sent tobacco prices surging. Prices were at an all-time high as Henry pulled his wagon into the yard at the Planter's Warehouse that day.

Their tobacco was unloaded and laid in piles amid long rows already crowded with the tobacco of other farms. A knot of farmers followed the grader who moved down the rows, inspecting and assigning a quality grade to each pile of golden leaves. Another group followed behind an auctioneer, who walked down the rows leading a handful of buyers, auctioning off the piles.

In the past, it had sometimes taken two days or more to complete a sale. But as the warehouses competed for farmers' business they had steadily improved the sales process, speeding it up. By 1918 farmers could expect to have their tobacco sold the same day they brought it in. Often they could be back on their farms that very night.

Henry did not want to stay overnight in Danville, so he was pleased to see the sales proceeding quickly. Jim found the process fascinating and he drank it all in, encouraged by Henry to watch carefully "so you can handle this for me someday."

Tobacco was selling briskly that afternoon, and at good prices. The sweet aroma of the cured leaf, the chatter of the farmers, and the hum of the auctioneer were all enchanting to young Jim. The only evidence of war and plague was the improvised face mask the auctioneer was wearing—a handkerchief wrapped across his face, which caused his chant to sound strangely muffled. Jim laughed at the sight of the man's beard bouncing up and down as he called out bids, hanging a foot below the handkerchief that concealed his mouth. For a while that day, the sadness was gone, without any effort on his part.

~~~

Every Thanksgiving, one of Henry's many relatives in the community would invite him and Caroline to join their family for dinner. It was never the same family in consecutive years, and Caroline sometimes wondered how they decided whose turn it was. Of course, the invitations were given out of kindness, so the old childless couple wouldn't have to be alone on the holiday, but for Caroline the dinners were poignant affairs. On those days, in homes brimming with children and grandchildren, she felt as if the word "BARREN" was stitched across her chest.

When the usual invitation came that year, she declined politely. "We're just going to enjoy a quiet family dinner at home this year," she said, her heart aglow. She put a feast on the table that day, the first Thanksgiving of her life on which she could play the role of mother.

Jim's heart was not entirely healed—it never would be. But he felt the warmth that day too. And when he looked at the food on the table, knowing that he had helped raise and harvest nearly all of it, it gave him a satisfying feeling he'd never experienced before. And he thought of something his mother used to say: everything's going to be all right.

~~~

Then it returned, worse than before. In December, a second wave of the Spanish flu swept across the area. More emergency hospitals opened. Even the city's most famous landmark, the old mansion where the last Confederate cabinet meeting had occurred, was converted into a temporary hospital as the others were overrun with patients.

This time, Maple Grove wasn't spared. First it struck the Fields family, who lived about a mile down the road from Henry and Caroline. Five-year-old Frances Fields was the first to die. Two days later her mother Katherine joined her, within hours of the death of the infant girl she was still nursing. His wife and daughters hadn't even been buried yet when Daniel Fields died two days later. Only a three-year-old son remained, and he never had so much as a sniffle.

Maple Grove, like Danville, was on lockdown now. The school, the depot store, and the churches all closed. Neighbors spread the news of the tragedy in the Fields family to one another, by shouting it from a distance. Caroline fried a chicken, and Henry and Jim carried it to the Fields' home, along with a pan of cornbread. They stopped about 50 yards from the house, where members of the immediate family were gathered on the porch. Recognizing Daniel's father Ira, another of the original Maple Grove Riflemen, Henry sat the basket on the ground and shouted to them, "We're terribly sorry for your loss. God bless y'all." Ira never heard him, having been left nearly deaf from artillery fire all those years ago. But one of the ladies on the porch answered with a nod of her head and a slight wave, and Henry and Jim returned home.

Soon afterwards the word spread that Richard Otis, having survived the trenches in France, had died of the disease on his way home.

Dorothy Atwell was the next Maple Grove victim. Only 24 years old, she died on Christmas Eve, as her husband and three young children watched in horror.

Dozens were sick. The disease, which was being called "the grippe," attacked quickly and seemingly at random. Sometimes within hours of the appearance of the first symptoms—a headache or a fever—the victims would be dead, literally drowning as their lungs were flooded with blood and mucous. There was no known cure or preventative. And it was vicious. Whereas previous flu outbreaks tended to claim mostly the old and the weak, this one seemed to prefer children and otherwise healthy young adults. So, Caroline and Henry watched Jim and Pearl's faces carefully, looking for signs and praying they wouldn't see any, in an atmosphere of dread and helplessness that they shared with households all across the world that year.

~~~

Despite the gloom in the air, Caroline Wrenn was determined that they would have an enjoyable family

Christmas together. Truth be told, she admitted to herself, for her it was a dream come true.

Henry cut down a small cedar tree and on Christmas Eve they all decorated it with homemade ornaments. Caroline baked sugar cookies and a sweet potato pie. She read the Christmas story aloud and they sang carols together. Even Pearl seemed to get into the spirit.

Because of the epidemic, it had not been possible to go shopping that season, so there were no store-bought toys on Christmas morning. But Caroline had made a ragdoll for Pearl and Henry gave Jim a pocketknife he'd had since he was a boy. Jim carried that knife the rest of his life.

That night, after the children were asleep, Henry and Caroline rocked before the fireplace, as they did most nights. But this night Caroline left her knitting in the basket on the floor. They rocked in silence for a while, then she reached over and took Henry's hand. "It's been a beautiful day, Mr. Wrenn," she said, her voice quaking with emotion.

~~~

The next morning, Henry awoke with a headache. He went about the morning chores, as usual. But as he and Jim were returning from milking, he felt weak and had trouble carrying the pail. By the time they got back to the house, Henry was bathed in a cold sweat.

"Caroline," he said, standing in the kitchen doorway, "I'm not well."

Despite wanting, with every fiber of her being, to wail and moan, Caroline kept calm. She knew there was no point in sending for a doctor. He probably couldn't come, and even if he did, there was nothing he could do in any event. So, she became a nurse. She put Henry to bed and forbade the children from entering the room. She made soup and hot tea. She bathed his aching sweaty body and she kept his chamber pot emptied and clean. She knew Henry had the grippe, there was no doubt about that. Although she didn't know the survival rate, she knew that most of its victims survived. She was determined to see Henry through the trial, and equally determined to keep the children safe.

Caroline stayed by Henry's side, leaving only when absolutely necessary. Meanwhile Jim kept the fire going and kept the animals tended. When not working outside, he stood anxiously outside the bedroom door, awaiting instructions from Caroline.

After three days, the symptoms began to abate. The fever was gone and Henry began to recover his strength. He was able to sit up in bed and take solid food. Caroline still wouldn't let the children into the room, but she allowed them to speak to him through the open door. "What do you want me to do, sir?" Jim asked him nervously. The old man's bushy mustache lifted, betraying a hidden smile. "Look after things till I'm better, Jim. You know what to do. Just do whatever needs doing." Holding his hand, Caroline smiled too.

~ ~ ~

Unlike the previous year, which had ended in snow and record-breaking cold, the last day of 1918 arrived warm and sunny. Henry felt well enough to get out of bed, but Caroline disagreed. "Not yet, Mr. Wrenn," she insisted. "One more day."

To humor him, she did consent to his request that the shutters be opened. From his bed, Henry drank in the sunshine, feeling relieved and refreshed. Not since he was six years old had he gone five straight days without working, and he didn't care for it. "All right, Caroline. One more day. But I'm tired of being spoiled and babied like this. There's work to do and I aim to get back to it tomorrow."

But Henry's apparent recovery was just the eye of a fatal storm passing over him. As was so often the case with the grippe, the lull portended not that the disease had fled the field in defeat, but rather that it had merely paused, reforming for a final savage charge. Instead of joining the rest of the family at the supper table that evening, as Henry had planned, by dark he was having trouble catching his breath. When he breathed deeply, there was a piercing pain in his chest. When he tried to breath more shallowly, he felt like he was choking. The fever had returned, worse now than before. And the cough which tortured his tender throat brought with it vile greenish-yellow clumps of slime, physical evidence of the war his lungs were losing.

Henry Wrenn was as strong as most men half his age, but no amount of human strength was sufficient to overcome this virus once it had chosen a victim. The end came quickly. By midnight his wheezing attempts to breathe were slowing. He had long since lost consciousness. Stroking his hair and squeezing his hand, Caroline whispered softly, over and over, "My darling Henry," her tears dropping onto his face like a soft summer rain.

Standing outside the doorway to the room, Jim wept with her—his 8-year-old heart crushed yet again.

~~~

That morning, from across the road, their neighbor Odell Maxey had hollered the news that Ruby Forrest was sick, as Caroline, Jim, and Pearl were sitting silently around the kitchen table. Without lifting her eyes Caroline spoke, "Jim, please tell Odell that the grippe has killed Mr. Wrenn." Obediently, the boy stepped out onto the porch and yelled out, like a lament, "The grippe has killed Mr. Wrenn." Odell snatched the cap off his head, said something Jim couldn't understand, then hurried away.

And so the news of Henry's death spread throughout Maple Grove. Neighbors brought food, leaving it by the road that ran in front of the house, shouting their condolences from there. A few of Henry's cousins came to the door, prepared to put themselves at risk for the sake of comforting their friends. Caroline thanked them warmly, and politely turned them away. "We're thankful for your kindness, but it's not safe here. We'll appreciate your visit when this has passed," she told them.

Old Ira Fields wouldn't be deterred so easily. Standing before the door and yelling, as the hard of hearing sometimes do, he hollered, "You let me in, Caroline! There ain't nothing in this house that can hurt me and I intend to pay my respects!" Worn out by grief, it was a struggle for Caroline to yell back loudly enough for him to hear her, "Thank you kindly Mr. Fields, but we're not receiving company right now." He stamped his foot in protest, but eventually marched away.

Some of the men in the community dug a grave next to those of Henry's parents and brother, careful to leave sufficient room for Caroline when her time came. There were no more coffins at the depot store and, with the businesses in Chatham and Danville closed, it was impossible to get them. So the gravediggers fashioned one from some milled pine lumber one of them had, leaving it on the bed of a wagon they positioned conveniently against the front porch. The preacher helped Caroline and Jim put Henry's body in it, and Buck pulled his old friend to the family graveyard.

There was no funeral. Though technically not banned, as they were in much of the country during the crisis, it was commonly believed that the bodies of flu victims were especially contagious, and the people of Maple Grove would not jeopardize their neighbors for the sake of a ceremony, however important. So only Caroline and the children were present as the preacher and his helper lowered Henry's coffin into the waiting grave. Jim helped as they shoveled in the dirt, covering Henry in the ground he loved.

~~~

After a few more weeks, the crisis had passed. Like animals who had been hiding from a predator, people began to peer cautiously out of their safe places, and to creep gingerly back into normalcy.

Caroline bore her grief with strength. She and Henry had not been apart for more than a day in nearly 53 years and the wound of the loss would never heal. But, like Henry, she valued practicality. She would grieve, but she would grieve while going about the life they had built for themselves, just as Henry would have wanted.

Nothing was said by Caroline or Jim about what the change would mean for him. Jim understood the responsibility that now fell onto his eight-year-old shoulders without being told and he carried on as before, now doing alone the things Henry had taught him. There would be no childhood for him. He was now, in some sense, a head of household.

Most of the difficult winter work had been finished before Henry fell sick. The hogs had been slaughtered and the tobacco had been stripped and tied. But the hardest work of winter remained undone.

Keeping the curing fires going in the tobacco barns required lots of wood. Less wood was needed for cooking and for heating the house, but a substantial amount nonetheless. Because the wood needed to season and dry for a year, it had to be cut a year in advance. This was the major work of January and February—felling and sectioning the trees, splitting the wood. It meant long hard days, hands blistered by ax and saw.

Jim tried. Henry had taught him how to keep an ax oiled and sharpened, how to fell a tree safely, how to section and split the wood. He knew what to do and he wanted desperately to do it. His spirit was willing, but his flesh was weak. He went out every morning after breakfast and gave it his best, coming home dead tired every day for evening chores. However hard he tried, however, there was no escaping the fact that his eight-year-old arms couldn't swing an ax with the strength needed to generate a year's supply of firewood.

On a mild sunny Monday morning in mid-January, just after sunrise, Jim was sharpening his ax for the day's work when he heard the sound of an approaching wagon. Turning toward the rising sun, looking down the road that runs through Maple Grove, he saw not one, but three wagons approaching, filled with men and boys, laughing and boisterous. One by one they turned off the main road and parked, about 50 yards away. As they descended from the wagons Jim saw that they were carrying axes, saws, and mauls.

They worked all day, stopping only to enjoy the pans of hot food that Caroline brought them at dinner time. By the time the sun set that day, and they climbed back into the wagons, the Wrenn farm had a year's supply of firewood laid by. Jim didn't cry, but only because he knew he shouldn't.

~~~

There were other times that year that neighbors helped Jim, invaluable help that he never asked for but gratefully received and, over time, dutifully returned. But on most days in 1919, Jim Wrenn performed the jobs that had been Henry Wrenn's in 1918. He made mistakes, but he learned from them. And it all got done—the hogs got butchered, the gardens got harvested, and the tobacco got cured.

That spring Caroline planted a dogwood by Henry's grave, where it still stands today. Every day she milked the cow, churned the milk, cooked the meals, and tended the chickens, pigs, and gardens. She washed, made and mended their clothes. In the heart of the summer she strung the tobacco Jim pulled. She was 72 years old, with a 150-acre farm, a five-year-old girl, and an eight-year-old boy, to whom she was deeply and increasingly devoted.

In August Caroline told Jim that she needed to measure him for the school clothes she was going to make. Had Henry been alive and well, Jim would not have objected. But he knew that he could not both go to school and take care of the farm. So he begged Caroline to let him wait another year, pretending that he didn't want to go, and insisting that the farm couldn't spare him. Torn between her maternal responsibility to see to Jim's education and her tender regard for his feelings and preferences (both springing from the intense love she now felt for him), Caroline eventually relented. Jim could stay home one more year.

With the help of a neighbor, Jim sold the tobacco crop in Danville that year. Once again prices were at an all-time high, hitting a peak that wouldn't be seen again for more than 30 years. As he rode home on a cold December evening, carrying in his pocket the reward for his work, Jim felt a confidence that Henry somehow knew, and that he was pleased.

~~~

Within a few months of their arrival, Pearl had begun calling Caroline "Ma." But she had been only four years old. For Jim, the situation was much more difficult. Even as his devotion to Henry and Caroline had matured into love, he was still carrying the pain of losing his parents. They were his Mama and Daddy, and he felt it would dishonor their memories to share those names with someone else. Henry and Caroline sensed his discomfort so they never asked to be called by any term of endearment. But neither were they willing to foreclose that possibility, so they never asked to be called anything more formal either. There was an awkwardness about the situation, but Jim had never called them anything other than sir and ma'am.

After breakfast on a warm morning in May 1920, Jim was walking toward the stable to retrieve Buck, so they could begin shaping the beds for planting. On his way, it occurred to him that he had forgotten to tell Caroline that he would need her help drawing the plants. Returning to the house, he found her bent over a flower bed, planting bulbs, with her back to him.

"Mama," Jim said, the word surprising him as it escaped from his mouth.

Startled, she stood quickly, then spun around to face him. Dropping to her knees Caroline took the boy by the shoulders and looked straight into his eyes. Anxiously, her voice cracking with emotion, she asked, "Did you call me Mama?" Jim glanced down at his feet, a lump rising in his throat, then lifted his eyes slowly to meet hers. Caroline studied his face, reading on it a pained request for permission. Sobbing, she threw her arms around him and pulled him tightly to her, repeating through her tears, "Thank you, Jesus. Thank you, Jesus."

~~~

The second winter after Henry's death, the men of Maple Grove had again come to the Wrenn farm to cut wood, once again rescuing Jim and once again finishing the job in a day.

The following year the wagons arrived again, unloading their cargo of woodcutters on a cold sunny morning in January. But as they began to assemble, one of the men said, "Well I'll be damned," capturing the attention of the others. He was looking at the Wrenn woodshed, stacked nearly to the top with freshly cut wood. In the distance, at the edge of the woods, they could see Jim, swinging his ax as vigorously as any of them could. Another man laughed and said, "That boy is a chip off the old block." "Looks like Jim don't need no help from us this year," someone else remarked, as the men began climbing back into the wagons, laughing and chatting.

Old Ira Fields stayed behind. "Go on without me, boys," he shouted to them. "I'll walk home."

Jim put his ax down when he noticed Mr. Fields approaching. Walking briskly, though with the aid of a stick, Ira Fields was tall and thin, wearing baggy clothes and the big bushy beard that his generation had favored, his hanging two feet below his chin, snow-white save for a long brown tobacco stain down the middle.

"Good morning, Mr. Fields," Jim hollered.

"Jim, you done finished cutting wood early this year. We was gonna help you cut it so we could have some of Caroline's pecan pie," Mr. Fields answered with a smile, talking loudly, as he always did.

"Yes, sir," Jim replied, "I'm just about done this year."

"Your Pa would be mighty proud of you boy. Mighty proud," the old man said as he lowered himself slowly to a seat on a tree stump. Jim could see that he intended to stay a while, so he sat down on the ground facing him.

"I knowed Henry Wrenn his whole life, boy. We played in them woods yonder when we was just chaps—me, him, and Asa," he said, pointing in the distance with his walking stick. "Raised us all kinds of sand in them days."

After a pause the old man asked, "Did Henry ever tell you about what he done at Five Forks?"

"No, sir," Jim answered, shaking his head.

Ira Fields bit a chunk off of the plug of tobacco he had taken from his breast pocket. He chewed thoughtfully for a few seconds, spit a stream of juice through his teeth and continued, a distant look in his eyes.

"We was whipped that day and whipped good. The generals had done left us out to hang while they was off somewhere eating shad. We was all running." He paused, spit again, then resumed.

"A few of us Maple Grove boys had done hightailed it into the woods. We outrun Henry, but he was coming too. Him and Thomas Bedford. I was looking at 'em running when Thomas fell. He won't nothing but a boy. He had done took a ball in the knee." Ira was pausing thoughtfully after each sentence, as if calling to mind and reviewing each memory before speaking. And he was no longer shouting.

"Henry was close enough to the woods to make it easy if he kept on running. But when Thomas got knocked down, Henry dropped his rifle and picked that boy up. Threw him over his shoulder like a sack of feed and started toting him." Ira smiled at the memory. By now it seemed as if he was talking to himself.

"And right then some Yankee cavalry come out and was riding down on 'em. Henry coulda dropped that boy and made it to the woods. But what he done is he set Thomas down and he pulled a pistol outta his belt that he done picked up when the lines broke. Damned if Henry Wrenn didn't stand right in front of that boy and commence to unload that pistol at them Yanks." Ira stopped for a few moments, eyes twinkling.

He laughed and continued. "Henry never could shoot worth a damn. He didn't hit nothing. But he run 'em off. I reckon them Yanks figured it weren't worth getting shot to try to get them two ragged scarecrows."

After another long pause, Ira spoke again. "It was one the bravest things I ever seen a man do."

He stopped again, staring into the distance. After a few minutes, Jim began to wonder if he had said all he was going to say. But then Ira started up again, this time shouting as usual.

"After that me and William Davis went out there and helped Henry get Thomas to the woods. To tell you the truth, I was feeling a little bit ashamed. If it had been me, I woulda kept on running." Another long pause. "We all took turns toting that boy until we found what was left of the regiment that night." Another pause, longer still. "He died while they was cutting his leg off. He was hurting real bad, since there weren't nothing to numb him." The old man's cloudy eyes were misty now and he was speaking slowly, the volume fading. "He won't nothing but a boy. A damn shame and a waste. A damn shame."

After a quiet minute, Ira spoke again.

"A few days later they c'aht the whole lot of us at Sailor's Creek. More fine work by our fancy generals. Me and Henry was sitting there that night and he said to me, 'Ira, I don't see no sense in us staying here.'" The old man chuckled at the memory. "There won't but a few guards on us. So me and Henry slipped on out when it was real late. Took us a couple of days, but we just walked on back home to Maple Grove."

Ira sat quietly a few more minutes. Then suddenly, as if the spell had broken, he slapped his knee and pushed himself up with his walking stick.

"Henry Wrenn was a fine man. As good a man as there ever was." Turning to face the boy he said, his voice rising again, "He'd be right proud of you, Jim."

~~~

After one more attempt, Caroline gave up trying to get Jim to go to school. He carefully hid his desire to go behind the reality that his responsibilities on the farm didn't permit it. Caroline, unwilling to force him, acceded on the condition that she would teach him to read at home.

On the night of what was to be their first lesson, Caroline sat beside Jim, her Bible on the table before them, lit by a lantern. She opened it and told Jim to follow along as she drew her finger across the page, beneath the words she was slowly reading and carefully enunciating.

"In the beginning God created the heaven and the earth."

She was astonished when Jim interrupted her and began reading aloud, "And the earth was without form, and void; and darkness was upon the face of the deep."

"Well I declare!" Caroline exclaimed. Then, eyes narrowing, she said, "Maybe you already know these verses." Flipping randomly to a page near the middle, she pointed to a sentence, slid the book toward Jim and asked, "What does this say?"

He read aloud: "He raiseth up the poor out of the dust, and lifteth the needy out of the dunghill." Looking up and into Caroline's widening eyes, Jim said, "I already know how to read, Mama. I learned a long time ago. Reading ain't hard."

"But how, Jim?" she asked.

"When I realized what was on the fans, I just figured it out from there," he answered.

Puzzled, Caroline asked, "The fans?"

"The fans in church. You know, with the picture on one side and writing on the other. I already knew how to say the Lord's Prayer and the 23rd Psalm, I just didn't know what the words looked like. When I figured out that the Lord's Prayer was on the back of a fan, I just matched the writing to the words I knew. I learned a lot that way. Same with the hymnal. I just looked at the words and matched them to what the folks was singing. Once I figured out what sounds went with what words, it was easy."

Caroline sat silently a few moments, looking at Jim in wonder.

"Well shut my mouth. Don't that beat all! Bless your heart, Jim. I reckon you don't need this old woman to teach you after all," she said, beaming.

~~~

By the time he was 12 years old, Jim had already grown as tall as his father had been. He had Lillie's brown eyes and Fuller's sandy blonde hair. No one in Maple Grove would ever know the resemblance, however, as no one in Maple Grove had ever seen his parents. Over time Jim's origin was forgotten, or dismissed as unimportant. As he grew into his teens, what the people of Maple Grove recognized in him were his broad shoulders, the determination in his eyes, the strength of his bearing. It was not uncommon for old-timers to tell him that he favored his father. They meant Henry Wrenn.

~~~

Pearl was a filly who wouldn't be broken. The fussy disobedient child grew into a rebellious young woman. At first Caroline attributed the difficulties with Pearl to the trauma the child had endured. Then, over time, she began to blame herself, alternately believing she should have been more, or less stern with Pearl. At times, she punished the child in the conventional ways. Other times she tried to reason with her, allowing misbehavior to go unpunished. Neither method produced any discernable change in Pearl. The girl was consistently sullen and disrespectful, nearly always wearing a scowl.

At 6 years old, Pearl began attending school, walking each day to the two-room schoolhouse a mile away. Always a poor student, she nevertheless enjoyed school, perhaps because it increased her opportunities for corruption and rebellion.

Over the years Jim had exchanged the mountain twang he had arrived with for the softer drawl of the Piedmont. He softened his vowels, and instead of emphasizing or adding r's, he dropped them. So, for example, "tobacco" had been "tabakker" but was now "tabacca", "tired" had been "tarred" but was now "tie-ud," and so on. City people might find fault with his grammar, but he spoke as his neighbors did. It was different with Pearl. As she grew older her manner of speaking became increasingly rude and rough. She imitated the speech of the most vulgar people, those who country folks sometimes called "white trash." She seemed to delight in speaking loudly and crudely. "Why do you insist on trying to sound common?" an exasperated Caroline once asked her, drawing a wry smile from Pearl.

At home Pearl increasingly took over the responsibilities of the aging Caroline. She could cook and sew and churn and pickle and clean. She could milk a cow, dress a chicken, string tobacco, and make sausage. But there was an attitude of resentment in all she did. She never seemed happy.

As she began to pass into womanhood she wore her dark brown hair cut short, flapper-style. She might have been pretty, had she ever smiled. She accepted the cigarettes offered by the bad boys attracted to her foul mouth and her blossoming figure. And she discovered the affinity for alcohol that had been lurking in her genes.

~~~

By November, what Jim and Caroline had been suspecting for a couple of months was no longer in doubt. Caroline's denial was rapidly turning into distress. Jim, troubled deeply, recalled his mother's words from that fateful night long ago: "Look after your sister, Gem."

He caught up with Pearl as she was walking to school, making sure they would be out of sight and earshot of Caroline. She gave him the information he requested, showing no remorse or concern, lighting a cigarette as he marched away.

Ben Rowlett lived on a farm on the eastern edge of Maple Grove. Like Jim, he was eighteen years old, three years older than Pearl. Jim knew him, but had never enjoyed his company, so they had never become friends. He was shoveling out a barn stall, when Jim walked up, surprising him.

"Morning, Ben."

"Morning, Jim," Ben answered, somewhat apprehensively.

"I come to congratulate you, Ben," Jim said, drawing closer.

"Congratulate me? What for?"

"Your marriage, of course. You and Pearl will make a good couple," Jim said, eyes burning.

"What the hell are you talking about, Jim. I ain't getting married," Ben said dismissively, moving toward the stall door.

Jim stepped forward, blocking the door. "Oh sure you are, Ben. I stopped at the preacher's house on the way over here to confirm it. Saturday at one o'clock. Pearl says it's going to be a small, family-only wedding. I think that's a good idea."

Ben grunted, avoiding eye contact. "Suppose I don't want to get married," he said disdainfully.

Jim took another step forward, noticing that Ben flinched and inched backwards as he did. "You're marrying Pearl this Saturday, Ben." He paused, sensing Ben's fear. "Of course, if something should happen to you before then we would have to move the date back. Like if you had a broke leg, or if your head was to get bashed in." After giving Ben a few moments to reflect on that, or to answer the challenge, Jim continued. "But as long as nothing like that happens to you between now and Saturday, I reckon you'll be getting married."

It was a simple ceremony, attended only by Ben's parents, Caroline, and Jim; Pearl scowling throughout. When the preacher declared them man and wife, Ben looked like a criminal defendant, having his sentence pronounced.

Three months later, on February 5, 1930, Dottie Rowlett was born, launching Pearl on what was to be a prolific maternal career.

~~~

In the decades to come, the people of Maple Grove called them "the Hoover days." There was no money. For two years in a row, Jim took his tobacco crop to town to sell, then brought it back home unsold. There were no buyers, at any price.

Having purchased his guano on credit (as they always had), now he was unable to pay for it. Wyatt Challis, the store owner, sent out hand-written pleas to his customers: "I know times are hard, but without some payment we cannot meet our obligations to our suppliers. If you cannot pay your bill entirely, please pay what you can."

Humiliated, Jim went to see him, intending to offer his labor as a partial payment, only to learn that four local farmers had already made the same offer. Over the next few days, even more would. The worry on Mr. Challis' face was unsettling. "Mr. Challis, you have my word that I will pay you in full as soon as we can sell some tobacco," Jim told him, burning with shame.

That evening during supper there was none of their usual chatter about the day's events. Deep in thought, Jim's despondency shaded the room as they ate silently. Then Caroline noticed him look up quickly, staring off into a corner. After a few seconds, he put down his knife and fork, took a long drink of milk and looked toward her, announcing, "I will never buy anything on credit again." Caroline blinked, sensing he had more to say. He continued, "From now on if we don't have the money for something, we'll have to make do without it. I will never borrow money again. Ever."

The next spring Jim spread onto his fields the bedding from the coop and barn stalls, together with all the manure he could gather from the pastures. He raised his crop without guano.

~~~

On the farms that were self-sufficient, there was no money, but enough to eat. On the farms that were not, there was neither money nor enough to eat.

The Wrenns had always prioritized food production, so even in the darkest days of the Depression, they didn't go hungry. Some of their neighbors were less fortunate. Often during those years Jim would pay with food for help he didn't need, as a way to share with his neighbors, while guarding their pride. Other times he'd deliver milk, eggs, or baskets of produce to needy families, with stories like, "We ended up with more than we know what to do with and just wondered if y'all could use it."

Nearly every Sunday after church and dinner, Jim took Caroline to visit Pearl's growing family, always leaving behind food.

They were lean years, and some families lost their farms to creditors. But there was no hoarding and there was no starvation. The community stepped up to help each other, and together they rode it out.

~~~

For Jim, the Depression years were proof that growing food was more important than growing a "cash crop." In hard times, people can do without tobacco, he realized, but they cannot do without food. And, he asked himself, what good is a cash crop if no one has any cash, especially if it takes borrowed money to make the crop? He went so far as to suggest to Caroline that they quit growing tobacco, but the idea so distressed her that he let it drop. She had known no other way for over 80 years. He would continue, for her sake.

With each year the situation worsened. Farmers, pressed for cash, increased production in an effort to make up for their losses in the previous year. So, with demand dropping, supply was ever increasing. Even when there were buyers, prices plummeted. It was a death spiral.

Relief came in 1933, with the Agricultural Adjustment Act. In order to stabilize prices, the federal government made cash payments to growers who restricted production. It wasn't much money, but to cash-strapped farmers and businesses, it was a godsend. Jim gave his payment directly to Wyatt Challis, clearing his debt and removing a weight from his shoulders. Two years later the Supreme Court declared the act unconstitutional, and Congress quickly substituted legislation that provided payments based on soil conservation practices. Finally, in 1938 a quota system was implemented. Growers were told at the beginning of each year how much they could grow, thereby assuring that production would reflect demand and that prices would stabilize at pre-Depression levels.

Jim found it all distasteful. After one of his many trips to the county seat to fill out forms, he said to Caroline, with disgust, "Mama, this ain't farming." But, farming or not, the program had helped the community survive.

~ ~ ~

Because he was a coward, Ben Rowlett made a good husband for Pearl. She bullied and badgered him, and he tolerated it. Not that standing his ground would have made any difference in the end. Trying to tame Pearl would have been like trying to tame a tornado. So every evening he braced himself with a long drink from a jug of whiskey he kept hidden in the barn, before coming inside to face the storm.

Pearl produced a new baby every two years, like clockwork. By 1938 there were five of them, with another one on the way.

Jim found the chaotic Rowlett household maddening—babies crying, toddlers and older children fighting, his sister's rough voice raised even higher than usual to be heard over the racket. But he dutifully took Caroline to visit them every Sunday after dinner. She enjoyed the company of her grandchildren, no matter how unruly they were. Sometimes Jim would wait it out in the barn with Ben. He always declined the jug when Ben offered it, but he had no trouble understanding its appeal to Pearl's beleaguered husband.

~~~

Buck was slowing down, and Jim knew he would soon have to be replaced. Buck number four had been a gelding, bringing to an end the stud-services-for-colt arrangement that Henry had made over 40 years earlier. If there was to be a fifth Buck, Jim would have to buy him.

His boyhood friend Allen Lightfoot, now the county extension agent, urged him to get a tractor instead. "A tractor can do the work of 12 horses for the cost of four."

"Well Allen, I don't need 12 horses. I don't even need four. All I need is one good one, and he'll keep me for 20 more years," Jim replied.

~~~

Clark and Myrtle Robertson bred Clydesdales on their farm about four miles from the Wrenn place. It was Clark's father who had made the deal with Henry Wrenn all those years ago, and the Robertson farm had been the source of the last four Bucks. In March 1939 Jim rode out to their place, to have a look at a colt they were willing to sell.

Clark Robertson was a pleasant man, in his mid-60s. A tobacco farmer of only average ability, horses were his passion. He greeted Jim with a smile and a friendly handshake. "He's a beauty, Jim. Gonna make a fine work horse. Comes from the same line that all y'all's horses have come from," Clark said, his enthusiasm sincere, as he led Jim into the stable.

The barn was lined with stalls down both sides. Clark stopped before the first stall on the right. In it stood a big bay Clydesdale gelding, his head hanging over the stall door, gazing curiously at the visitor.

"He's halter broke already, and I've started training him to the harness. He's got a good temper and is coming on fine. You'll need to work with him, but he'll be ready for the field in another year," Mr. Robertson said as he rubbed the horse's head.

Sliding open the stall door, Clark stepped inside saying, "Come on in and have a close look at him."

Jim stepped into the stall and pulled the door closed behind him while Mr. Robertson continued chattering excitedly about the horse. But Jim was having trouble following what he was saying, having become distracted by a creature in the opposite stall, who he had noticed as he was closing the stall door. There

139

was a nice-looking quarter horse in the stall across the way, but what had grabbed his attention was not the horse, but rather the young woman who was grooming it.

"Well, Jim? Do you?"

Returning his attention to Clark, Jim realized he was waiting for an answer to a question Jim hadn't heard. "I'm sorry, Mr. Robertson. I didn't hear you."

Had Jim been looking at the girl, he would've seen a slight smile spread across her face.

"I said do you want to take him out for a walk," Clark answered.

"Oh. Yes, sir. That would be good," Jim said, feeling foolish and keenly aware of it.

Speaking over Jim's shoulder, Clark said, "Julia, bring me a lead rope for this colt."

Jim had always found the feeling of being in a small stall with a big horse unsettling, but when the girl reached in to hand the rope to Mr. Robertson, he pressed back against the stall wall, never having felt more confined and anxious than then. "Open the door Jim, and I'll bring him out," Clark said as he fastened the rope to the halter.

The girl had not returned to the other stall, but was standing in the aisle watching them as Mr. Robertson brought out the horse. Wearing an apron over a light blue dress that fell to the ground, thick brown hair hung over her shoulders, framing a thin face anchored by dark brown eyes. Trying to force himself to concentrate on the horse, Jim fought the urge to stare.

140

As if suddenly aware that the two hadn't met, Mr. Robertson abruptly interrupted his Clydesdale monologue. "Jim, have you met our daughter Julia? Julia, this is Mr. Wrenn."

Startled, Jim pulled off his hat, nervously fumbling it so that it dropped to the barn floor. As he bent over to pick it up, mumbling some incoherent greeting as he did, the Clydesdale took a step, planting an enormous feathered hoof directly atop the unfortunate hat.

"How do, Mr. Wrenn," Julia said, laughter sparkling in her eyes.

Jim had never felt more ridiculous in his life.

~~~

Julia Robertson was an only child, and an improbable one at that. Myrtle Robertson was 42 when Julia was born, having become pregnant long after she and Clark had concluded that they were fated to be childless. Julia grew up living the rigorous life of a farm girl, even if a little spoiled as a child of old age. Her father's love of the outdoors and passion for raising horses passed easily onto her, her mother's snobbery and affectation did not.

For all of her 19 years, Julia had lived only about four miles from the Wrenn's farm. But because they didn't attend the same church or family reunions, her path had rarely crossed Jim's, and when it did, the nine-year difference in their ages had meant he didn't pay her any mind.

But after seeing Julia in the barn that day, Jim began to pay her a lot of mind. He was so consumed by her, in fact, that he was having difficulty thinking about anything else.

Caroline began to notice odd changes in Jim's behavior. Suddenly he seemed to be concerned about his appearance, a subject that had never before been of any interest to him. Having inherited his father's thin wispy beard, Jim had only shaved on Sunday mornings. But after the visit to the Robertson farm, Caroline noticed that he began shaving every day. And for the first time in his life, he made a clothing request, asking Caroline if she would please make him a new "Sunday shirt." With a little triangulation, she determined that the object that had appeared so unexpectedly on her maternal radar screen must be Clark and Myrtle Robertson's daughter.

The discovery came as a great relief to Caroline. For several years now she had been suffering the anxiety common to mothers with an unmarried adult child. Jim's highest priority, in her opinion, should be the pursuit of a wife, a matter to which Jim himself seemed utterly indifferent. She had found the situation exasperating, unsure which bothered her more—Jim being a 28-year-old bachelor, or his evident satisfaction with that state of affairs.

Caroline considered the matter sufficiently urgent to warrant the exercise of what she regarded as a maternal privilege under such conditions—she nagged her son. Sometimes she merely needled him, and other times it felt more to him like a harangue.

But after seeing Julia in the barn that day, Jim began to pay her a lot of mind. He was so consumed by her, in fact, that he was having difficulty thinking about anything else.

Caroline began to notice odd changes in Jim's behavior. Suddenly he seemed to be concerned about his appearance, a subject that had never before been of any interest to him. Having inherited his father's thin wispy beard, Jim had only shaved on Sunday mornings. But after the visit to the Robertson farm, Caroline noticed that he began shaving every day. And for the first time in his life, he made a clothing request, asking Caroline if she would please make him a new "Sunday shirt." With a little triangulation, she determined that the object that had appeared so unexpectedly on her maternal radar screen must be Clark and Myrtle Robertson's daughter.

The discovery came as a great relief to Caroline. For several years now she had been suffering the anxiety common to mothers with an unmarried adult child. Jim's highest priority, in her opinion, should be the pursuit of a wife, a matter to which Jim himself seemed utterly indifferent. She had found the situation exasperating, unsure which bothered her more—Jim being a 28-year-old bachelor, or his evident satisfaction with that state of affairs.

Caroline considered the matter sufficiently urgent to warrant the exercise of what she regarded as a maternal privilege under such conditions—she nagged her son. Sometimes she merely needled him, and other times it felt more to him like a harangue.

Clark and Myrtle Robertson bred Clydesdales on their farm about four miles from the Wrenn place. It was Clark's father who had made the deal with Henry Wrenn all those years ago, and the Robertson farm had been the source of the last four Bucks. In March 1939 Jim rode out to their place, to have a look at a colt they were willing to sell.

Clark Robertson was a pleasant man, in his mid-60s. A tobacco farmer of only average ability, horses were his passion. He greeted Jim with a smile and a friendly handshake. "He's a beauty, Jim. Gonna make a fine work horse. Comes from the same line that all y'all's horses have come from," Clark said, his enthusiasm sincere, as he led Jim into the stable.

The barn was lined with stalls down both sides. Clark stopped before the first stall on the right. In it stood a big bay Clydesdale gelding, his head hanging over the stall door, gazing curiously at the visitor.

"He's halter broke already, and I've started training him to the harness. He's got a good temper and is coming on fine. You'll need to work with him, but he'll be ready for the field in another year," Mr. Robertson said as he rubbed the horse's head.

Sliding open the stall door, Clark stepped inside saying, "Come on in and have a close look at him."

Jim stepped into the stall and pulled the door closed behind him while Mr. Robertson continued chattering excitedly about the horse. But Jim was having trouble following what he was saying, having become distracted by a creature in the opposite stall, who he had noticed as he was closing the stall door. There was a nice-looking quarter horse in the stall across the way, but what had grabbed his attention was not the horse, but rather the young woman who was grooming it.

"Well, Jim? Do you?"

Returning his attention to Clark, Jim realized he was waiting for an answer to a question Jim hadn't heard. "I'm sorry, Mr. Robertson. I didn't hear you."

Had Jim been looking at the girl, he would've seen a slight smile spread across her face.

"I said do you want to take him out for a walk," Clark answered.

"Oh. Yes, sir. That would be good," Jim said, feeling foolish and keenly aware of it.

Speaking over Jim's shoulder, Clark said, "Julia, bring me a lead rope for this colt."

Jim had always found the feeling of being in a small stall with a big horse unsettling, but when the girl reached in to hand the rope to Mr. Robertson, he pressed back against the stall wall, never having felt more confined and anxious than then. "Open the door Jim, and I'll bring him out," Clark said as he fastened the rope to the halter.

The girl had not returned to the other stall, but was standing in the aisle watching them as Mr. Robertson brought out the horse. Wearing an apron over a light blue dress that fell to the ground, thick brown hair hung over her shoulders, framing a thin face anchored by dark brown eyes. Trying to force himself to concentrate on the horse, Jim fought the urge to stare.

As if suddenly aware that the two hadn't m Robertson abruptly interrupted his Clydesdal monologue. "Jim, have you met our daughter Julia, this is Mr. Wrenn."

Startled, Jim pulled off his hat, nervously fur it so that it dropped to the barn floor. As he b over to pick it up, mumbling some incoherent greeting as he did, the Clydesdale took a step, p an enormous feathered hoof directly atop the unfortunate hat.

"How do, Mr. Wrenn," Julia said, laughter spa in her eyes.

Jim had never felt more ridiculous in his life.

~~~

Julia Robertson was an only child, and an improbable one at that. Myrtle Robertson was 42 when Julia was born, having become pregnant long after she and Clark had concluded that they were fated to be childless. Julia grew up living the rigorou life of a farm girl, even if a little spoiled as a child of old age. Her father's love of the outdoors and passio for raising horses passed easily onto her, her mother' snobbery and affectation did not.

For all of her 19 years, Julia had lived only about four miles from the Wrenn's farm. But because they didn't attend the same church or family reunions, her path had rarely crossed Jim's, and when it did, the nine-year difference in their ages had meant he didn't pay her any mind.

Just a few days before he was smitten by Miss Robertson, for example, Caroline had delivered a broadside at breakfast: "Why ain't you courting yet, Jim? It's time you got married. Pearl's got five babies already and another one on the way, and you ain't even got a girl!" Jim sighed deeply and got up to make his escape. "Well, Mama" he answered, pulling on his boots and stepping out onto the porch, "If it's a contest, I reckon Pearl's gonna win."

So naturally the prospect of Jim love-struck and altar-bound delighted her, giving her hope that she might yet live to see a Wrenn grandchild. She resolved to do her best to facilitate the transaction.

~~~

While Julia Robertson had been unknown to Jim before meeting her in her father's stable that morning, the opposite was certainly not true.

In the fall of 1933, having just dropped off a basket of apples at the home of a needy neighbor, Jim encountered Clark Robertson and his 13-year-old daughter at the gate as he was leaving. The men exchanged pleasantries, chatted briefly, and then Jim went on his way. "Daddy, who was that man?" Julia asked her father, as they continued on toward the house, bearing a basket of their own. "That's Jim Wrenn," he answered. "They live out on Clouded Hills Road. His Daddy died when that boy was only 8 years old and he's run that farm mi' near by himself ever since."

Being at the age when some girls begin to long for a romantic hero to adore, Julia was captivated. Although she didn't know Jim, and rarely saw him, in her imagination he grew ever more handsome, kind and generous. Her image of him became the standard by which she judged the local boys who sought her attention—and none of them measured up. In the language of a future generation, she had a crush on Jim and it had never gone away.

It was no accident that she had been in the barn that morning when Jim arrived. It was a moment she'd been waiting six years for.

~~~

Jim went back to the Robertson's farm two more times, ostensibly to look at the colt, and on both occasions he exchanged a few words with Julia, while a flight of butterflies danced in his stomach. Clark Robertson was only slightly annoyed at the second visit. But when Jim came a third time "to look at the horse," Mr. Robertson took offense.

While Jim pretended to be carefully examining the horse, buying time before he could speak to Julia on the way out, Clark lost his patience. "Are you seeing something wrong with that horse, Jim? Do you doubt I'm being honest with you?"

Jim recognized his blunder immediately. He had been so anxious to concoct an excuse for seeing Julia that he hadn't considered how Mr. Robertson might interpret his repeat visits. Fortunately, he had a legitimate means of escape.

"No sir, Mr. Robertson. This is as fine a horse as I've ever seen and I entirely trust your judgment of horseflesh." Jim paused before continuing, "But there is a problem, sir, and I've been hesitant to tell it to you."

"A problem? What problem?" Clark quickly asked.

"Well sir, this horse is worth every penny you're asking for him. But, well, I ain't got it. I want to buy him, but I won't have the money until we sell our crop this year."

"Oh hell, Jim! Is that all?" Clark brightened, relieved and amused. "Go on and take the horse. Just pay me when you can."

"I'm much obliged Mr. Robertson, but I reckon I'd rather wait till I have the money," Jim said, hoping Clark wouldn't be offended at his answer.

"All right Jim, I understand. This colt will be here when you're ready to come get him. And if you change your mind and want him sooner, you can go on and take him home and pay me later."

"Thank you, sir. I hope to get him this fall. Of course, if someone else comes along before I have the money, then…"

Clark interrupted him. "This horse will be here when you want him, Jim. As far as I'm concerned, he's yours."

Nodding to Julia as he left, Jim said, "Nice seeing you again, Miss Robertson."

Watching as he mounted Buck to leave, Clark remarked to his daughter, "That's a fine young man. Raised right."

Julia turned away, hiding her flushing face.

~~~

Now Jim found himself in a distressing situation. He ached to see Julia again, but could no longer visit her farm on the pretense of looking at the horse. It was enough to make him wish he was Baptist.

Other than occasional visits to the store or grist mill, and a once-a-year trip to Danville to sell tobacco, the only time Jim left the farm was to go to church. Church attendance was not optional in Maple Grove. Other than a handful of rebels and reprobates, everyone went.

But while Jim, Caroline, and Pearl's family dutifully attended services each Sunday at the Maple Grove Methodist Episcopal Church South, as the Wrenns had done since the church was founded, over 150 years earlier, the Robertsons were faithful members of the Mt. Sinai Baptist Church, located on the other side of Maple Grove. Absent a radical change in ecclesial loyalty, unprecedented in the community's history, the Wrenns and Robertsons would not see each other in church.

Thus, the only social excursions in Jim's life simply were not going to bring him into contact with Julia, something he wanted as much as anything he'd ever desired.

~~~

"I believe I'd like to go hear them make music over to the store this evening, Jim," Caroline said, lowering herself cautiously into a chair at the kitchen table.

"Do what, Mama?" Jim asked, as he filled his plate.

"I said, I believe I'd like to go over to the store tonight to hear the music. I hear tell Jimmy Craig and some of them Starks boys play real good and I've never heard them play."

Looking up from his dinner, Jim laughed. "Merc᾿ Mama. Why in the world would you want to go t᾿ some foolishness like that?"

"Well, I'm only 92 years old. Maybe I'll᾿ somebody there who wants to dance with᾿ answered playfully.

Jim snickered and shook his head. Spooning moᵉ potatoes onto his plate, he stopped abruptly when she continued.

"I hear tell everybody is going to see them play lately. I reckon we might be the only two people in Maple Grove who ain't been going."

~~~

Jim hitched the horse to a post, then helped his mother down from the wagon. A few dozen people had gathered already, some sitting on blankets in the grass, as four men tuned their instruments on the porch of the country store.

As Jim led Caroline toward the crowd, John Starks hurried over with a chair. "Evening Miz Wrenn," he said as he set the chair down and offered it to her. "Why thank you, Mr. Starks. You are a gentleman," she said kindly to the blushing young man as she took a seat.

From the moment they had arrived, both Jim and Caroline had been searching the crowd for Julia Robertson, while pretending to do nothing of the sort. When it was clear that she wasn't there, Caroline was nearly as disappointed as Jim.

Jimmy Craig stepped forward, his fiddle tucked ⬛ his arm, and addressed the audience. "We sho' ⬛ 'all coming out this evening. Me and the ⬛ g to play a few old tunes and we hope ⬛ em." Clean-shaven, tall and skinny, ⬛ was in his 50s but looked much older. Standing behind him were three younger men, holding a banjo, a guitar and a bass fiddle. Jimmy always had some combination of the Starks clan playing with him, but folks never knew which ones it was going to be. Esther and Harvey Starks had 13 children, eight boys and five girls, and there wasn't an instrument any of them couldn't play. Jimmy drew his bow across the strings sharply, as the Starks brothers joined in, the one playing guitar singing, "In the days of eighteen and one, peg and awl…"

It was a warm spring evening, the dogwoods and redbuds lining the road were blooming, and crickets and peepers were clamorously competing with the musicians. Under normal conditions, Jim might have enjoyed himself. But he'd only agreed to come in order to see Julia. Because she wasn't there, he didn't want to be there either. How soon can I suggest leaving without upsetting Mama, he wondered.

Distracted, he almost didn't hear Caroline when she spoke. "Jim, isn't that the Robertsons coming up yonder?"

~~~

Jim had looked up eagerly when Caroline spoke, seeing Mr. Robertson hitching his horse next to theirs. The Robertsons, like the Wrenns, still relied on horses for transportation in 1939, Clark continuing to insist stubbornly and defiantly that automobiles "won't last." Seeing Julia smoothing her dress after climbing down from the carriage, Jim felt an exhilarating rush, followed immediately by a knotted stomach. His heart racing, he defeated the powerful urge to stare at Julia, by concentrating instead on Jimmy Craig's hat, so nervous he was almost trembling. He found himself simultaneously hoping fervently that she would walk in their direction, and (imagining all the ways he might embarrass himself if she did) that she wouldn't.

"Evening, Myrtle. Hello, Clark," he heard his mother say.

Jim turned to face them, removing his hat and gripping it tightly. "Throw your blanket here and sit with us if you like," Caroline said.

Julia had not expected to see Jim. Trying not to blush, she mentally critiqued her appearance, wishing she'd worn a different dress. As Clark spread the blanket on the ground and Myrtle chatted with Caroline, their eyes met briefly, her quick glance satisfying her that Jim was not disappointed. The apparently new shirt he was wearing wasn't flattering—it looked stiff and uncomfortable on him—but choosing to believe he wore it for her benefit made Julia's heart glow.

Jim spent the next hour pretending to be interested in the music, from time to time stealing glances at Julia, who had settled onto the blanket next to her mother. Just as he was wondering if it would ever end, the musicians stopped playing and said goodnight, while one of the Starks clan passed a hat among the crowd.

Rising slowly from her chair, Caroline said, "Well I've had a fine time. Those boys are certainly talented."

"They sure are," Julia said. "Lately they've been playing at the ball games too."

"Oh? What ball games do you mean, honey?" Caroline asked her.

"At the baseball games over at the ball park on Lewis Road. There is a game every Saturday afternoon," she answered.

"Goodness. I didn't know so much was happening around here these days," Caroline said with a smile.

As they were riding home that evening Caroline remarked to Jim, "Well that girl Julia has certainly grown up to be a pretty young woman." He just grunted and shrugged.

~ ~ ~

The following Saturday morning at breakfast Caroline announced that she'd like to go the baseball game that afternoon. "I don't know what's gotten into you lately Mama, but if you want to go I reckon I can take you," Jim said, concealing his excitement.

By the time the Wrenns arrived the game had already started. Taking a seat on a makeshift bench along the first-base line, Jim reflected on the absurdity of the situation—he was sitting at a baseball game with his elderly mother, neither of them having any idea how the game was played. Turning to one of his neighbors, seated beside him, Jim said, "Hey Isaac. Who's playing?"

"That's Oakton in the field. We're batting," Isaac answered. Jim nodded, assuming that "we" meant Maple Grove.

For the sake of his mother, he feigned interest in the game. Although he couldn't make much sense of what was happening on the field, the crowd's reaction told him whether it was good or bad. Frustrated and disappointed that Julia wasn't there, he kept thinking of all the work back home that he should be doing.

After a few minutes, Caroline spoke. "Jim, would you please go get me some peanuts," motioning toward a boy who had leaned a hand-painted sign against a stool, upon which he had set a bucket of boiled peanuts. "Yes, ma'am," he answered, relieved to have something to do.

Caroline's timing had been perfect. Just as Jim reached the line forming before the peanut vendor, Julia Robertson arrived from the opposite direction.

"Well howdy, Mr. Wrenn," she chirped.

"Good afternoon, Miss Robertson," he replied, heart racing.

"Getting some peanuts?" she asked.

Jim nodded. "Yep. For Mama."

After a pause Julia said, "I'd be pleased if you would call me 'Julia.'" Adding quickly, "As long as you don't mind."

Jim beamed. "I don't mind at all, as long as you're willing to call me 'Jim.'"

She returned his smile, "Thank you, Jim."

"Thank you, Julia," he said, as they both laughed.

Once they had their peanuts, and were preparing to leave in opposite directions Jim said, "It's been nice talking with you, Julia. I'm sure glad to have seen you today."

Julia pursed her lips, as if thinking, then said, "I hope you won't think me too bold, Jim, but we're having a picnic after church tomorrow and I'd be mighty pleased if you would come."

Taken aback, Jim stammered for words, then she continued, "Oh, I'm so silly to have put you on the spot like that. Never mind, Jim. I'm sure I'll see you again sometime."

"Wait, Julia." Jim composed himself. "I'd be very pleased to come to the picnic."

Julia smiled, tilting her head to one side. "Good! I'll see you there. At noon, right after service, beside the church." Looking behind her, then back at Jim she said, "Gotta go now. Bye, Mister… I mean, bye Jim." Calling back to him, as she skipped lightly away, "See you tomorrow!"

~ ~ ~

At supper that night, Myrtle Robertson stared at her daughter across the table, brow furrowed, eyes storming. "My word, Julia! You don't just go inviting men to picnics."

"Well for goodness sakes Mama, I could hardly expect him to invite me to *our* picnic," Julia answered cheerfully, drawing a smile from her father.

"It ain't proper, Julia!" Trembling with anger now, Myrtle continued. "Folks are going to think he's courting you!"

"Well, maybe he is," Julia said with a smile.

Myrtle turned to her husband, challenging him. "Did you know about this? Are you going to allow it?" Clark just shrugged and reached for a plate of biscuits, fueling Myrtle's fire.

"Julia Anthony Robertson, your behavior is very unladylike!"

"Oh, Mama…," Julia said with a sigh.

"This is unacceptable! Clark, you must forbid her from seeing that boy!" Myrtle was now red with rage.

"Forbid her? Why?" Clark responded, puzzled.

153

"Why? Why??" Her voice rising, "That man is nothing but an uneducated farmer. Julia deserves better in her life than that."

Clark lifted his eyebrows, his occupation and educational achievements being identical to Jim's.

"Besides that," Myrtle continued, delivering what she considered the decisive punch, "he isn't even really a Wrenn."

"What do you mean, Mama?" Julia asked, her eyes clouded with concern.

"That boy and his wild sister just showed up here one day, and Caroline and her husband took them in. It's no telling where they came from, and who knows anything about their family. He is almost surely ill-bred."

Clark had been willing to endure the dig at uneducated farmers, but now his wife had crossed a line he would not yield.

"Now you hold on, Myrtle! He damn sure is a Wrenn and there ain't nothing about his family that you need to know that you can't see from looking at Caroline and Henry Wrenn."

"Mr. Robertson, I would appreciate it if you wouldn't use that tone of voice with me," Myrtle replied curtly.

Clark banged his fist down on the table, his uncharacteristic passion shocking his wife and daughter. "I'll use whatever tone of voice I damn well please, Myrtle!" Shouting now, "Jim Wrenn is a good man and he comes from good people. You got no

154

right to criticize him that way and I won't stand for it!"

An uneasy silence settled over the room, Myrtle turning away and shedding a tear. Lowering his voice, Clark continued, "I don't know if Jim is courting Julia or not, but if he is then there'll be no objection from me."

He turned to face Julia, her eyes widened by the rare confrontation. "You can't undo what you already done, Julia, but your mother's right. It ain't proper for you to invite a man that way. It's unbecoming. Reflects badly on you." He paused as the hurt gathered on his daughter's face. "From now on, you just wait for him to invite you. If he wants your company, you won't need to wait long."

"Yes, sir," she said, dropping her head—a somber face disguising her blissful heart.

~~~

Myrtle Robertson was among that breed of Southern women, all too common in her day, who took comfort from the perceived injustices in her life by imagining aristocratic origins and a past to which she rightly belonged. Although fate had placed her on a modest farm, Myrtle insisted that her people, the Anthonys, had descended from knights and cavaliers, living on large verdant plantations, attended to by hordes of loyal servants.

It was mostly nonsense of course. Myrtle's family was no wealthier before the War than after it. But she lightened the burdens of her life with the sincere conviction that the humble station she now occupied was attributable to the Yankees and General Longstreet.

Myrtle's delusions grew grander with time. It wasn't enough that she had some French ancestry; she invented connections to Lafayette. It wasn't enough that her grandfather had served honorably in the ranks; she made him an officer, promoting him ever-higher as the years marched on (by 1939 Private Anthony had evolved into Colonel Anthony).

As a young girl, Julia had found her mother's tales of their distinguished past enthralling. But as she grew older, and the stories grew increasingly implausible, Julia became skeptical. By the time she had matured into a young woman, Julia recognized her mother's fantasies for what they were, and she pitied her for them. But whatever her family and neighbors thought of Myrtle's myths, they were convictions that Myrtle herself held as absolute indisputable truths.

Fate may have required that she live as a farmer's wife, enduring life among the peasants, but Myrtle took solace in the belief that her daughter was destined to someday reenter the privileged class, reclaiming the social position to which her noble blood entitled her. As she watched Julia, bubbly and radiant, flirting with an admiring Jim at the church picnic, she saw her long-cherished dream vanishing. And she imagined dozens of whispering voices, enjoying her comeuppance.

~~~

Jim began to visit the Robertson farm once or twice each week, where he and Julia would sit on the porch till dark, Myrtle watching through the window with cold and disapproving eyes. And every week he rode to the store for the music-making, sitting beside Julia on her blanket, her nearness thrilling him. Caroline no longer accompanied him. "I'm too tired, son. You just go on without me," she had told him.

As they were all preparing to leave the store grounds, four weeks after he had first begun join the Robertsons on their blanket, Jim finally found the nerve to ask Clark's permission to bring Julia home. His daughter's pleading eyes causing him to chuckle, Mr. Robertson readily assented. "Of course, Jim. But y'all come on directly," he said, as he and his sullen wife walked away. Then stopping, so that there could be no mistaking his meaning, he turned back around, looked Jim squarely in the eyes and said firmly, "By that I mean, y'all come *straight* home." Julia nodded as Jim quickly answered, "Yes, sir."

Julia, who had ridden her mare to the store that day in the hope that Jim would offer to ride home with her, pulled up alongside Jim as he mounted his horse, and they fell in behind her parent's carriage. A clear warm evening in early summer, they rode side by side down the old country road that winds its way through Maple Grove, following the very same path the Saponi and Occaneechee had trod hundreds of years earlier. Serenaded by whippoorwills, they rode silently, pulling back on their reins to slow their mounts, putting distance between themselves and the carriage ahead of them.

When they reached the Robertson house, Clark had already unhitched the carriage and was walking his horse into the stable. Julia and Jim dismounted, just outside the gate to the iron fence that surrounded the front yard.

"I had a real nice time tonight, Julia," Jim said.

"Me too, Jim." Julia paused, waiting. Looking at him with a devilish twinkle in her eyes she said, "Well Jim, are you going to kiss me goodnight?"

Jim was caught entirely by surprise. "Well, um, I mean…" he stammered.

Julia giggled, rose up on her tiptoes, leaned forward and planted a kiss on his flushing face. "Goodnight, Jim," she said, her eyes sparkling. As she turned toward the barn, Jim reached for her reflexively, grabbing her by the wrist.

Julia turned back toward him, with an inquisitive and teasing look.

Dropping her wrist, with embarrassment, Jim spoke urgently, "I love you, Julia."

A wide smile brightened her face. "Yes, I know you do. Isn't it graaaand?" Holding her arms out wide, she twirled around once, then ran away laughing, pulling her horse along behind her, leaving Jim wondering what in the world had happened to him.

~~~

Jim had been seeing Julia as often as he could for four months, and Caroline was becoming impatient. Over breakfast, on an early morning in June, she playfully asked, "Jim, when are you going to marry that Robertson girl? I'd like to attend the ceremony and I'm not getting any younger."

The troubled look that spread across Jim's face surprised her.

"What's the matter, Jim? Is everything all right?"

~~~

Everything was not all right.

For over half her life, Julia had found her mother's unmerited snobbery offensive. One of her most painful childhood memories was of her mother saying of some of her dearest friends, "We're a higher class of people than them." But, of course, she nevertheless loved her mother, and it pained her to see that as her love for Jim grew, so did Myrtle's distress.

Julia felt confident that Jim would soon propose. And when he did, she was resolved to marry him whether her mother liked it or not. But she continued to hold out hope that Myrtle's opinion of Jim would change and that she could get married with her mother's blessing. So, to slow his pace, Julia told Jim that her mother did not approve of their relationship. "I don't need her approval Jim, but it does hurt my feelings. She doesn't want me to marry a farmer."

Julia said nothing to Jim about her mother's other objection. Instead of being dissuaded by her comment about Jim's unknown origin, as Myrtle had intended, to Julia it only made Jim even more mysterious and appealing. Intrigued, she had later asked her father about it, and he had confirmed that Jim and Pearl were not Caroline's natural children. "The way I remember it," her father told her, "they were orphans—children of one of Caroline's cousins in Tennessee I think they said. But I don't think anybody really knows for sure. They were just young'uns when they came here."

But Jim didn't have to be told. He had gotten to know Myrtle Robertson well enough to suspect that it wasn't just his livelihood that she found objectionable.

"Well, Mama," Jim said, answering her questions, "Mrs. Robertson doesn't think I'm a suitable husband for Julia." After a long sad pause he added, "And she's probably right."

Jim rose gloomily from the table and stepped outside as Caroline, shaking with anger, wondered whether at age 92 she was still fit enough to give Myrtle Robertson the thrashing she deserved. "My boy not 'suitable'?" she fumed. "Not suitable? What the devil does she mean by that?" Then, as she recalled her experiences with Myrtle over the years, the picture in her mind became clearer. "Of course," she thought, a wry smile cracking her wrinkled face.

Jim ate supper quickly that evening, as he always did on the days he visited Julia. After shaving on the back porch, he stepped inside to get his hat and was surprised to find Caroline standing at the door, dressed to go. "I haven't seen Myrtle Robertson in a long time Jim. I'd like to pay her a visit tonight, so I hope you won't mind bringing me along."

~~~

"Aren't these new ice boxes the most wonderful things?" Myrtle said as she handed Caroline a glass of lemonade. Electricity had arrived in Maple Grove in 1937, followed soon by refrigerators. Mrs. Robertson was proud of hers and liked to draw attention to it. "I just love having these little ice cubes now."

"What will they think of next?" Caroline answered, taking a sip.

Instead of inviting her guest into the parlor, as she would normally have done, Myrtle had seated Caroline at the kitchen table, so that she could keep an eye on Jim and Julia through the window.

Noticing them walking slowly across the yard, seemingly deep in quiet conversation, Myrtle shouted through the open window, "Julia! Don't wander off, honey. Stay close, in case I need you."

Caroline glanced out the window to see Julia raise her hand slightly, in acknowledgment of her mother, without ever breaking eye contact with Jim.

"Those two seem to be sweet on each other," Caroline said.

"Seems like it." Myrtle paused, gathering her strength for the battle she expected. "And I don't approve. I don't think it's a good match at all," she said firmly.

"I'm interested to hear you say that, Myrtle. I must confess that I do wonder if Julia is the right girl for my Jim," Caroline said with a casual air, taking another sip of lemonade.

The words took Myrtle by surprise. "Well, yes," she stammered. "A lifetime commitment is such an important decision."

Caroline continued, nonchalantly. "Julia is such a pretty girl, it's easy to understand why Jim is attracted to her. But I wonder if someone like Judith Flournoy might not make more sense for him. That would sure make Theodocia happy, I imagine." Caroline had chosen her words carefully. She had no reason to think that either Judith or Theodocia Flournoy had ever given a moment's thought to a union with Jim, but the words "wonder" and "imagine" afforded her considerable latitude in meaning.

Myrtle flared like a racehorse in the starting gate at the mention of Theodocia Flournoy, the woman she regarded as her chief rival for the status of grand dame of Maple Grove. She and Theodocia had been skirmishing for decades, in an apparent contest to see who could be the more pretentious. Still smarting over Theodocia's most recent subtle snub, Caroline's words had stung her.

"Judith Flournoy," she said indignantly. "Why would anyone prefer her to my Julia?"

"Oh dear, Julia is a fine girl," Caroline said, her voice dripping with condescension, "and you should be proud of her. But she and Jim are so…dissimilar. With Judith, there would be less of an age difference, for instance. And I'm sure the match would have made Mr. Wrenn proud. Wash Flournoy rode with Colonel Munford, you know. I just wonder if Judith might not be more…suitable."

"Any man should be proud to marry into my family, Mrs. Wrenn," Myrtle replied sharply, in a huff. "My grandfather was on General Pickett's staff and was cited for gallantry at the battle of Gettysburg. The Anthonys were the wealthiest landowners in the Tidewater. My great-grandfather…."

As Myrtle rattled on, calling upon Pocahontas, Sir Walter Raleigh, Charlemagne and all the rest of her pantheon of imaginary ancestors, Caroline tuned her out, satisfied that the victory was won. Through the window she saw Jim reach out and take Julia tenderly by the hand, warming her heart and carrying her mind deeply into her past.

~~~

Still seething as the Wrenn's wagon pulled out of the drive, Myrtle was muttering to herself. "Judith Flournoy. Hmff! And how dare that old woman come here and put on such airs!" Then, suddenly, she was stricken by the horrifying thought that her daughter might be jilted in favor of Theodocia Flournoy's daughter, a humiliating defeat from which Myrtle could never hope to recover. The prospect was so frightening that it made her unsteady on her feet.

Sitting down to regain her composure, the solution quickly came to her—the way to foil Theodocia and Caroline both. Yes, she thought, smiling as she imagined how much she was going to relish the triumph.

As Julia came inside, closing the door behind her, Myrtle spoke quickly. "Julia, dear. When are you going to invite your beau to have supper with us? I would enjoy getting to know him better," smiling warmly at her astonished daughter.

~~~

Clark Robertson swelled with pride as he walked his daughter down the aisle of Mt. Sinai Baptist Church on a hot Saturday afternoon in July 1939. Julia was radiant, wearing her mother's wedding dress. When she reached the altar and turned to look into Jim's suntanned face, she felt as if a dream had come true. Jim took her hand, his heart bursting with joy, as Caroline Wrenn looked on, tears streaming down her face.

After the ceremony, the guests gathered outside the church, clustering around tables that had been set up for the event, enjoying cake and punch, while Jimmy Craig and the Starks family played music, and Pearl scandalized the Baptists by dancing. When Myrtle saw Theodocia Flournoy approaching in the small receiving line that had formed before her, she loaded double canister, correctly anticipating that Theodocia had already done likewise.

"What a pretty wedding, Myrtle," Theodocia said, grasping Myrtle's hand between her own. "Julia looked lovely. It's so refreshing to see a girl who isn't afraid to wear such an old-fashioned dress."

"Why thank you, Theodocia," Myrtle answered. "It was my mother's dress. She had a very talented seamstress. Chantilly lace can be awfully difficult to work with, you know, especially when it's so old."

Parried, Theodocia withdrew her hands and changed course. "You must be very proud, Myrtle. I understand that Jim has turned out to be quite an industrious young farmer, bless his heart."

"Oh, but Theodocia, it's so easy to make crops on that farm. It's the best part of old Peter Wrenn's homeplace you know—the finest piece of land in the county they say." Looking around, Myrtle continued, "I'm sorry that Judith isn't here. Is she indisposed?"

"Indisposed? Oh, no. Not at all, Myrtle. Judith would have enjoyed being here—our little country weddings are so charming. But she's in Richmond this month visiting her Talbot cousins. My guess," Theodocia said, smiling and lowering her voice as if to share a secret, "is that it is Mr. Edward Wells who is keeping her there. He seems to find her company most agreeable."

"Oh now Theodocia, don't you let that worry you at all," Myrtle replied. "I'm sure you can count on your brother and his wife to see that Judith's reputation is kept intact."

Theodocia blinked, then said pleasantly, "I do so enjoy chatting with you Myrtle, but I absolutely must go have a closer look at your new son-in-law, before he whisks his bride away to his moth…," stopping, as if to correct herself, then continuing, "to Mrs. Wrenn's house."

The women exchanged mocking smiles before Theodocia strutted away.

~~~

The crowd of well-wishers cheered as Jim lifted his bride into the carriage her father had loaned them. Walking around to the driver's side, he waved good-naturedly to a small group of hooting young men.

The band struck up one last tune as the carriage pulled away, draped in garlands of flowers, ribbons streaming behind it.

Earlier that evening Clark Robertson had pulled Jim aside, telling him very earnestly how proud he was to have him in the family. "She's a good girl Jim, and I believe you will make her a good husband," Clark said, his eyes damp with emotion.

"I will do my very best, sir," Jim answered.

"Well, son," Clark said, smiling, "that colt is in a stall in your stable. Take good care of him too."

"But Mr. Robertson, as I told you, I…"

Clark interrupted him, "He's our wedding gift, Jim. I'm mighty glad to be giving him to you."

~~~

Julia transitioned smoothly and gracefully into the Wrenn household, relieving Caroline of many of the jobs that were becoming increasingly difficult for her. Impressed with Julia's housekeeping and farm-wife skills, Caroline yielded to her without complaint, her opinion of Myrtle considerably softened.

Jim had never been happier. The tender curves and folds of Julia's soft, warm body had awakened within him a voracious appetite—and she was keeping him well-fed. In the weeks following the wedding, Jim went about his days with a spring in his step and a gleam in his eyes, energized and glowing with satisfaction, even if sleep-deprived.

~~~

Every Sunday morning on the way to church, Clark Robertson stopped the carriage at the Wrenn place to pick up Julia. It was a concession the couple had made to appease Myrtle.

Neither Julia nor Jim were particularly pious, and neither felt any great denominational allegiance. But Myrtle, a zealous Baptist who was of the opinion that Methodists were all Hell-bound, had been horrified at the prospect of Julia attending a Methodist church. So when the couple announced their engagement, Myrtle had demanded that they pledge to attend church at Mt. Sinai. Jim gently replied that while he would be satisfied to attend any church Julia chose, his mother had faithfully attended Maple Grove Methodist for over 70 years, and was too old to take herself. It was his duty, he said, to take her to church. Grudgingly, Myrtle acknowledged the merit in Jim's position and proposed a compromise—Jim would continue to attend the Methodist church with his mother, and Julia would continue to attend the Baptist church with hers. For the sake of familial peace, Jim and Julia agreed, awkward as it was.

So every Sunday morning Julia climbed into her parent's carriage for the ride to Mt. Sinai Baptist, while Jim helped Caroline into the wagon that would take them to Maple Grove Methodist.

~~~

Over dinner, Julia spoke. "Tomorrow is the day to sow the sallet, Jim. I hope you'll disk the patch for me this afternoon."

He knew that she was right about that. Turnip greens are sowed on the first full moon of August.

"Yes, ma'am," he answered with a smile. "I'll do it as soon as I finish housing the tobacco."

In the post-marriage division of labor, Julia had taken over primary responsibility for the vegetable gardens, leaving Caroline as the principal cook; just as she had taken over the chore of milking, leaving Caroline responsible for churning. Jim handled the tobacco and livestock, with the women's help as necessary. When there was any plowing or disking to be done, it was Jim's job to do it.

In mid-afternoon Jim brought Buck around, harnessed and hitched to the disk. Normally disking required a team, but Jim preferred working with a single horse whenever possible, and because the sallet patch wasn't very large, he knew that Buck could handle it alone. Not disappointing him, Buck pulled the implement spritely, breaking the dry and clodded ground into a bed. As he turned to make a final pass, Jim saw Julia approaching, carrying a bucket.

Jim stopped the horse, got down off the disk and walked to a shade tree where Julia awaited him, handing him a dipper with a smile. It was a hot and steamy afternoon. A dog day. "Thank you, dear," he said, filling the dipper with cool water, then chugging it down. "I sure needed that, Julia," he said as he filled the dipper again. Looking up to the sky, Jim closed his eyes, tipped the dipper and poured the water over his head. Then, laughing, he shook his head vigorously, scattering his sandy blonde hair and flinging droplets onto his giggling wife.

"Whew!" he said, grinning broadly.

Julia stared back at him, her mouth drawn into a thin tight-lipped smile. She leaned back against the ancient oak, her twinkling eyes locked on his, issuing an invitation. Jim dropped the dipper into the bucket and stepped toward her.

~~~

By November Julia was certain of what she had suspected a month earlier. To the delight of her parents, Caroline, and Jim, she proudly announced that she was with child. Pearl, who had given birth for

169

the sixth time a few days earlier, was pleased, but unimpressed.

Fall gave way to winter, then winter to spring, as the baby inside Julia grew. Jim loved to lay his hand across her tightly stretched belly, Julia laughing as he marveled, overjoyed by the tiny kicks. In the days following the wedding, Jim had believed he couldn't possibly be any happier. Now, his wife swelling with new life as nature awakened around them, he saw that he had been mistaken. It was the best of times.

~~~

Julia's pregnancy was remarkably docile—no morning sickness, no weakness, no nausea. "I feel better now than I did before getting pregnant," she told Jim on a warm May night, as they sat rocking on the porch, fireflies lighting up the air as a million stars shined down on them.

Jim smiled. "Mama says that means you're having a boy," he said teasingly.

"Oh, Jim. That's just an old wives' tale. I keep telling you, it's a girl. I just know it."

It was true. Julia had told him, at least a dozen times over the past seven months, that her baby was going to be a girl. Whenever he asked how she knew, she had no answer other than, "I just do. It's a girl."

He had hesitated before, but now, feeling intoxicated by the evening, Jim introduced a subject they had not yet discussed.

"Julia, if it is a girl, I'd like to name her Lillie."

"Lily?" she answered sweetly. "What a pretty name Jim. I like it."

They sat silently a few moments, the chirp of crickets and the creaking of their rockers the only sounds.

"I love the name Jim, but I must admit I'm surprised. I would've guessed you would want to name her after your mother."

Jim thought back on his life's journey, his mind wandering through paths marked by heartbreak, shame, fear, love and redemption. He remembered the tear-streaked face of a frail and defeated woman, surrendering that which was most precious to her; trusting, because she could do nothing else. And another woman, on her knees, hugging him tightly and sobbing with joy—her heart melted by a single word, her prayers answered.

After a while he broke the silence. "Lillie Caroline. Would that be all right?"

~~~

Jim rose from the breakfast table and kissed the top of his wife's head.

"Just leave the milk in the barn, dear. You probably shouldn't be toting it anymore. I'll bring it up when I come back from the pasture."

Julia smiled sweetly back at him, as he stepped out the door into the predawn morning.

The full moon shone so brightly that morning that Julia didn't need a lantern. She carried the empty pail from the back porch to the well and pumped once, adding just enough water to cover the bottom. It was her favorite time of day, the time just before dawn, when nature is awakening—a songbird symphony filling the air, punctuated by rooster crows, anticipating the sun. The dew-soaked grass cool between her toes, she called out as she neared the barn—as her mother had taught her, "Coo-way! Coo-way!"— answered by the clanging of the milk cow's bell as she lumbered toward the barn, lowing in response.

The old Jersey entered her stall, as she had every morning and evening for over 10 years, just ahead of Julia. "Good morning, Bessie," Julia said, petting the cow's rump before dumping a scoop of sweet feed into the head-high trough. With the cow's attention on the feed, Julia pulled a squat three-legged milking stool from the corner of the stall and positioned it alongside the cow's swollen udder, beneath which she sat the milk pail. After rinsing the teats, she dumped the rest of the water onto the ground, then leaned her head into the cow's soft fawn side. Humming a song, Julia wrapped her fingers around the nearside teats, pulling down and squeezing them gently, hearing the familiar ring as the streams of milk struck the bottom of the pail. For both of them, the old cow and the young woman, the routine was nearly as natural as breathing.

After a few minutes Julia shifted to the farside teats, her seasoned hands sending thick jets of milk swooshing into the pail, kicking up froth. To chase away a fly that had lighted on her side, the old cow swished her long thin tail, sending it brushing across the top of Julia's head. "Now you stop that, Bessie," Julia said playfully.

It was a horsefly, determined to taste the cow's blood. Upon returning and finding a place safe from the swinging tail, the fly bit deeply into the old cow's tender flesh. Stung sharply, the cow stamped her leg, shaking away the fly, and knocking over the milk pail as she did. The pail tumbled over onto Julia's foot, splashing her with milk and causing her to pull back reflexively. When she did, she lost her balance and spilled backwards off the stool, her knee rising swiftly, jabbing sharply into the cow's soft belly. Frightened suddenly, the cow kicked violently and began backing out of the stall in a thousand-pound panic, trampling Julia's prostrate body.

~~~

The sky was beginning to lighten as Jim entered the barn. Seeing the overturned pail, he wondered why Julia had left it that way.

Then a chill ran up his spine, a wave of fear rushing over him. He ran out of the barn and looked anxiously toward the house. Halfway there, bathed in moonlight, his wife lay sprawled on the ground.

~~~

"Goodness! What happened, Jim?"

Caroline dropped the dishcloth and hurried to the door, as Jim entered, carrying Julia.

"Julia honey, are you all right? Jim, what has happened?" There was a frightened urgency in her voice. "Put her on my bed!"

"I don't know what happened, Mama. She's hurt." As Jim laid Julia down on the bed, Caroline saw that his shirt was bloody.

"Run over to the Bryant's house Jim and have them call Dr. Moseley!" Momentarily paralyzed with fear, Jim stood staring down at his unconscious wife. "Go, Jim! Hurry! I'll take care of her."

Suddenly alert, Jim turned and bolted out the door, the screen door slamming behind him, as he sprinted toward the closest telephone.

His lungs were burning when he leaped onto the porch of their neighbors' house, a mile away. Eliza Bryant swung open the door. "What's the matter, Jim?" she asked with concern in her voice.

Gasping for air, Jim spoke, breathing deeply and rapidly, "Please call Dr. Moseley. Emergency. Julia's hurt. Please call him. Please."

"Yes, of course. Of course," Mrs. Bryant said, as she quickly stepped inside and picked up the telephone, Jim turning and running back toward home.

~~~

"She's hurt bad, Jim." Caroline turned a frightened face to him as he burst back into the room. "The cow must have kicked her."

Jim fell to his knees beside the bed, choking back tears. "Julia, dear. Julia," he said softly, stroking her hair. "It's going to be all right, dear. The doctor's on his way."

Caroline stood, scooping up a handful of bloody cloths. "I'm going to get some more cloths, Jim. I'll be right back," she said as she left the room.

"Oh, Julia. Please be all right. Please be all right, Julia," Jim pleaded as he wept, laying his head on her chest.

~~~

A half hour later, George Moseley stopped his car in front of the Wrenn's home, parting a small group of people gathered in the yard as he hurried inside. Entering the room, he assessed the situation quickly. "Jim, please step outside. Mrs. Wrenn, stay please. Jim, please shut the door."

Eliza Bryant was policing the front door as neighbors continued to arrive—in cars, on horseback and by foot. After calling the doctor she had followed Jim, finding Caroline at the sink rinsing cloths. "What can I do to help you, Mrs. Wrenn?" she asked. Noticing two men in the distance, running toward the house, Caroline answered, "Thank you, Eliza. Will you please keep people out of here? Tell them we're grateful for their concern but to please stay outside."

Eliza had nodded and stepped out onto the porch. Periodically she addressed the growing crowd, "The family is very grateful for y'all's concern. If there is anything you can do, we'll let you know. Please pray for Julia."

Jim waited outside the room for a few minutes, tortured with worry, before Dr. Moseley emerged, his face grave.

"She's hemorrhaging, Jim, and she's in labor. She's trying to have the baby. I'm giving her something for her pain. It's a serious situation. Wait here. I'll call you in shortly."

As the doctor stepped back into the room, Jim buried his face in his hands, sobbing and whispering, "Please…please…please."

Sometime later, Caroline opened the door, her face ashen and tear-streaked. She motioned Jim inside.

As Jim entered the room, Julia rolled her head toward him. When their eyes met, she offered a weak smile. His heart lifted to see her awake, Jim dropped to his knees by the side of the bed and took her by the hand, struggling to stay composed as he stared into her clouded, unfocused eyes. The doctor approached from the other side of the bed, holding a tiny, red-stained baby boy, which he placed gently on Julia's chest, lifting and laying her limp left arm over the child. Very slowly, Julia's weary eyes turned to the baby, which gave a feeble whimper, then fell silent. Looking back toward her husband, she said faintly, the light fading from her eyes, "She's beautiful. Oh, Jim. I am so…happy."

Then she was gone.
And Jim came apart.

~ ~ ~

The weeks that followed were dark and grief-soaked. Jim, inconsolable, would not eat and could not sleep. He spent entire days deep in the woods, in anguished solitude.

Steeling herself, Caroline took control. She saw that Julia was buried in the Wrenn family cemetery, holding her ground firmly in the face of Myrtle's bitter objection. The baby was buried with his mother, Julia's arm enfolding the child in death, just as she had in the few moments of his life. Myrtle insisted that the boy be named Billy, and Caroline didn't have the energy or desire to fight her over it. Jim would say nothing on the subject, or on anything else. He avoided all those who came to pay respects, declining even to make eye contact. Only out of a sense of duty to Caroline, who begged him, did he attend the funeral, his heart-wrenching suffering multiplying the community's grief and loss.

A neighbor took away the cow. As May matured into June, crucial days for a farm, the community stepped up, tending Jim's crops and livestock while he mourned. Pearl and the neighbors wouldn't allow Caroline to cook or clean, until she kindly insisted they stop bringing food and leave her to her housework.

On a Saturday in mid-June, as Caroline was sitting on the front porch at sunset, her Bible in her lap, Clark Robertson rode slowly up to the house. He dismounted, tied his horse to the post, then stepped onto the porch, where Caroline had risen to greet him. They stood facing each other, with quivering lips and tear-filled eyes, unable to speak. After a few moments, Caroline opened her arms and drew him to her hug. They wept together, mourning doves calling in the distance.

~~~

Eventually Jim emerged from the darkness, forever changed. On a Monday morning in late June he took his place at the breakfast table and ate a few bites. When he rose to leave he looked into Caroline's sad and troubled face. "Thank you, Mama," he said.

In time, once he could bear it, he would visit the homes of every person who had helped him through his grief, thanking them for their kindness. But, for now, all he could do was put his hands to the plow. Word spread, and he was left to tend his farm, as he had always done.

~~~

In October 1940, five months after Julia's death, Jim reported to the county seat, as required by law. A month earlier Congress had passed a law requiring every man between 21 and 36 years old to register with their local draft board. Never before had conscription occurred in peacetime, but war clouds were gathering.

Jim slid the paperwork across the desk to a young clerk from the War Department, who scanned it, flanked by the other two board members. "Birth certificate," he said curtly.

"Ain't got one," Jim answered.

Looking up at Jim, the young man pushed his steel rimmed glasses up his nose with a forefinger, then said, "So how am I supposed to know if this is your true age?"

Eyes narrowing at the accusation, Jim looked back at him crossly, holding his stare until the young man blinked. "Well, I reckon you could cut me down and count my rings," Jim answered. Seeing the young man squirm, he added, "Or you could assume I've given you an honest answer to a simple question."

The man looked back down at his papers, took up a pen and said dismissively, "One H. Deferred. Over age 28."

~~~

Caroline broke her hip, four days before her 94th birthday.

She had lost her balance while descending the steps into the cellar to get a jar of pickles. Jim found her, six hours later and in great pain, lying at the base of the steep and narrow steps that he had been begging her to stay away from for the past five years.

Jim carried her to her bedroom, astonished at how light she was. Caroline winced as he settled her gently onto the bed Julia and the baby had died in almost a year earlier. It was the first time Jim had entered the room since that brutal day.

"I'm going to call the doctor, Mama. Can I do anything for you first?"

Seeing the concern and apprehension on Jim's face, she tried to conceal her pain. "I'm so clumsy, Jim. I'll be all right."

"I'll be right back, Mama," Jim said as he stepped into the kitchen.

A few months after Julia's death Caroline had a telephone installed in the house. She had done it without asking Jim's opinion, haunted by the fear that something would happen to him and she would have no way to summon the doctor. Using the phone for the first time, Jim called the operator and asked her to send Dr. Moseley over right away.

~~~

"Her hip is broken," the doctor told him as they stepped out onto the porch.

"How long will it take to heal?" Jim asked with concern.

"Jim, at her age it's not going to heal," the doctor answered grimly.

Jim was stunned. "What do you mean, doctor?"

"I mean I doubt she'll ever get out of that bed again. She may be able to sit up eventually, but it's highly unlikely she'll ever walk."

Jim's head dropped, his gaze falling to the floor.

"I'm going to leave you something to give her for pain." After a pause he added, "Get someone to help you look after her, Jim." He set a bottle on the kitchen table, then shook Jim's hand firmly, saying, as he turned to leave, "God bless you, son."

~ ~ ~

Neighbors kept Caroline company during the day, bringing meals despite her protests. Pearl, nine-months pregnant with her seventh child when Caroline fell, was in no position to help, but 11-year-old Dottie, Pearl's oldest, came after school each day to sit with her grandmother. On Sunday afternoons the pastor visited, praying with Caroline and sharing an abbreviated version of his sermon.

Through it all she remained friendly and warm, but her bright cheerfulness was gone. The idleness drained her and her strength faded.

Caroline had been bedridden for a month when Pearl brought over her new two-week-old baby girl for a visit. Holding the baby lifted her spirits, as Jim had hoped it would, but the next day the decline continued—she seemed weaker than before.

Dr. Moseley came by every couple of weeks to check on her. After a visit in mid-May Jim told him he was concerned that Caroline seemed to be getting weaker. "Jim, she's tired," he answered. "She doesn't seem to be in much pain. If she is, give her one of the pills I left you. Otherwise, my advice is to just keep her comfortable."

"Is she going to get better, doctor?" Jim asked.

"Maybe, maybe not. It's impossible to say. Just keep her comfortable Jim. Get some help if you can."

Jim sat with her every night. When Caroline had the energy, and was in the mood, they talked about the farm, about the weather, about the news of the community. Jim was aching to spill out his heart to her. Every day while working he rehearsed in his mind the ways he would tell her how much he loved her, and how grateful he was for all she'd done for him. And every day Caroline thought of all the things she wanted to tell Jim—how much she loved him, and how grateful she was for all he'd done for her. But they spent their time together on small talk, and the conversation they both ached to have, never happened. They kept putting it off till the next day, until there was no next day.

One morning Caroline didn't wake up as usual. She'd been sleeping a lot lately, so Jim wasn't alarmed. He quietly left to do his chores. When he returned, Pearl was waiting for him. "She ain't waked up yet, Jim."

Caroline was breathing normally, but they couldn't wake her. Jim called Dr. Moseley whose only advice was, "Just keep her comfortable."

Pearl stayed with her all through the day and Jim slept in her room at night, getting up to check on her every couple of hours. One night, a few days later, he woke suddenly at the sound of Caroline's voice. Hurrying to her bedside he spoke softly into her ear, "Mama, can you hear me? Is everything all right, Mama? Do you need anything?" She was mumbling, but her eyes remained closed. "I can't understand what you're saying, Mama. Can you hear me?"

"Yes, Jim. Of course, I can hear you," Caroline said, wondering why Jim looked so worried and why he kept repeating himself. She sat up, then glided out of bed, smiling as she saw that she was wearing her favorite dress, the blue one her mother had made for her at Christmas. She crossed the room to the door. Looking back, she saw Jim on his knees, squeezing an old woman's hand and whispering into her ear. Such a kind boy, she thought, as she moved into the parlor and toward the front door. But it wasn't a door. It was a beautiful gate, swinging slowly open as she approached. So lovely, she thought, looking out onto a field of wildflowers, glowing in sunlight. And there, smiling, waiting for her at the edge of the field, were Luke and Henry. She smiled back and stepped toward them, into the light.

~~~

They buried Caroline next to Henry, one year and two days after they had buried Julia.

Jim and Pearl lingered at the graveside, after the others had begun to leave.

Looking down at the grave, Jim said softly, "Do you remember, Pearl? Do you remember it all?"

"I remember a right smart more than you think I do, Jim," Pearl answered roughly. "You ain't the onliest one in this family with good sense."

Looking down, but far into the distance, Jim said, "Sometimes I don't know if I remember it or not, Pearl. Sometimes I wonder if my memories are real."

Pearl was silent for a moment, then she snorted and said, as she turned to walk away, "Well, Jim, maybe you just wonder too damn much."

~~~

Jim was alone now, hollowed out by the losses in his life.

In the months leading up to Caroline's death he had gradually assumed her work, facilitating his transition into solitary bachelorhood. In addition to his other work on the farm, he washed clothes, cooked simple meals, canned and preserved food. He learned to restructure his days to accommodate his new responsibilities. In due course, there was a new rhythm to life on the farm. Even though always quiet and often sad, it sustained him and he settled into it. But his ultimate sense of purpose was gone, and that troubled him. He spent long hours sitting in the graveyard, searching for meaning in it all, struggling in vain to understand his powerful conviction that, despite everything that had happened, he should continue.

He had wanted to think deeply, to remember, to grieve; but he was restless. So on Sundays he began to walk the farm, with no destination or purpose in mind. Sometimes, to clear his mind, he would stop and look around him, studying carefully the things and places he'd come to take for granted. In time, he became aware that the living and ever-evolving world surrounding him was even more complex and marvelous than he'd ever before imagined. He came to realize that he and his place were not separate things, one was not an instrument of or for the other. He sensed, in a deeply profound way that he would not have been able to articulate, that he was merely a component part of a larger organism—the farm, the place, the world. Nothing dies forever and is gone. Instead, he came to understand that just as the place transitions, as through seasons, seemingly changing but at its essence remaining the same, so the particular identities of the creatures crawling around on the place may seem to change as they come and go, are born and die, but in truth they never leave. The appearance that the lives of the creatures on the place are transitory, was, he came to understand, merely an illusion. Instead, the ultimate truth is that so long as the place survives, so do the creatures who have inhabited it.

He imagined an hourglass, the sands of the future crowding through the tiny opening that was the present, and dropping into the cavern of the past. And in his mind, he saw a vision of the hourglass turning over onto its side, blurring the distinctions of

185

past, present, and future, the sands flowing freely back and forth among them. Reflecting on that vision often as he grew older, Jim recognized that it could not be called an epiphany. Meaning and purpose had not declared themselves to him suddenly and dramatically. Rather, like the change of seasons, the answer had arrived naturally and gradually. He still harbored a deep bitterness that he would never completely surrender—his memories of Lillie's shame and humiliation, and of the senseless death of Julia and his son, would never permit that. But he learned to separate that pain from his surroundings, to find in them not hurtful reminders of the loss, but instead comforting assurance of a more profound and permanent reality. He had long loved the farm, as a father might love a child, but now he projected onto it the loves that had been taken from him. He came to understand that the farm, the place he loved, did more than just remind him of Henry, of Caroline, of Julia, and of Fuller and Lillie, whose journey had brought him here. In some mysterious way that he could not express in words, the farm was them, just as it was all others who had gone before him, and just as it would someday be him. The land—the place— absorbed all of his love. As it served him, he would serve it. And in so doing, he would serve those who had come before him, and those yet to come. He loved the land, and it loved him back.

~~~

Once again, the world had gone to war, and in December 1941 America was dragged into it. In the days and weeks following the attack on Pearl Harbor, men across America rushed to volunteer, and Congress began to expand the pool of those subject to conscription.

Being 31 years old, Jim was now eligible to be drafted, although also eligible for an agricultural deferment. His Sunday meditations now turned to war and his answer wasn't long in coming. The thought of a lengthy separation from the farm pained him, but likewise he felt a powerful sense of duty. So, he resolved to volunteer for service, as soon as he was satisfied the place would be well-tended in his absence.

But, as with all human plans, Jim's were made without complete knowledge of all relevant circumstances. The universe at large had not been consulted. With the arrangements nearly complete, on January 15, 1942, he received a letter from a childhood acquaintance that would alter the course of his life.

~ ~ ~

Burr Capshaw was a Maple Grove boy who had, in the words of the country folks, "done well for himself." A farm boy with the right combination of intelligence, determination, and ambition, he had attended the state university and later its law school, ultimately graduating sufficiently polished to win the hand of the daughter of a prominent Danville attorney, thus securing his professional future. Handsome, articulate, and possessed of an uncanny ability to recall names and faces, he had won the favor of both the local judiciary and the local corporate elite. His bright future a certainty, the only question his admirers debated was whether he was destined for the bench or for congress.

But back when Jim Wrenn had come to know him, Burr was just another one of the boys in Mrs. Mitchell's Sunday school class at Maple Grove Methodist. Mrs. Mitchell, a kindly but flighty old woman, had been assigned the responsibility of trying to keep two dozen 7 to 12-year-old boys under control for an hour every Sunday, ostensibly while giving them Bible lessons. Burr was the ringleader of the handful of boys who made that assignment most challenging.

Mrs. Mitchell required the boys to choose and memorize a Bible verse each week. Every Sunday in class, each boy would stand and recite the verse he had memorized, and Mrs. Mitchell would thereafter expound upon the moral and theological significance of the chosen passage. Torture for some of the boys, for Burr and his co-conspirators it was an irresistible opportunity for mischief. They would deliberately choose verses they found strange or funny, in order to see what Mrs. Mitchell would make of them.

Having become bored with the bizarre exegetical wonders Mrs. Mitchell performed with verses like "Cush begat Nimrod," "Cretans are always liars," and

"Let beer be for those who are perishing," in the summer of 1919 Burr and his pals hit upon the idea of using the exercise as a way to befuddle the teacher, while simultaneously getting away with saying words otherwise forbidden to them. For weeks on end one of the boys (alternating responsibility, in the belief that this would decrease their chance of being caught and punished) would stand and solemnly recite a verse containing a "cuss word," whereupon the class would watch as Mrs. Mitchell attempted to unravel the divine lesson in the text. So the boys listened, suppressing giggles, while she expounded upon the whore of Babylon, coveting the ass of one's neighbor, generations of vipers damned to hell, and so forth.

None of it had amused Jim. Still uncomfortable over a year after his sudden appearance in Maple Grove, he spoke only when required to by the teacher. By then the boys had stopped trying to pry his mysterious past out of him, but the rumors persisted—some plausible, some ridiculous, one of the more persistent being that he and his sister were the illegitimate offspring of someone in Caroline's family. Jim simply stayed quiet, keeping his distance from the other boys.

Until one Sunday that summer when the distance between him and Burr Capshaw precipitously closed. That day, one of Burr's accomplices rose and recited the verse he had chosen, saying solemnly: "Deuteronomy 23:2. A bastard shall not enter into the congregation of the Lord; even to his tenth generation shall he not enter into the congregation of the Lord." He sat down and all eyes turned expectantly to Mrs. Mitchell.

"Well, yes, um, yes…" she sputtered, the familiar confusion spreading across her face.

"What does it mean Miz Mitchell?" one of Burr's friends asked, mocking sincerity.

Mrs. Mitchell thought for a second then said, "Well, you see, the children of adulterous unions are called 'bastards,'…."

Burr interrupted her. "Sometimes they're called 'orphans,'" he said.

Someone snickered. Someone gasped. Most squirmed uncomfortably.

Jim looked up quickly, eyes flashing. He had been sitting quietly at the end of the table, enduring the nonsense and waiting patiently for class to end when Burr spoke. His eyes met Burr's long enough for Burr's sneer to confirm that the remark had been aimed at him. Firing across the table like a bullet from a gun, Jim drove the boy out of his chair and onto the floor, furiously kicking and punching him. Despite being three years older and much bigger than Jim, Burr never had a chance. As some of the other boys dove in to try to separate the two, Mrs. Mitchell screamed for help and the pastor rushed into the room and pulled the still-flailing Jim away. Once Jim had settled down and Burr had recovered his wits, the pastor ordered them to apologize to each other. Burr sheepishly complied, Jim refused. "Then go outside!" the pastor shouted at Jim. "You will not be allowed back inside this building until you have apologized."

Without saying a word, Jim marched out the door and out the building, leaving behind him a room of astonished boys, who had never before seen anything but meekness from him.

When services ended, Caroline found him there, waiting outside. As much as he didn't want to disappoint her, Jim told her that he would not apologize. Once Caroline had heard the story of what had happened, and confirmed it from another source, she loaded the children in the wagon and drove home, telling Jim on the way, "You will not apologize to that boy, Jim. You did the right thing."

A few days later she called upon the pastor at the parsonage. "I understand that you ordered my son out of the sanctuary unless he apologized to the boy who insulted him."

"Mrs. Wrenn, it has always been our policy to require both boys to apologize under such circumstances. We can't have them fighting in church and it is the right and Christian thing to do for them to apologize to each other," the pastor said, with an air of authority.

Caroline stood, saying, "Well sir, if an apology from Jim is a condition to his being allowed back into the building, then we shall find a different church to attend."

Taken aback, the preacher beat a hasty retreat and the matter was dropped.

No one ever again dared to tease Jim about his parentage. And among the children of Maple Grove, the story of the day Jim Wrenn whipped Burr Capshaw in church became legendary.

Jim and Burr got alone fine after that day. They were never close friends, but they never again fought. They became cordial neighbors.

And then, over 20 years after their famous tangle on the church floor, Jim opened a letter from Burr Capshaw, attorney at law.

~~~

It was just a note. "I need to see you about an important legal matter," it read. "Please come by my office at your earliest convenience."

For the second time ever, Jim used his telephone. "I have a letter asking me to come to Mr. Capshaw's office, but why can't I talk to him on the telephone instead?" he asked the secretary who would not put him through without knowing the reason for the call. Momentarily she came back on the line, "Mr. Capshaw says he's sorry, but the discussion must be in person."

Jim was sorely tempted to ignore the letter, but after stewing over it for a few days, he reluctantly saddled his horse and rode the 15 miles to Danville, on a very cold day in January. Much had changed in the years since Jim had first made that trip. Gone were the days when horses ruled the highways, accommodating the occasional automobile. Now it was the horse and rider who were the interlopers, intruding on space now commanded by motorized vehicles. And there were no longer hitching posts along Main Street, making it difficult for him to find a place to tie his horse. Jim found these conditions exceedingly disagreeable.

"Well, Burr, here I am," Jim had said upon being seated in the lawyer's office, making no effort to conceal his annoyance.

"Thanks for coming in, Jim. I'm sure it was inconvenient for you, but it is an important matter," Burr said from behind his large desk, his tweed suit and silk tie contrasting sharply with Jim's attire—a white shirt crumpled by the journey and a pair of gray trousers that he reserved for church or visits to town. Jim just nodded in response.

"Let me get right to it, Jim."

Burr leaned forward, hands clasped, his elbows on his desk, revealing the gold cufflinks that fastened his starched white shirt at his wrists. "Did you ever meet Mrs. Wrenn's brother Webster?"

Jim shook his head. He'd heard Caroline mention her brother Webb, but there had been little contact with her family over the years. None of them had come to her funeral.

"Well," Burr continued, "he passed away a couple of months ago, in Florida. Evidently he made himself a small fortune down there. Never married. The last of his siblings to go. Died without a will."

Burr paused as Jim looked blankly at him, waiting for the relevance of it all.

"His nieces and nephews in Tennessee are probating the estate, to establish his legal heirs," the lawyer said. "Because the children of his brothers and sisters are entitled to Webster Adams' estate, they've had to determine Mrs. Wrenn's heirs too."

After another pause, Burr continued. "Jim, did Mrs. Wrenn have a will?"

"No," Jim answered. "A few years back she sat down with me and Pearl and told us what she wanted done after she died, but as far as I know she never wrote it down."

"Damn," Burr said, straightening in his chair. "Jim, there's no easy way to tell you this. You and Pearl are not the legal heirs of Mrs. Wrenn. You're not her natural children and you were never formally adopted. In the absence of a written will, you have no rights to her estate."

Jim thought for a few seconds, then answered, "I don't care about that, Burr. I don't want any of that man's money."

"That's not what I'm trying to tell you, Jim." Burr lit a cigarette and blew the smoke toward the ceiling. "Damn. On days like this I hate being a lawyer. I'm talking about the farm, Jim. Legally it passed from Mr. Wrenn to Mrs. Wrenn. And when she died, it passed legally to her heirs."

His stomach tightening, Jim said uneasily, "The farm? *My* farm?"

"What I'm trying to tell you, Jim, is that it ain't your farm. It belongs to those greedy bastards in Tennessee."

Stunned, Jim's head swam as the words sank in.

"You see, Jim, under the Virginia law of intestate succession, the property of a decedent passes first to her spouse, if married, then, if not, to her surviving children per stirpes…." Burr proceeded to explain the law, but Jim didn't hear him. The thought that he was losing the farm, his beloved farm, so fully occupied his mind that there was no room for anything else.

Eventually the lawyer stopped talking. Jim was staring at him, pale-faced.

"What does it mean for me, Burr?" Jim asked him, hating how helpless asking the question made him feel.

"Look Jim, they don't really want the farm. All they want is money. I recommend you negotiate a price and buy it from them. They'll probably sell cheap."

"I don't have any money, Burr," Jim answered.

"I've got contacts at the bank. They'll loan it to you, Jim. You're good for it," Burr answered. "Of course, you'll have to give them a mortgage on the place," he added.

"I don't want to do that, Burr. I ain't borrowed a nickel from nobody in ten years," Jim said.

"I don't see that you have much choice, Jim, if you want to keep the place." Burr stood, straightened his tie and walked around the desk toward Jim.

"You think about it, Jim. If you want me to, I'll find out from the Adams clan's lawyer what his clients will take for the place, and I'll help you get a loan to buy it." Burr extended his hand, signaling the end of the meeting.

Jim rose, shook his hand and answered, "Thanks, Burr. I'll let you know." As he was about to open the door, Jim turned back and asked, "How did you know all this, Burr? I ain't heard a thing about it."

"Their lawyer is an old friend of mine. I went to school with him. He contacted me about representing them on this. I'm not going to do it of course," Burr answered.

Jim nodded and left the room.

~~~

HUDSON & CAPSHAW
1101 Main Street
Danville, Virginia

January 27, 1942

Henry W. Reeves, Esq.
213 Georgia Ave.
Chattanooga, Tennessee

Re: Adams Estate

Dear Hank:

Enclosed herewith are the materials you sent me in connection with the above-referenced matter. As I mentioned to you in our telephone call of this morning, I am unable to represent your clients in this proceeding.

The tract in issue is known to me and I believe your agents will be able to confirm that it is of no great value. I am of the opinion that the farmer living there now (having been raised on the place by Mr. and Mrs. Wrenn) would pay a fair price for a quitclaim deed, relieving your clients of the expense and inconvenience of any ancillary probate proceedings in Virginia. If you would like to pursue resolution in this manner, please advise and I would be pleased to facilitate it.

Give my love to Nancie.

Very Truly Yours,

E. Wilbur Capshaw

~~~

Jim had spent much of the week after his meeting with Burr Capshaw angry at the injustice of it all. What kind of law would take away the farm his Pa and Mama had given to him, the farm that he hoisted onto his eight-year-old back and had carried through the Great Depression, the farm he loved to the marrow of his being, and give it to people who hadn't even bothered to attend his mama's funeral? The more he thought about it, the angrier he became— until a familiar image came to mind, settling him on the course he had to take.

He remembered, as a young boy, watching ants building an anthill, stacking sand one grain at a time.

He had kicked the anthill, because that's what young boys do, destroying the structure the ants had so patiently and slowly built. But the ants didn't flail and moan in protest. They didn't quit in despair. They just started over again, bringing out the grains of sand at the same steady pace as before. And now, Jim realized, he was the ant whose anthill had just been kicked down. The anthill had been built, and now it had been destroyed. Complaining wouldn't bring it back. The only way to get it back was to start building it again, one grain at a time.

And so, having once vowed never again to borrow money, Jim signed a promissory note obligating him to pay $6,000 to the First Danville Bank, with interest, secured by a mortgage on the Wrenn home place.

~~~

Joining the army was now out of the question. Instead Jim had to find a way to earn enough money to keep up the payments on the note.

Many of the men in Maple Grove had already enlisted. Even Pearl's cowardly husband had joined up, although in his case it was probably not patriotism that motivated him—but rather the chance to escape Pearl and the seven children. It soon became apparent that the rush of enlistments was a threat to the workforce, so much so that within a year the President would sign an executive order prohibiting any further volunteers and requiring the military to rely solely on conscription. Thanks to the war, industry was booming and jobs were plentiful.

Staying out of the army wasn't the hard part—Jim was eligible for an agricultural deferment. The hard part was coming up with a way to earn $6,000, something he knew he couldn't do farming.

It was an agonizing decision, but, in the end, he felt he had no choice. The prospect of losing the farm was crushing. Not only would walking away be a betrayal of those who had preceded him, he and the place had fused together over time. He could no more imagine being separated from the farm than he could imagine being separated from his head. A man's got to do what a man's got to do, he told himself. He took a job at the mill.

Riding back home after filling out his application and being hired on the spot, Jim couldn't shake from his mind the memory of his mother, coughing the last bits of life out of her frail body on that brutal winter night twenty-four years earlier, as she told him the story of her life. Of all the things she told him on that long and painful night, there were words that especially haunted him now: "Your Daddy always dreamed of coming to work in this mill and now it done killed him, and I'm next. I ain't but 22-years-old Gem, and look at me. I knowed women back home what lived to be a hundred or more. Slaving for those machines and sucking in that fouled air kills us. If'n it don't, then living all crammed together like this will. I'll say straight out I'm sorry to have left the mountains where the air was clean and if you tended

199

the ground you ate good. We was poor, but we could take care of our ownselves there."

Sinking back into sadness on the long ride home, Jim felt as if the steady clip clop of the horse's hooves was beating out a funeral cadence. "I'm sorry, Mama. I'm sorry," he said. "It's only for a little while."

~~~

Dramatic changes had come to the mill over the past 20 years. Wages and working conditions were better. Children no longer worked on the mill floor. Instead of one ten-hour shift, the mill now operated twenty-four hours a day, with three eight-hour shifts.

Jim was hired to work as a card hand at the so-called "Long Mill," a series of four connected mills sitting below a bluff on the north side of the river. Old Mill Number One, where his parents had worked and where he had spent most of his first seven years, was across the river to the east, still operating. On the south bank of the river, directly across from the street where he had once lived, the company had constructed a massive new facility called Mill Number Eight, or more commonly "the White Mill." All told, Dan River Mills had become the largest cotton mill in the South, with over 14,000 employees, and over the past 20 years the population of Danville had doubled to approximately 40,000.

Jim's job was to feed sheets of cotton into steel-teethed carding machines, which ripped and cleaned it, converting it into rope-like slivers of fabric that

200

coiled into large cans, which were in turn sent to the spinning rooms. It was a dirty job, kicking up lint that clogged the air, hair, and skin of the workers, finding its way into their eyes and throats as well.

Jim worked the third shift, meaning his workday started at midnight and ended at 8 a.m. Third shift is always disconcerting, no matter how long a person endures it. Many of the workers kept alert by downing Pepsi's all night, often with a packet of BC or Goody's headache powders dumped in for an extra lift. Being too frugal to buy soft drinks, Jim just labored on, even as his body insisted that nighttime was for sleeping, not for carding cotton. At first he had trouble getting to sleep in the afternoons, but eventually he wore his fatigued body down to the point that it would accept the opportunity for sleep, whenever offered. In time, he adjusted to the pattern of it, but he never felt fully rested.

Every night at 11 p.m., a neighbor who also worked third shift and who had an automobile, would pick him up in front of his house. When his shift was over they would ride home together and, after his breakfast/supper, Jim would work on the farm until about 4 p.m. After about six hours of sleep, he'd start over again, day after day, month after month, year after year.

Meanwhile, across two oceans, the war raged on. And with the United States military as its principal customer now, the mill's business was booming. Jim was safe from conscription, now having a deferral for employment with an industry essential to the war effort, but he was not safe from feelings of guilt, nor from the judgments of those who didn't know or appreciate his story. The neighbor whose car he shared every day had two sons in harm's way. During their nightly commute she spoke often of them, sharing her pride and her fear, and leaving Jim feeling ashamed at his relative safety. In time, he tamed his guilt, reminding himself that a man can't be in two places at one time. But he still sometimes felt the sting of judgment. One day, standing in line to draw his pay, he overheard a woman behind him saying something about the men "who get to stay home and make lots of money while others do the fighting and dying for them." And when he passed by the War Bonds table without stopping, his salary in hand, angry eyes stabbed at him.

There was a reason Jim didn't buy War Bonds. It was the same reason he endured the judgment and guilt. The reason he had taken the wretched job, the only reason, was to earn the money he needed to save his farm. He considered his wages blood money and he would use them for nothing else—Caesar's silver was given back to Caesar. Every penny he earned at the mill went straight to the bank to pay down the debt, with his food and modest living expenses coming from the farm.

~~~

The war ended eventually, and the men began to come home. But not all of them. Just a few months before it was over, Pearl's cowardly husband was killed in Italy and was thereafter awarded a posthumous medal for bravery. As a result, Pearl got a flag, a widow's benefit of $100 a month, and the freedom to select a new victim upon whom she could commit matrimonial malpractice.

After being drafted and sent to Washington to do legal work at the War Department, Burr Capshaw had his promising career cut short by a colleague who had come home for lunch unexpectedly, finding his wife and Burr in bed, enjoying a degree of intimacy that he found objectionable. The widow Capshaw received neither a flag nor a pension.

But most of the men came home safely, now forever members of a fraternity to which Jim could never belong.

~~~

In 1946 Pearl married Charlie Garrett, a nervous, wiry-thin, chain-smoking mechanic and childless widower, twenty years her senior. Within a year, she had delivered child number eight.

"Well, Pearl," Jim said when he visited her and the new baby, "you are, above all else, fecund."

"What the hell are you talking about, Jim?" Pearl shot back. "You ain't no better than me."

"No, Pearl, I'm not," he answered sincerely. "Not by a long shot."

~~~

There were two books that could be found in nearly every rural household in those days—the family Bible and the Sears, Roebuck and Company catalog. One collected dust, opened on special occasions, if at all. The other was pored over regularly, like a family treasure, and was known universally as the "Wish Book."

There was a new Wish Book every year. In many rural homes, when the new one appeared the old one was relegated to a place of honor in the outhouse, where it would not only keep the occupant entertained, but, page by page, would assist in one of nature's most delicate tasks.

On Jim's farm the Wish Book proceeded directly to the outhouse. His relationship with the book was an ambivalent one. On the one hand, he looked contemptuously upon what he regarded as an effort to persuade people to desire things they didn't need, which he saw as a program designed to transform contentment into dissatisfaction. On the other hand, he appreciated the functionality and utility of the book, and considered its ultimate use an appropriate response to its creators.

On a Sunday afternoon in the summer of 1942, having completed the mission that had brought him into the facility, Jim reached for the Wish Book lying beside his seat. Throwing open the book and preparing to rip out a page, something caught his attention. Soon he was engrossed. On pages 710-716 he had made a discovery that was destined to imprint deeply onto his life.

~ ~ ~

The sun was shining brightly when Jim walked out of the mill on a Friday morning in April 1949. "Go on without me, Mary," he had told the neighbor who he had ridden to work with the previous night. "I've got business in town."

Halfway across the bridge Jim stopped and looked around. To his left was Mill Number One, the place where his parents had worked and where most of his first seven years had been spent. To his right he could see the three-room mill-house on Floyd Street where they had lived. Below him, sprawling massively along the river was Mill Number Eight, "the White Mill," crowned for the past year with a giant electric sign reading "Home of Dan River Fabrics." Behind him was the "Long Mill," where he had spent the first 8 hours of every weekday for the past seven years. Ahead of him was Main Street. And on Main Street was his destination: The First Bank of Danville, an imposing brick neo-classical structure within whose walls lay documents that for the past seven years had put a claim on his life and had hung threateningly over his farm.

Open for business by the time he arrived, Jim entered the bank, found the right teller, and endorsed his paycheck, the last one he would ever draw, to the bank, as he had been doing on every payday for the past seven years. This time, in exchange for the check, he received a promissory note marked "Paid in Full."

Then, on a beautiful spring day, he walked the fifteen miles from Danville to Maple Grove.

Arriving home that afternoon, Jim pulled a box from beneath his bed and from within it took out a large black Bible. He opened the Bible to the middle, removing from it a yellowing newspaper clipping. After staring for a few moments at the clipping and then at the pencil-written names on the Bible's center page, he sighed deeply before placing the clipping and the paid note inside the open pages. Then he closed the book and returned it to its box.

Part Three

Gravel crunched under the tires of his 25-year-old Chevy Nova as J.B. Wainwright turned onto the drive leading up to a simple white farmhouse, shaded by oaks on a hot summer afternoon. He climbed the steps of the front porch, and stood before the front door, flanked by a rocking chair and an antique refrigerator. Not seeing a doorbell button, he knocked.

He had only been waiting at the door a few moments when a voice came from behind him, in the familiar unhurried drawl of the area. "What can I do for you?"

J.B. turned around and found himself facing a broad-shouldered old man wearing a faded blue cap and denim overalls over a white shirt. Beside him sat a large black Labrador with a gray beard, both old dog and old man looking inquisitively at the visitor.

"Good afternoon, sir. I'm J.B. Wainwright, the new pastor at Maple Grove UMC. I'm just going around the community and introducing myself."

After studying him silently for a moment, the old man spoke, "The new pastor? You don't look like a pastor."

J.B. chuckled and answered with a grin, "So I've been told."

After a reflective pause, the man spoke again. "No offense intended, young man." He extended his hand, "Jim Wrenn."

Shaking it firmly, J.B. said, "Pleased to meet you, Mr. Wrenn. I've heard a lot of nice things about you. I won't take up much of your time, sir. I just wanted to say hello and invite you to join us on Sunday mornings. We would be especially honored to have you come, Mr. Wrenn. I understand that it was your family that donated the land for our church all those years ago."

Jim did not answer immediately. He had that way of speaking that was common to the older people of Maple Grove, and discomforting to those unaccustomed to it. It seemed as if he only spoke after first thinking through the words he was about to say, making sure they were exactly the ones he wanted.

"Well sir, I believe my family is already well-represented in your congregation."

~~~

Jim's family was indeed well-represented at the Maple Grove United Methodist Church. His sister Pearl hadn't missed a Sunday service since her last child was born, nearly 50 years earlier, and had missed precious few prior to that. She was a fixture on the front pew, her extended tribe occupying the pews behind her and typically filling half the church.

Pearl was, however, something of a mystery to the young pastor, as she had been to all his predecessors. She never attended Sunday school, never joined the women's group, never served on a committee, and never seemed to show any interest in the politics or management of the church. Yet week after week she would crush out her cigarette on the church steps, march down the aisle and take her seat on the front pew, which she always had completely to herself, occupying it like a throne. Whether due to inattention or deliberate provocation, she wore clothes that most conventional church-goers would deem inappropriate (on J.B.'s first Sunday she wore gray sweat pants and an airbrushed "Myrtle Beach" t-shirt). She sat through each service, seemingly bored, chewing gum and adjusting her mountain of wild red hair, while in the rows behind her three generations of her progeny (as unlikely a conglomeration of church-goers as one would ever expect to see) fidgeted, whispered, and battled unruly children.

Pearl was not a pious woman, by any means, and the days when the entire community turned out for church every week were long gone. So no one knew why she so faithfully attended, and why she bullied the rest of her clan into doing likewise. Perhaps it was just another of the eccentricities in which she seemed to delight. But, whatever her motivation, week after week, there she was, front and center, and woe be to any of her descendants and in-laws who were not there with her.

"Yes, sir," J.B. answered with a smile. "Mrs. Humston and her family are some of our most loyal congregants. Nevertheless, we'd be pleased if you would join us as well."

Jim nodded in response.

"Well, sir, I'll be on my way," J.B. said. "But would you mind if I ask you a question before I go? Why do you have a jar of money on your porch?"

J.B. gestured toward a mason jar, stuffed with bills, sitting on a bench beside an old refrigerator.

After a moment, Jim answered. "There's eggs, vegetables, and sausage in the fridge. Folks take what they want and leave their money in the jar."

~~~

Jim raised vegetables, pigs, chickens, and sheep. He sold produce, meat and eggs at the farmers' market in Danville, to a few local stores, and to neighbors. He hadn't raised a crop of tobacco since 1940, fifty-five years earlier.

Folks knew him as an honest, reliable neighbor, albeit something of an eccentric. He lived alone and always seemed to be decades behind the time. He drove a 40-year-old pickup on those few occasions he left his farm, never exceeding 25 miles per hour. He had no television. It wasn't until the 1970's that he added an indoor bathroom to his place. Few could recall ever having seen him wearing anything other than brogans, denim overalls, a white work shirt, and a cap, all of which he bought at the local feed store.

214

He'd never been more than 20 miles from his farm,
and he never went to church. A big black Labrador
retriever named Buck was his constant companion.
He lent a hand when one was needed and he stayed
clear of controversy and scandal, usually.

Many in the community could recite some version
of a locally-famous incident from 1956, which had
served to discourage any attempts to discern or
cultivate Jim's political opinions. Over the years the
story had been repeated so many times that most of
the essential facts had been replaced by mistakes and
inventions, causing the original context to be lost in
the fog of the past. Contrary to what many now
believed, Jim hadn't chased anyone off his farm at
gunpoint and he hadn't declared himself to be
sympathetic to communism. Beyond the mists, myths
and misremembrances, however, there was a story—a
true one.

Jim was sitting on his front porch on a Sunday
afternoon in October that year, reading a book, when
a car carrying a handful of local men turned into his
drive. Setting the book down, he met them as they
exited the car. "Afternoon, Jim," one of them said.
"We're going around the community on behalf of the
White Citizen's Council to make sure people know
who stands for us in the election this year." The man
handed Jim a flyer, which he scanned quickly.

"Well thank you, gentlemen. I appreciate your
concern," Jim said, handing it back.

The men seemed puzzled. Then Ray Saunders, the
youngest man in the group spoke up. "What does that

mean, Mr. Wrenn? Us white men have to stick together these days. Are you for us or not?"

Jim's eyes narrowed and he stared intensely into the young man's eyes for a few moments. Sensing his mistake, the man stammered, "I mean, what I'm trying to say is…"

Jim interrupted him. "Did you know your granddaddy?" he asked pointedly.

"My granddaddy?" Ray replied, puzzled.

"Yes. Your granddaddy. Mr. Elmer Saunders. Did you know him?"

"I was a young'un when he passed, I don't…"

Jim interrupted him again, "Well, I knew him. He helped me make my crop the first two years after my Pa died, when I won't nothing but a chap. And he wouldn't take nothing for his work. He was a good man."

Jim paused, Ray's eyes darting about as he tried to figure out where Jim was going.

"Mr. Saunders—your granddaddy—he'd a been the first one to tell you he was no genius. But he worked hard, he knew what he could do, and he did it the best he could."

Jim stopped again. "Yes, sir, but…" Ray began cautiously, before again being interrupted.

"I was unloading my crop one year—I won't as old as you are now—when I saw your granddaddy pull his wagon up across the way. He was having some trouble lining up the wagon when one of the warehousemen standing next to me laughed and said to his buddy, 'Hey, look yonder. It's Elmer Saunders.'

They both got to laughing and the first one said, 'Ain't none of them Saunders boys got sense enough to pour piss out of a boot.'"

At that Ray's eyes flashed. He straightened his shoulders and was about to speak when Jim continued.

"That man was a damned fool and I told him so. I woulda whipped him, or been whipped, if he hadn't backed down."

Ray settled and by now all in the group were shuffling uncomfortably.

Jim continued. "The warehouseman who said that about your granddaddy is one of the same men whose name is on that paper y'all are handing out. See, to men like him we ain't nothing but a bunch of clod-kicking hicks. They don't give a shit about us, except when they want us to tote their water for them." After another long pause, Jim added, "I got no fight with any man who is honest, works hard, and does the best he can. I don't care what color he is. That's how I judge a good man from a sorry man. And that's the only way I judge it."

"All right, Jim. I reckon we'll just be moving along now," the first man said.

"Y'all are all welcome here anytime, Jeff. I consider every one of you a friend," Jim said to him. "But I'll ask you not to come around here with any more papers like that. You men are welcome here, but I don't need any 'Citizen's Councils' on this place."

"Understood, Jim. We 'preciate your time," Jeff said as they all climbed back into the car to leave.

~~~

"I like the way you do business, Mr. Wrenn. But are you telling me that that old refrigerator still works?" J.B. asked.

"Runs just as good today as it did the day I bought it in 1952. Back then, things were built to last."

"Well I'll be doggoned," J.B. said, opening the doors and looking inside. Egg cartons were stacked in the refrigerator and packets of sausage were in the freezer. "How much are your eggs?"

"Eggs are a dollar a dozen. Sausage is three dollars a pound. When I have honey and produce there's usually a sign out with a price. If I forget to put one out, folks just leave whatever they think it's worth."

J.B. smiled. "Nothing beats farm eggs and homemade sausage, Mr. Wrenn. I expect I'll become one of your regular customers."

"That's fine, parson. The store's always open."

~~~

On a Sunday morning about two months into his stint in Maple Grove, J.B. stood in the pulpit to deliver his sermon. A center aisle led from the front door to the altar, with rows of pews on each side. Looking down from the pulpit, on his right he saw Pearl sitting alone in the front pew, wearing a garish dress and fuzzy pink slippers, chewing gum, her restless tribe occupying the pews behind her. On his left sat the non-Pearl portion of his flock—mostly old women, with a few old men sprinkled among them, all in their Sunday best. On most days a few of them would be snoozing by the time he finished speaking.

"Good morning, everyone. Most of y'all will be pleased to hear that today's sermon is going to be shorter than usual. This week I got an unexpected letter from the District Superintendent, passing along an anonymous letter he received, and I thought I'd share it with y'all before the sermon."

J.B. cleared his throat, looked down at the lectern, and began reading.

"Dear Sir, I am writing to complain about the new preacher you have sent to us in Maple Grove. Since we're just a country church we know you always give us your leftovers, but this young man is the worst one you've ever sent. First of all, no man of God would ever have a beard and long hippie hair like his."

J.B. paused, looked back over his shoulder at the painting of Jesus hanging on the wall behind the pulpit, then looked out at the congregation, eyebrows arched, before looking back down at the letter and continuing to read.

"But the worst thing is when he puts down the Bible and picks up that guitar of his."

J.B. pronounced "guitar" with the emphasis on the first syllable, the way the letter writer would have.

"This young man is not fit to be our preacher and you should replace him with a decent-looking man of God who has respect for our church."

J.B. folded the letter and set it aside, then looked out at the congregation.

219

"I want to thank the writer of this letter for taking the time to share these concerns with the D.S. When y'all have concerns, it's appropriate to make them known. And I don't think you should have been afraid to put your name on it, but I respect your wish to remain anonymous.

"Let me just say a couple of things about this letter. First of all, if y'all think my hair is long now, you should have seen me in college. As for my beard, trust me, y'all don't want to see any more of my face than you have to.

"Anyhow, I promise to do my best to be as 'decent-looking' as I can, considering what I have to work with.

"I have to say, though, it was the comment about my guitar that bothered me the most."

J.B. picked up his guitar and slung the strap over his neck.

"I love this old guitar. It's just a cheap Japanese model, but it means a lot to me. My mama bought it for me. She couldn't afford it, but she knew how much I wanted one, so she bought it for me at a pawn shop and made me a very happy boy. I played this thing every day for years, then took it off to college with me. This guitar was with me when I got my call to ministry. It has helped me through a lot of rough times.

"Now I reckon I have a confession to make. I wanted a guitar because I wanted to learn how to play like Lynyrd Skynyrd. But I let my mama think I wanted to play like John Denver. I'm not sure she would've bought it for me if she'd known my true ambition." J.B. smiled at the memory.

"I never did figure out how to play like Lynyrd Skynyrd," he added, strumming a chord.

"Anyway, I'm not going to bring my guitar to church anymore. We'll just leave the music in Mrs. Anderson's very talented hands." J.B. nodded toward the octogenarian sitting on a bench in front of the upright piano beside the choir pews.

"But in honor of my mother, I hope y'all will indulge me one last song."

With that, J.B. began to play "Amazing Grace," beautifully and with unconcealed emotion. After a verse and chorus, Pearl stood up and began to sing, surprising J.B. and the rest of the congregation, and prompting her side of the church to rise obediently and join in. Then a few on the other side stood, prompting a few more, until the entire congregation was standing and singing along. When he finished, J.B. set the guitar aside, looked out at the still-standing congregation with tears in his eyes and said, "Thank you. Thank you."

There were no more complaints about the preacher.

~~~

J.B. began to shop regularly at Jim's old refrigerator. A country boy himself, he appreciated the fresh produce, farm-raised eggs, and homemade sausage. He also appreciated the neighborliness of the honor system method of payment.

He came in the mornings, and for several weeks he stopped by without seeing Jim. But on a late Saturday afternoon he pulled in after visiting a homebound congregant and Jim was sitting on his porch swing, his dog at his feet.

"Evening, Mr. Wrenn. Just stopping by for next week's breakfast."

"Howdy pastor," Jim replied. "I understand somebody took exception to your beard and your guitar," he added with a chuckle.

J.B. laughed with him. "Yeah, and my hippie hair too."

"Don't mind 'em too much young man. Folks here are good. They just prefer change to come real slow." Jim chuckled again.

"Oh heck, I know that, Mr. Wrenn. I come from a place a lot like this."

"So why don't you cut your hair? Waiting for Delilah to come along and cut it for you?"

"Well that would spice up my life some, wouldn't it? No good reason really. I let it get long when I was a teenager, just to be rebellious. After that, it kinda grew on me, if you know what I mean." Both men laughed.

"Have a seat if you like, pastor." Jim motioned to a rocker.

"Thanks, Mr. Wrenn. I wouldn't mind sitting a while."

Jim took a sip from a mason jar, then said, "If you're a backsliding Nazirite, you're welcome to some homemade watermelon wine. Just step in that door yonder and pour you some from the jug. There's cups next to it."

"Much obliged Mr. Wrenn. Don't mind if I do," J.B. answered as he opened the door, returning soon with a mason jar about a quarter full.

"On Saturday evenings me and Buck like to watch the sun set, and he gets to watch me have a little wine. It's a kind of celebration for another week's work done," Jim said before taking another sip. "There was a time when a dozen or more folks would come and sit here with us on Saturdays. But it seems like everybody is too busy now. Either that or too old. Or dead. So usually these days it's just me and old Buck."

Jim rubbed the old dog's head.

"This is good," J.B. said after taking a sip. "Did you make it?"

"Yes sir, I did. Raised the watermelons too. Had to buy the sugar though," Jim said with a smile.

After about an hour, with a little small talk and a lot of sitting quietly, the sun had slipped below the horizon and J.B. rose to leave. "Reckon I need to go polish up tomorrow's sermon. Thanks for the wine and the company, Mr. Wrenn."

"My pleasure, pastor," Jim said, standing as well. "Time for me and Buck to go put the chickens to bed and call it a night."

The men shook hands and left in opposite directions.

~ ~ ~

Gripping the handles of the post hole digger, Jim lifted his hands above his head then drove the blades deep into the red clay. After rocking them back and forth to loosen the soil, he pulled up on the handles, but the blades were stuck. So he yanked harder, this time dislodging the digger so easily that his pull sent him sprawling backwards, dropping him painfully onto his rear. Sitting there chagrined, he said to himself, "Jim, you're getting too damned old to do this by yourself."

Jim was in excellent shape for his age. But digging post holes by hand is a lot to ask of an 85-year-old man, no matter how fit.

"C'mon, Buck. Let's go see if we can find some help."

He knew that wouldn't be as easy as it had once been. Most of the neighborhood farmers who had once pitched in to help each other were now old or gone. Gone too were the days when the children of the community did farm work in the summer to earn money. By then, in the summer of 1995, the few farmers that remained hired seasonal labor from Mexico. Instead of a large farm family all working together and making a decent living off of a few acres of tobacco, now the typical farmer raised hundreds of acres and one or both spouses had full-time off-farm jobs in order to keep the bills paid. And children didn't do farm labor any more.

But he recalled an odd-looking kid coming up to him during the chaos that was Pearl's Fourth of July party and saying, "If you ever need any help on your

farm Uncle Jim, I'd be happy to help." He had asked
Pearl about the boy later and she identified him as
one of her nearly innumerable mob of great-
grandchildren. "His name is Bobby Hendricks," she
told him, adding, "He's one of Charlie's grand
young'uns. His daddy ain't worth a damn and his
mama ain't much better. They live out on
Humphrey's Road, not too far from your place."

~~~

Jim turned his old truck off the paved road and
onto a rutted drive at a sign that read "Humphrey's
Landing." Whatever the creator of that name had in
mind, there was nothing about the scene that
suggested a landing. Mobile homes flanked the dirt
road, their yards accented by battered vehicles and
satellite dishes. About a mile down the road, in a
clearing in the woods, he found the place he was
looking for—a single-wide trailer with cardboard
duct-taped over one of the windows, a rusting old
Ford and a truck on blocks in the front yard. As he
pulled off the road and stopped in front of the trailer,
a pack of barking mutts surrounded his truck.
Because Buck was snarling back at the dogs, and
because he wasn't sure if he could safely leave the
truck, Jim honked his horn.

Presently a man emerged from the trailer. Unshaven
and with disheveled hair, the man was barefoot,
wearing overalls over his bare chest. He approached
the truck, yelling and kicking at the dogs as he came,

"Shut the fuck up! Quiet down! Get the hell out of here!"

Jim rolled down his window and the man greeted him with a big smile, revealing his few remaining teeth. "Hey Uncle Jim! Come on in the house! These damn dogs won't bother you."

Jim answered calmly, "I'm not your uncle."

"That's right!" the man said with a laugh. "What can we do for you, Uncle Jim?" It was nine o'clock in the morning and the man smelled like beer.

"I could use some help on my place and just come over to see if Marilyn's boys want to give me a hand," Jim said, glancing around the trash-strewn yard.

"Well I doubt it, Uncle Jim. They're playing with their new Game Boy." Then the man paused, as if thinking. "But you know, Bobby might want to. He keeps on saying he wants to earn some money. Let me go check."

Jim nodded and the man returned to the trailer.

After a few minutes a teenage boy emerged, wearing cutoff shorts, an oversized t-shirt and tennis shoes. Tall and thin, the boy's face was speckled with acne, his shaggy hair curling upward at his ears and eyebrows. It was the boy Jim remembered from Pearl's party.

"Hey, Uncle Jim," Bobby said. "Tony says you need some help today."

"That's right," Jim answered. "I'm putting in a new section of fence. If you want to help me I can pay you a little."

"Yes, sir," the boy said with a beaming smile, a smile that proved he came from a family unable to afford orthodontics.

"Then hop in."

As the boy walked over to the passenger side and opened the door, Jim turned to his dog and said, "Slide over, Buck." The boy climbed in, reeking of cigarette smoke, and Jim backed the truck out the drive.

"Who is Tony?" he asked.

"Mama's boyfriend. Fiancé. Whatever," the boy replied, not hiding his disgust.

Jim grunted.

~~~

Seventeen years old, Bobby Allison Hendricks was the oldest of Marilyn Rowlett Hendricks' four children. Like his 15 and 16-year-old brothers, Bobby had been named after a Nascar driver. As much as his name embarrassed him, he was thankful that it hadn't been worse: his brothers Richard Petty Hendricks and Dale Earnhardt Hendricks were known as "King" and "E" respectively.

Bobby's parents had split up when he was seven years old, but they had never formally divorced. He rarely saw his father, who contributed nothing to his sons' support. Bobby's five-year-old half-sister Ashley also bore the Hendricks surname, although her father was a seasonal farm worker who had returned to Mexico blissfully unaware of the seed he had planted.

His mother worked as a cashier at a convenience store on the edge of town, her $4.25 per hour wages being all she had to support herself, four children and, lately, Tony.

Bobby, like many kids in his class and social location, grew up immersed in shame and ignorance, a fate made worse by his precociousness and intellectual curiosity. He was determined to escape, but his path out was blocked by his poverty. Without a car, he couldn't get to town to get a part-time job. And without a part-time job, he couldn't afford a car.

When Tony told him Uncle Jim was outside, looking for farm help, Bobby was thrilled. He'd been hoping for a chance like that all summer.

~ ~ ~

"Now look here, Bobby. I ain't gonna pay you the so-called minimum wage. I'll pay you what you're worth."

Jim hated the thought of hired labor. He'd avoided it all his life, always making sure he took on nothing on the farm that he couldn't do alone if necessary, and bartering labor with his neighbors when he needed it. But nowadays folks didn't build fences for one another and they didn't take turns killing hogs. He had become an old man with no other options. The fence needed building, so he'd have to hire this boy to help him.

Bobby answered quickly, "Yes, sir. Totally understood. I'm a quick learner and a hard worker. I'll do the best I can."

Impressed by the answer, but skeptical, Jim just grunted.

~~~

Bobby had never before dug a post hole or stretched wire. He was weaker than he ought to have been and he bent too many staples when hammering them in. But he never once complained, even after hammering his finger. Despite his rookie mistakes, the fence was up in less than half the time it would have taken Jim alone.

At the end of the day, over nine hours of hard labor behind them, Jim handed Bobby a $20 bill, and the boy seemed delighted to have it. "I appreciate your help, young man," he said.

"I'd be very happy to help you more Uncle Jim. You can pay me less if you want to. I really do need a job."

Jim just grunted as they climbed back into the truck for the ride home.

"What you need money for, Bobby? You courting a girl?" Jim asked, trying to lighten the mood.

"I owe Mama $25. She loaned me the money to take the SAT test and I need to pay her back," Bobby answered.

"SAT test? What's that?" Jim asked.

"The college entrance exam. I'm hoping to go to college next year."

"College?" Jim said. "Well I'll be damned." The comment was sufficiently ambiguous that Bobby dropped the subject.

They rode in silence until Jim stopped in front of the trailer, and once again was surrounded by the mob of yelping dogs. Over the cacophony he said, "I'll pick you up tomorrow at 7:30."

Bobby smiled and leaped out the door.

~~~

Bobby worked on Jim's farm every day for the next two weeks, until school started, and then on Saturdays after that. As he had told his uncle, he was indeed a hard worker and a fast learner. In time his aching muscles and sunburned neck accustomed themselves to the situation, and he began to settle comfortably into the flow of farm life. And the end of each long hot day, his uncle gave him twenty dollars. By November he had accumulated nearly $400, more money than he'd ever seen in his life.

When his college board scores arrived, Bobby took them to the school guidance counselor. He'd never met her, but needing some guidance and counseling, it seemed the right thing to do.

"Your score is surprisingly high," she told him as she looked over the letter he handed her.

"Surprisingly?" Bobby asked.

"Well, I mean, you know, you did very well," she stammered.

Of course Bobby knew exactly what she meant. Sitting in her office in his second-hand clothes, reeking of second-hand smoke, he was painfully aware that white trash trailer-dwellers like him weren't expected to be good students.

"And you have an excellent GPA as well," the woman continued, looking at papers inside a manila folder on her desk. "Your lack of extra-curricular activities is a negative though."

Extra-curricular activities, Bobby thought contemptuously. They all require money. Money for dues, money for uniforms, money for field trips, money for transportation. Hell lady, he ached to tell her, I can't even afford lunch money. How am I supposed to have "extra-curricular activities?"

The woman looked up at him and asked, "Have you considered the state university?"

Embarrassed, he answered, "I don't know anything about colleges, ma'am."

"Well it's a very fine school. I think you'd like it. With your grades and scores there is a possibility you could be admitted early-decision, but if you want to try you have to apply by next Friday." Reaching into her desk she brought out an envelope and handed it to him. "This is the application. I recommend that in the essay you emphasize your under-privileged background. It would help to mention that you have participated in the free lunch program."

Burning with shame and anger, Bobby took the envelope, muttered thank you, and left the office. I'll be damned if I will do that, he thought to himself, recalling what it had been like in homeroom class every Monday, when the teacher called roll—students answering "present" when their names were called and carrying their lunch money up to her desk, except for the handful of kids who, like Bobby, were required to answer "free" and remain in their seats, announcing their poverty to their classmates every week. Furious at being reminded of his humiliation, and at the notion that he should seek favors from it, a dark bitter cloud shaded him for days.

Bobby took the envelope home and laid it on the dresser by the bed he shared with his two brothers. Still stewing over the guidance counselor's advice, he was tempted to throw it away, twice resolving to do just that. But finally, after a few days, he opened the envelope, took out the application, and began filling it out. The application required a 250-word essay on the topic "If admitted, how do you expect to contribute to the university's academic community? Why, specifically, do you believe both you and the university will benefit from your attendance?"—a problematic task given that he knew virtually nothing about the state university. So he just winged it, emphasizing his desire to learn and to be in the company of others who shared his interests, while saying nothing about being poor and "under-privileged." Letters of reference were optional, fortunately, given that he knew no one to ask for one.

Then, at the very end of the application he came to something that might have put his dream to rest: "Please submit along with your $50 non-refundable application fee."

But for once in his life, the obligation to pay a fee didn't disqualify him. He opened the dresser drawer that was "his" drawer, the place where he kept his socks, his underwear and, for the past two months, the envelope containing the money he'd earned on his Uncle Jim's farm. But it wasn't there. Digging around the drawer, at first anxiously then frantically, Bobby came to the sickening realization that his money was gone. His ears were ringing so loudly he felt as if his head was going to explode.

~~~

Things were slowing down on the farm. The market was closed, the gardens were fading away and it was too soon to kill pigs. "I don't reckon I'll need any help next week, Bobby," his uncle had told him the previous Saturday. "Take the week off."

But when Jim came out of the house after breakfast that Saturday morning, he was surprised to see Bobby walking up the drive. "Did you walk here, Bobby?" he asked, puzzled.

"Yes, sir," the boy answered.

"Well, there ain't much needs doing today. That's why I said I wasn't coming to get you today," Jim reminded him.

"Yes, sir. I know you did. But I'd really appreciate it if you'd let me work today. In fact, I need three days' work this week," Bobby was speaking anxiously and uncharacteristically.

"Three days? Ain't you still in school?" Jim asked, still puzzled.

"Yes, sir. But I'm going to skip a couple of days this week. See, I have to earn $50 by Friday."

Suspicious now, Jim pressed. "Why do you need $50 by Friday?"

"I need it for my college application," Bobby answered, his tension palpable.

"You've already spent the money you earned? I thought you were saving it for college."

Bobby couldn't contain himself any longer, exploding in a torrent of words, trembling with anger and his eyes filling with unshed tears, "I did save it, Uncle Jim! Every penny of it except for the $25 I owed Mama! But that asshole Tony stole it and now I gotta have $50 for my application by Friday!"

"Son of a bitch," Jim muttered, his fists clinching.

"I'll work all week, Uncle Jim. I'll do anything you need. You can pay me less, just so long as I can work enough to earn $50." Bobby was struggling to stay composed.

Jim thought a moment, then said, "All right, Bobby. How about I advance you the $50 and you make it up to me later?"

Bobby shook his head. "I'd really rather not take the money till I've earned it, Uncle Jim."

Jim nodded slightly. "Well, how 'bout I give you a $50 project to do today?"

"You ain't never paid me but $20 a day Uncle Jim, and that's all I expect to earn."

Jim looked carefully at the boy, who was still trembling with rage and frustration. I would've said the same thing, he thought to himself.

"All right, Bobby. One thing about a farm—there's always something needs doing. I'll work you today, Monday, and half of Tuesday. Then you tell me who to make the check to and I'll write it straight to them. Deal?"

"Deal," Bobby answered feeling a great sense of relief flowing over him.

"To start with, we got a lot of sweet potatoes to get up. Might as well get started now. Come on."

~~~

Jim had just returned from taking Bobby home and was settling into the porch swing with his jar of wine when J.B. pulled into the drive. He stopped in front of the house and walked up to the porch, carrying a brown paper sack. Taking a seat in a rocker, he pulled a can of beer out of the sack, then opened the refrigerator door and put the sack inside it.

"Evening, J.B."

"Evening, Mr. Wrenn."

For the past few months J.B. had been showing up every Saturday evening for Jim's sundown ritual. A couple of times another old man had joined them, but most weeks it was just the two of them.

"The sun's going down a little bit sooner every day," J.B. remarked.

"Yep. That's nature's way of resting, and her way of giving us farmers a little rest too," Jim answered.

"What do you do when it gets too cold to sit out here?" J.B. asked.

"It never gets too cold, preacher. If it's raining or snowing, I just sit at the kitchen table and look out the window."

The familiar silence settled over them as the sun sank toward the horizon, setting the sky ablaze and bathing the trees in a soft light that seemed to make them glow.

After a while J.B. spoke, "It's the prettiest time of the year. I never get tired of it."

Jim nodded and replied, "Nature paints us a picture every fall, but we're only allowed to see it for a little while, then it's gone. Then the next year comes around and we get a brand-new painting, but again only for a little while. No two years are the same. They're gifts, I think. Temporary beauty. It's a shame that some folks never even slow down and look. How many of these paintings do we get to see in a lifetime? Not many. And every one could be our last one. This one could be my last one. Would be a damn shame to miss it."

J.B. nodded. It was more than he'd ever heard Jim say at one time during a porch-sitting.

Once the orange began turning purple, Jim spoke again, "Well J.B., are you ready to face your flock tomorrow?"

J.B. laughed and took a sip of his beer, "As ready as I'm gonna be I reckon. As usual, I don't expect any fire to rain down from heaven on us."

After another long pause, he asked, "Why don't you ever come to church, Mr. Wrenn? Legend has it that you were a regular way back in the day."

"Hmmf," Jim snorted. "I been asked that question a hundred times over the years and I ain't never answered it yet."

"Fair enough," J.B. said with a shrug. "At least I can take comfort in believing it has nothing to do with the deficiencies of the current pastor."

Jim took a sip from his mason jar and stared off into the sky, the evening star beginning to brighten into view. After a few moments, he gave a deep sigh, then took another sip.

"What the hell. I reckon I might as well tell you. Ain't no point in carrying it with me to my grave."

Taken by surprise, J.B. looked up expectantly.

"After my wife and son died, the preacher and everyone else in the community came to comfort me. I was hurting so bad then that I wanted to die too. Over and over again, here's what they told me: 'The Lord gives and the Lord takes away,' 'His ways are not our ways,' 'God is in control,' 'He just wanted another angel in heaven.' In a dozen different ways I was told repeatedly that God killed my wife and child, for some good reason that was just too damn mysterious for me to understand. Now, mind you, these were good people telling me these things. When I was in so much grief I thought I was going to die, my own mama told me, 'Jim, the Lord don't put nothing on you that you can't handle.' And I decided right then that I didn't want anything to do with an institution that would teach good people to believe such horrifying things. I've never believed that God killed my wife and son, but I knew that if he did, then I didn't want anything to do with him either. So, either way, I was done with church at that point. Out of my duty to my mama, I kept going with her until she died. But I haven't been back since the day of her funeral." After a long pause, Jim finished. "So there. You wanted to know and I told you."

They sat silently again, the sky continuing to darken.

Eventually J.B. spoke, "We cannot understand. The best is perhaps what we understand least."

"Oh, God!" Jim said quickly, his voice rising. "The preacher trots out C.S. Lewis. Who's next? Alvin Plantinga?"

J.B. was startled. "How do you…"

Jim interrupted him, "You mean, how does an ignorant truck farmer recognize something that you're only supposed to learn in preacher school?"

Recovering, J.B. said, "Come on, Mr. Wrenn. You're just being contentious now."

"No offense intended, pastor. But I don't need a lecture on the problem of evil. I've lived it," Jim responded firmly.

"You have suffered pain in your life. Yes sir, that's true. But we all feel pain and grief at some point Mr. Wrenn. You're not alone in that."

"You don't know the half of it, J.B." Jim answered, staring into the twilight.

"Maybe not. But those words that hurt you have comforted others. We just struggle with these things and try to get along," J.B. said with a sigh. He sat a few more minutes, then rose saying, "I reckon I better be getting back home. You've given me plenty to think about."

Jim rose too and they shook hands. "Thanks for stopping by, pastor. I enjoy your company."

~~~

You want to get a fat envelope, Bobby's friends at school had told him. A thin envelope is a rejection letter. A fat one means you've been accepted. So every day for a month, Bobby got off the school bus and went to his mailbox, anxiously hoping for a fat envelope from the state university.

Finally, on December 1, he opened the mailbox and there it was. A letter from the university. Was it fat? He wasn't sure. He only hesitated a few moments before tearing it open and locking in on the first word in the letter: 'Congratulations.'

~~~

Jim made his obligatory appearance at Pearl's home on Christmas Day. Still living in what Jim knew as Ben Rowlett's house, even though she'd buried three more husbands since Ben, the house was, as usual, overflowing with the families of her descendants. Her eight children had generated twenty-nine grandchildren, who had in turn produced a legion of great-grandchildren, some of whom were now beginning to spawn her great-great grandchildren. As vast as her troop had become, it would have been even more multitudinous but for the intervention of the Axis Powers, who had separated her husband from her womb for four years, while it was at the peak of its reproductive powers.

To all of her grandchildren and beyond, she was "Aunt Pearl," a title she had first claimed in 1947, when her daughter Dottie had presented her with her first grandchild. Pearl, 33 years old at the time and nursing her eighth child, had firmly declined the name "Granny," insisting instead upon "Aunt Pearl" (pronounced "Aint Pearl," of course). Dottie protested ("Whoever heard of anybody calling their Granny 'Aunt'"??), but Pearl's foot was planted firmly and she would not budge. As always, she got her way. So "Aunt Pearl" she became, to Dottie's baby and to all the others that followed.

Pearl was in her natural element on days like this, gliding through the house adorned in a Christmas-tree dress, complete with flashing lights, a cigarette in one hand and a high-ball cocktail in the other, the jostling mob parting on her approach to let her pass.

"Merry Christmas," Jim said, hugging his sister. Looking her over, he laughed. "Pearl, you are a scientific wonder."

"What the hell are you talking about, Jim? You don't never make no sense to me," Pearl said, taking a long drink.

"What I mean is that you've been smoking and drinking and raising hell all your life and you're as healthy as a horse and still going strong. You're set to outlive all us clean-living mortals," Jim said, his eyes still laughing.

Pearl snorted and answered, "Well then maybe you ought not be so clean-living."

People were continuing to arrive, all bearing cakes, pies, or covered dishes. From the kitchen came the smell of oysters frying. Years earlier Pearl had prohibited the exchange of gifts in her house ("Too damn many of y'all to keep up with," she had declared), requiring that the families bring something to eat instead. The result was an outrageous avalanche of food, which multiplied each year, filling every table and countertop in the place, including the many fold-up tables put out just for the occasion, all making the house feel even more crowded than it would have been otherwise.

Spotting Bobby across the room, Jim made his way to him through the crowd, extended his hand and said, "Congratulations, young man. I understand you've been accepted to college. As far as I know, that's a first in our family."

Bobby shook his hand, but his sullen face was not what Jim had been expecting.

"Thanks, Uncle Jim. But I ain't going."

~~~

The envelope was fat for a reason. Not only did it include the congratulatory cover letter and details about enrollment, it also contained information about the costs and about the availability of financial aid.

The cost to attend—tuition, fees, room, board and books—was approximately $10,000 per year. For Bobby, it may as well have been $10 million per year. He planned to get a job while in school, but he knew that wouldn't be enough. As much as he hated the thought of borrowing the money, he knew that was his only option.

But when he reviewed the financial aid application, his heart sank. It required a listing of his parents' income and assets, as well as their signatures. The requirement angered him. "I'll be eighteen when I start," he fumed, "A legal adult. Why should my parents' incomes matter?" His mother owned virtually nothing and was paid the minimum wage. He hated the idea of asking her to humiliate herself with a public confession of her poverty, but he knew she'd do it. It was his father that was the biggest problem. His parents had never divorced, neither of them being able or willing to pay for the proceeding. But Bobby rarely saw his father and couldn't bear the shame and pain of asking him for the financial details of his life and for his signature, which he'd likely be refused even if he did. So after a few tortured days, he surrendered his plan. He would not go to college. Not yet at least. Instead he would join the army. If college was to happen, it would have to wait.

~~~

"What do you mean you ain't going?" Jim asked with furrowed brow. "You've worked hard for this."

"I'm going to join the army instead," Bobby answered, looking away from his uncle, in order to conceal the hurt in his eyes.

"The army? They got plenty of soldiers already, Bobby."

"Well that's what I'm going to do," Bobby replied, still avoiding eye contact. "See you later, Uncle Jim," he said, walking away.

Eventually Jim found Marilyn and asked why Bobby had changed his mind about college.

"I don't know neither, Uncle Jim. We ain't got no money, so that might be it. I asked him ain't there no loan you can get, and he just told me he don't want to go no more," she told him.

Jim sought out the last piece of the puzzle, pulling Pearl aside and asking what she knew about Bobby's father. "Everett Hendricks. He's a sorry piece of shit. Makes my ass want to chew tobacco. If he was on fire I wouldn't piss on that lazy fool to put him out."

Jim stared at her for a second and replied, "Pearl, you sure do have a way with words."

"Well don't ask me nothing if you don't want to hear the answer!" she said heatedly, turning to walk away.

Jim reached out and caught her by the elbow, "Sorry, Pearl. Where does Bobby's daddy live now? What does he do for a living?"

"I ain't sure. He's back in Yanceyville I think—where he come from. And unless'n he done changed, his lazy ass ain't doing nothin' for a living."

By mid-afternoon there were enough rowdy drunks in the crowd to persuade Jim to leave. He sought out Bobby first.

"Military service is an honorable profession, Bobby. As you know, many of your uncles and cousins have served or are serving now. If you join up, I'll be proud of you. But I want to ask you a favor. Don't enlist right away. There ain't no rush. Just think on it a while longer. Will you do that for an old man?"

Bobby nodded, "OK. I ain't planning to sign up until spring no how."

"That's good," Jim said. "Time for me to get on back home, Bobby. I'll see you around."

~ ~ ~

J.B. banged his boots on the mat, then stepped through the doorway into the kitchen, carrying a six-pack.

Jim was pouring some homemade wine into a mason jar when he entered. "Happy New Year, Reverend. Wasn't expecting to see you this week."

"Doggone it, Mr. Wrenn. It's as cold as a witch's tit," J.B. said as he pulled off his coat.

Jim laughed, "I been hearing that expression my whole life J.B., and I still don't know what it means. Is it snowing yet?"

"Just a few flakes. Supposed to turn heavy tonight. I already cancelled services tomorrow. I'm not going to stay long. Don't trust my old tires on a slick road. But it wouldn't seem like Saturday if I didn't stop by for a little while."

"Glad you did, pastor." Jim took a seat at the table, the same table that had been there when he arrived, seventy-eight years earlier, where it had already been for two generations before that, ever since Henry Wrenn's grandfather had built it from wood he'd cut on the farm. "There's something I need to discuss with you."

J.B. looked up attentively. "Discussions" were not normally part of the Saturday evening porch-sittings.

"I'd like to make a donation to the church," Jim said, his voice even and unrevealing.

Caught by surprise, J.B. answered, "A donation? Well of course we're happy to receive them."

"There are some strings attached," Jim continued, silencing the pastor. "I would like to fund a scholarship, which you will award to a member of your congregation based upon the results of an essay-writing contest."

J.B.'s mind raced, "You want to do what? A contest for…"

Jim interrupted and continued, "The winner of the contest will be Bobby Hendricks."

"Hold on, Mr. Wrenn. You're going to have to back up and slow down. You want to sponsor a contest with the winner already decided? If you want to give Bobby Hendricks money for school, why not just do it?"

"Because he wouldn't take it, pastor. He's a stubborn boy. In a good way. He'll take the money if he feels like he earned it, but not otherwise."

J.B. was surprised at how little thought Jim seemed to have given to the idea. "But Mr. Wrenn, it doesn't make any sense. He'll know you're just giving him the money, albeit in an odd way. Besides, he's the only kid in the church graduating this year. It wouldn't be much of a contest."

"That's where I'm going to need a little help from you, J.B. You need to let him think that the denomination is sponsoring the contest as part of some state-wide competition. I don't want my name mentioned at all. He'll turn in his essay to you and after a while you'll announce that he's the winner."

J.B. pondered it all for a minute, sipping his beer. "It seems to me you're asking me to mislead the congregation, if not outright lie to them. I don't think I can do that. What is this all about anyway? What's the story?"

"Well sir, I don't see how you'd have to lie a'tall, but I'll grant you may have to do a little dissimulating. This is a smart boy in a tough spot. He's been admitted to college but can't afford to go. He either can't get a loan or won't ask for one. He wants to get a college education and he deserves one. This is his shot and a chance for his church to help make it happen."

J.B. sat deep in thought for a few minutes, then spoke quietly, "My church paid for my education, Mr. Wrenn. My mama raised us by herself and she didn't have any money. The people in our little country community sponsored me through college and through seminary. I couldn't have gone otherwise."

Waiting for more, Jim didn't respond.

"I'm going to have to think on this, Mr. Wrenn. How much are you planning to give him?"

"All of it. A full ride," Jim answered. "But only if the essay justifies it. You and I will be the judge of that."

"Well, I do want to help. And maybe the church owes you a favor." J.B. saw a stern look sweep across Jim's face and he immediately corrected himself, "I mean maybe it's the right thing to do."

Glancing outside he saw that the snow was starting to fall harder. "Dang, it's coming down hard. Reckon I better go," J.B. said, standing and reaching for his coat.

"J.B., I'm not going to press you and I'm not going to beg you. You think about it and let me know. But we're running out of time."

"OK. Understood." Motioning toward the old black telephone in the corner he asked, "Do you ever use that thing?"

"As little as I can, but you can call me when you like." Jim scribbled his number on a slip of paper and handed it to J.B.

"OK. I'll call you in a few days."

~~~

J.B. stepped out from behind the pulpit as the closing hymn ended, to the spot from which he always pronounced the benediction. After making sure Bobby Hendricks was still in the sanctuary he said, "One last announcement before the benediction. I've just learned of a college scholarship opportunity—a full ride for someone in the state. It requires an essay and the deadline is a couple of weeks from now. See me after church if interested."

Bobby hovered shyly nearby as J.B. shook the congregants' hands as they were leaving. As soon as he was able, J.B. stepped over to the boy and said, "Bobby, aren't you graduating this year? You ought to consider trying to win this scholarship. Looks like a great opportunity."

"Yes, sir. I might be interested. What's the deal?" Bobby asked, hiding his hope.

Jim had left the essay topic up to J.B. with only one caveat, "Don't make it some Sunday school bullshit. He shouldn't have to be insincere."

J.B. answered him. "Pretty simple. They want a two-page essay on the history of your church. There will be one winner. Essay deadline is Friday after next."

Bobby seemed to be pondering the matter, so J.B. continued, "This place has a pretty interesting history. How 'bout I come get you some afternoon this week and I'll let you dig into the archives. Maybe you'll get inspired."

On the one hand, Bobby sensed that he was probably just setting himself up for another disappointment, but on the other hand he had nothing to lose and he liked the idea of digging into archives. "OK. Might as well. Is tomorrow all right?"

~~~

J.B. smiled as he read, saying out loud to no one, "Not bad. Not bad at all."

Bobby had spent hours in the archives, every day after school for a week, while J.B. worked on sermons and lesson plans in his office next door. After church that Sunday, he surprised J.B. by handing him his essay, a week early, saying, "Here's what I wrote, Mr. Wainwright. I hope it's Ok."

J.B. had tucked the paper into his Bible, without looking at it, answering, "I'm sure it's excellent, Bobby. I'll deliver it and we'll just have to wait for an answer." Back now in the parsonage he'd read the essay twice, fully convinced that he'd done the right thing in going along with Jim's scheme.

He usually only visited Jim on Saturday evenings, but today he made an exception, pulling into the snow-cleared drive and trudging up to the porch, Buck loudly announcing his arrival. Jim threw open the kitchen door, "Come on in out of the cold, preacher. But if you're out visiting the sick and shut-in, no need to stop here."

J.B. laughed, kicking the snow off his boots before stepping in. "I'm not here to evangelize, Mr. Wrenn, although you might could use it."

Jim poured coffee for both of them and sat across the table from J.B.

"Bobby turned in his essay today. A week early. I brought it over so you could tell me if it's worthy of the scholarship." He handed the paper to Jim, who pulled a pair of reading glasses out of the breast pocket of his overalls and sat them on his nose. Opening the paper, Jim read the first paragraph:

Seedlings at the dawn of the Renaissance, the four-hundred-year-old pines that Peter Wrenn and his sons felled during their first winter on the southern Virginia frontier would become the floors upon which ten generations to follow would kneel for communion. From the maples which gave the community its name came pews, carved and ornamented by skilled, farm-roughened hands. A towering red oak gave its life to become a pulpit, its companion remaining to shade picnics for centuries to come...

He stopped reading, his mind and heart suddenly jerked back to 1918—to his dying, desperate, illiterate mother, and to the loving and kind-hearted old couple who had rescued him. He stood and turned his back on J.B., long enough to beat back the tears he had felt rising in his eyes. After a few moments, he walked to the cupboard and took out a checkbook and a pen, returning with them to the table.

"I'm much obliged for your help in this, J.B.," Jim said as he wrote out a check. "If I'm as good a judge of character as I think I am, this will be money well-spent."

He handed the check to J.B. who glanced at it, then did a double-take, looking up at Jim questioningly.

"I'm giving two scholarships J.B. One of these days another kid is going to come along who needs one. All I ask is that they're hard-working and honest."

The check was for $100,000.

~~~

Jim never earned much money, but he always spent less than he earned. He considered thrift and frugality primary virtues. And having lived through the Great Depression, he avoided dependence upon money, rarely paying for things he could grow or make himself. The money he earned at the market, from his farm stand, and from livestock sales, he stuffed into a can he kept in his bedroom. Once a year he took it all to town and deposited it into the bank, first into a savings account and later into certificates of deposit. After fifty plus years of living this way, his savings had swelled into a sizeable sum.

Now, with his account considerably lighter, he felt a sense of relief, the beginning of closure. After his evening chores, he walked over to the family cemetery, as he often did, to sit awhile and think. He closed his eyes and saw the hourglass turning onto its side. It's time, he realized. Time to start letting go.

~~~

"C'mon, Bobby. It will be fun. You have got to come. I'm not taking no for an answer."

It was the third-time Becky Wilson had asked him about coming to the school newspaper's awards banquet. Becky was class president, a cheerleader, and editor-in-chief of the school newspaper. Her parents worked at the mill. Now that the millworkers were earning enough money to afford middle-class lifestyles, the mill was doomed. Textile capital would soon be abandoning the southern United States, going abroad in search of the cheap labor that had brought it there a century earlier. But in the spring of 1996, the bankruptcy and closure of Dan River Mills were still a few years away, and in places like Maple Grove, kids like Becky were among the economic elite.

Bobby couldn't remember the girl having ever said more than a sentence at a time to him in the ten years he'd known her, and now, all of a sudden, she wouldn't stop pestering him.

"Thanks again, Becky, but I don't want to go," he said, feeling that awkward unease that beset him whenever he found himself one-on-one with someone outside of his socioeconomic peer group, all of his insecurities on full alert.

"But why not, Bobby? You've got to at least give me a reason. Give me a good reason and I promise to stop bugging you about it," she said with a playful whine.

Afterwards he replayed the scene in his mind dozens of times, thinking of all the good answers he could have given, answers that would have saved him a lot of embarrassment. But what he'd said was, "I don't have a car."

"Not a problem!" Becky said quickly with a perky smile. "I'll give you a ride. So there, it's settled and you're coming. I'll pick you up at 6:30." She turned and began to skip away. Stopping suddenly, she looked back at Bobby, who was still standing there, stunned and speechless. "By the way, it's semi-formal."

His stomach in knots, Bobby said meekly, "What does that mean?"

"It means wear a suit, silly!" Becky answered with a giggle.

~~~

Bobby didn't own a suit. For the rest of the school day he was nauseous. He felt like a trapped animal. Even though he was accustomed to the daily humiliations of poverty, the thought of having to tell Becky Wilson that he didn't own a suit ripped at his guts.

He had decided to just get it over with, to just take one more punch in his redneck gut and be done with it, when he hit upon an idea.

Intercepting Becky as she was walking toward the parking lot with a few of her friends, Bobby said, "Better give me your phone number so I can call you if anything comes up," drawing giggles from the other girls.

"Nothing is going to 'come up,' Bobby Hendricks. You are going to the banquet if I have to drag you," Becky answered with a friendly laugh. "But here ya go," she said, scribbling her phone number on a sheet of paper. "I will see you at 6:30," she said with a teasing firmness.

Bobby had lived his whole life in a no-man's land between two worlds. He didn't fit in with the roughnecks of his social class, who would typically pretend to be proud of their ignorance, and he didn't fit in with the kids in the middle class and above, who took for granted things that were alien to his world. So to both groups, he was a weirdo.

As a survival mechanism, he had learned to hide his intellectual curiosity. He read books, wrote stories, created and solved math problems, memorized poems and soliloquies, made lists from the dictionary of the words he didn't yet know, computed pi by hand to dozens of places, studied maps, dreamed of libraries and adventures—but all in secret. He imagined a time when he'd be free to pursue his interests openly and unashamedly. But if that time was ever to come, it was to be in the future.

The probability of eventual embarrassment was one of the reasons he had avoided extra-curricular activities (another being his poverty). He wasn't on the newspaper staff officially, but during the first semester of his senior year he'd begun submitting a few stories. He enjoyed writing and he liked the fact that it didn't cost anything to write for the newspaper. Had he known it might lead to being required to attend a banquet, he would never have written a story.

Bobby's plan was to phone Becky and make up some last-minute excuse—sickness, family emergency, alien invasion, whatever he could come up with. But when he got home, he made another mistake—he told his mother that he'd been invited to a banquet but couldn't go because he didn't have a suit, the pain and shame in her eyes reflecting back and stabbing him in his heart. "But I don't want to go, of course. I wouldn't go even if I had a suit," he said with a laugh, trying to salvage the situation.

"You can go, Bobby. You've got a nice sport coat and a tie. We'll just borrow some shoes and a pair of britches from your Uncle Allen—you and him are about the same size," she said excitedly. "I'll run over there right now and get them."

"No, Mama. Really, I don't want to go," he said desperately.

"It ain't no problem at all, Bobby. You ought to go," she said as she was gathering up her purse and keys. "Here you are fixing to go off to college and I ain't got you no suit. Shame on me. Well we'll take care of that after tonight," she said, hurrying out the trailer door.

Now Bobby's stomach was in a total uproar. He'd made the situation even worse. He seriously considered running off into the woods and hiding. He also considered trying to break a bone. But, distressed as he was, he knew that his only remaining hope was that Uncle Allen's clothes wouldn't fit him and that he'd still have time to call Becky and cancel.

His mother returned at about 5:30, with a pair of pants and a pair of shoes. Bobby's sport coat was brown corduroy, stylish twenty years earlier. His dress shirt was light blue, the sleeves terminating two inches above his wrists. His necktie was a dark blue clip-on. Uncle Allen's pants were far too big in the waist, a problem his mother addressed by pinning them in the back with a safety pin. He had no belt to wear, but if he kept his coat buttoned he could hide its absence. The shoes were much too large, so his mother stuffed paper into the toes. In any event, they were safely hidden by the trousers legs, which were so long on Bobby that they dragged the floor when he walked.

When she had finished helping him dress, Marilyn stepped back, looked him up and down and said proudly, "You look real good, Bobby." For her sake, Bobby tried not to show the shame the comical ensemble caused him.

"Thanks, Mama. I got to go. I told my ride I'd meet her at the road."

"Her? Oh, Bobby. You got a girl coming to pick you up?" Marilyn was obviously delighted at the prospect of Bobby going on a date. And now another wave of embarrassment washed over him, as his brothers and Tony began to taunt and tease him.

Bobby hurried out of the door, anxious to escape. In fact, he had not told Becky to pick him up at the road. He knew she had his address from the school directory and he desperately wanted to prevent her from seeing where he lived, so he planned to wait for her at the highway. Stepping out into the yard, however, he was horrified to see that she was early, her red Honda Prelude pulling into his driveway.

All the dogs rushed out of course, surrounding the car, barking and snarling. Then, as if it couldn't get any worse, Tony came out of the trailer, barefoot and wearing his bibs, a cigarette dangling from his mouth as he cursed and herded the dogs away. King and E followed him out the door, staring into the car for a look at "the girl," while Marilyn stood in the doorway of the trailer, waving and smiling.

Bobby opened the passenger door and climbed in, soaked in shame. "Sorry, Becky. Welcome to my neighborhood."

She answered with a friendly smile and said, "I'm just glad you're coming, Bobby."

~~~

Bobby had never been to a banquet of course and he struggled to conceal how much the affair intimidated him. He knew all the other students there and he managed fine until it was time to sit down for dinner. Becky motioned for him to sit next to her, and only then did he notice his name on the place card.

First there was a tossed salad. Bobby had never eaten one before, or even seen one for that matter. Of course he had never used a salad fork, so he got that wrong, as he realized when the waiters carried everyone's plate away with the fork on it, except for his—before carrying away his plate the waiter removed his fork, laid it by his dinner plate, then picked up and carried away his unused salad fork, all while Bobby was desperately hoping that no one had noticed and that the night would end soon.

Imitating the people around him, Bobby thought he was getting through the rest of the meal safely until Becky leaned over and whispered to him, "Put your napkin in your lap, Bobby." He shot a glance around the table and saw that everyone but him had put their napkins in their laps, something he'd never before done in his life. Grateful for her tact, he shook his head and smiled, as if to suggest he'd simply forgotten, while discreetly sliding the napkin off the table.

Feeling as if there was a spotlight shining on him through the entire meal, he felt a great sense of relief when it was finally over. Then, after some introductory remarks from one of the teachers, Becky went to the podium.

"As you all know, the awards are voted on by the editorial staff and the faculty sponsors. First of all, we want to thank every one of you for all your great work. There were so many excellent and amazing stories this past year that it was very difficult for us to choose the winners. But after a lot of agonizing and discussion we've done our best. So here we go.

"The first award of the night is for Best Feature Story, and the winner, for his outstanding piece bringing to light the scholarly achievements of some of our most talented teachers, is Bobby Hendricks."

Everyone began clapping and all eyes turned to Bobby. Smiling nervously, he had no idea what to do. He looked over at Becky and she smiled, crooking her index finger. Pushing back his chair awkwardly, Bobby walked toward the podium, his napkin dropping onto the floor after a few steps. He stopped, bent over to pick it up, then stopped again and straightened back up, wondering if he should just leave it there, all the while embarrassed to his core at being the center of attention. "Come on, Bobby," Becky said cheerfully. Blushing, he stepped to the podium where she handed him a certificate, while the newspaper's photographer snapped their picture.

He returned to his seat with relief, gathering up the napkin on the way back, wondering where he should put the certificate, as Becky continued to announce awards. "Best Sports Reporting, for his gripping story on the basketball championship, goes to Tommy Armistead," she said, the applause resuming.

Bobby's pulse was almost back to normal when, a few awards later, Becky said, "The award for Best Investigative Journalism, for his amazing story connecting last year's bathroom vandalism and locker thefts, goes to Bobby Hendricks." Once again, there was applause and all eyes turned to him as Bobby walked to the podium, again smiling nervously for a picture.

Bobby had not even considered the possibility that he would get an award. If he had thought about it he would have assumed he was ineligible, given that he had never officially joined the paper's staff. As much as he hated being there, the awards gave him an undeniable sense of satisfaction.

The night dragged on. There were awards for photography, for advertising salesmanship, for best editorial contributions, for faculty sponsor appreciation. He clapped at all the right times and hoped that there would be no further opportunities for embarrassment. Finally, and mercifully, Becky's words revealed that the event was coming to a close.

"The final award of the evening is for Best Overall Reporting and this year's winner is a very talented writer. He submitted eight stories this year and we published them all—features, news, and op-eds. And he never even came to one staff meeting," she added with a teasing laugh. "This is the first year he's written for the paper and we're just sorry we didn't snag him sooner. The winner is Bobby Hendricks."

Stunned, Bobby rose awkwardly from his seat to go back to the podium. As he did he saw two of the teacher sponsors stand as well, still clapping. By the time he reached the podium, feeling a strange combination of happiness and profound embarrassment, everyone in the room was standing and applauding. As she handed him the certificate, Becky leaned toward him and said quietly, "Now do you see why I nagged you so much about being here?"

~~~

At seven a.m., on the Monday following Bobby's graduation, Jim pulled up before the trailer, where Bobby stood waiting for him. Buck scooted over as Bobby climbed in the passenger door. "Good morning, Uncle Jim."

"Morning, Bobby." They rode in Jim's customary silence for a while, a few cars starting to back up behind the truck as he eased it down the country road at 25 miles per hour. "I don't think I've congratulated you yet on the scholarship. The preacher says it was a fine essay you wrote."

"Thanks. That scholarship was a lifesaver," Bobby said. After a moment he added, "But I'm going to pay them back someday. I'm treating it as a loan."

Jim grunted. "Good for you, Bobby. But here's some advice. When you do pay 'em back, make sure they're going to use the money for another scholarship. You don't want them spending it on stained glass."

Bobby nodded thoughtfully. "Yes, sir. Good point," he said.

When they arrived at the farm, and were walking toward the barn, Jim said, "I hope you're ready to work this summer. I'm planning to get my money's worth out of you."

"Yes, sir," Bobby said with a determined laugh. "I'm ready."

~~~

Jim stood and stretched, arching his stiffened spine, smiling with satisfaction as he noticed how much faster Bobby was picking the beans in his row, evidence of the advantages of a young man's back. Am I getting too old for this, he wondered?

"So, Bobby. You got a girl?"

It was just one of the things old people like to ask young people. Jim was making small talk, having forgotten how questions liked that had stabbed him sixty years earlier.

"Nope," Bobby answered curtly, not looking up from the beans.

"Why not?" Jim replied teasingly as he sat back down on his stool and resumed picking.

"Because I'm a freak," Bobby said, no tone of fun in his voice.

Sensing that the subject might be painful for the boy, but unwilling to drop it on such a sour note, after a pause Jim asked, "A freak? There's all kinds of freaks. What kind are you?"

Still not looking up from his work, Bobby answered quickly. "I'm the kind who doesn't care about football. I don't care about race cars. I don't care about deer hunting. I don't care about fighting or lying or smoking cigarettes or getting drunk or wrecking cars. Like I said, a freak."

Jim grunted and looked to change the subject. "Well that's plenty to not care about. So what *do* you care about?"

"I don't know," Bobby mumbled, still working.

"You don't know?" Jim said. "That's one thing a man ought to know before he knows anything else— what he cares about. I recommend you work on that. Everybody needs to care about something, and care about it a lot. Don't worry about what you *don't* care about, concentrate on what you *do* care about."

Emboldened, Bobby fired back, "What about you, Uncle Jim? What do you care about?"

"That's a fair question. Well, I care about this place mostly. I care about it in ways I can't even put into words. It's in my blood I reckon. I care about my friends, neighbors and family. There's some good people out in that graveyard yonder, and some elsewhere, that I still care about. Miss 'em every day."

Jim was speaking in the old way, slowly, pausing between his sentences, thinking first about his words. Bobby envied that way of talking—feeling a relative absence of control over his own words, which usually came pouring out of his mouth before his brain had signed off on them, often trailed by regret.

Jim continued, returning to the original subject. "Ain't there no girls in your school who like the things you like?"

Bobby answered sourly, "Yeah, a few. But they wouldn't be caught dead with a hick like me. And with no money and no car, I couldn't take a girl on a date even if there was one who would go."

There was a long pause, longer than Jim's normal thoughtful pauses. After a deep sigh, he spoke, seemingly to himself, "The whips and scorns of time."

Turning to Bobby he continued, "This is when I'm supposed to tell you there's no shame in being poor, right? Well that is bullshit, as you well know. Anyone who says there's no shame in being poor has never been poor. So you won't hear any lies from me on that subject.

"But I will tell you this Bobby, and it's the honest truth. When I was your age I didn't have a girl either. Truth is, I didn't have one for a long time after that. My mama rode my butt about it, and it hurt. But there just won't nobody for me. I'd honestly quit looking. Then one day she just showed up and knocked me over." Jim's voice cracked a little. He cleared his throat and finished. "I know it's easy for me to say, but be patient." After another long pause, "And don't mind old fools like me who ought to know better than to go popping off about young people's business."

~~~

As they were walking back to the house, the long first day of work coming to an end, Jim reached into his pocket and pulled out a roll of bills. "How about you just hold onto my pay for now and we can settle up at the end of the summer?" Bobby said.

Jim nodded and returned the money to his pocket. "Sure," he said.

~ ~ ~

Waiting outside as usual when Jim arrived to pick him up the next morning, Bobby tried to hide his black eye. Boiling with anger inside, Jim kept a calm face and pretended he hadn't noticed it.

They put in another long day on the farm, Bobby growing quieter as the time to go home grew nearer. As Jim pulled his truck onto the drive at the trailer, he broke the silence. "I'm getting tired of having to drive over here every morning to pick you up. It would be a lot easier for me if you just stayed at my house during the week. How does that sound to you?"

Bobby, trying not to sound as enthusiastic as he actually was, replied, "That would be fine by me."

"OK, then. Go on in and get your stuff. I'll wait here. We'll call your mama tonight when she's home from work. I'm sure it will be OK with her too."

Bobby hurried into the trailer, emerging a few minutes later with a grocery bag into which he'd stuffed his work clothes.

Back at the farm Jim led the boy into one of the two bedrooms in the house. "You can stay in here," he said. Looking around the room wistfully, he added, "There's a lot of history in this room."

Later that evening, after a simple supper, Jim spoke. "I need to go see Pearl for a few minutes. I'll be back soon. Make yourself at home, but I'll ask that you don't go in my room," he said, nodding toward a closed door. "I like my privacy."

"Yes, sir," Bobby answered. He paused, then added, "Thanks for letting me stay here, Uncle Jim."

Jim just nodded and grunted affirmatively.

~~~

Jim found Pearl sitting on a recliner, wearing a nightgown, drinking a beer and watching a game show—the television blaring. "Howdy Jim. What's up?"

Never able to understand how people could carry on a conversation with a television playing in the background, Jim shouted, "Could you cut that damn thing off so I can hear myself talk?"

Pearl lifted the remote control from the arm of the chair, killing the sound but leaving the television on.

"Much better. Thank you," Jim said.

"What's up, Jim? I know you ain't just come over to chat."

"What do you know about Tony, the man that's living with Marilyn?" Jim asked.

"He's a sorry piece of shit, that's what I know. She sure knows how to pick 'em," Pearl answered, turning back to the screen.

"Has he got a job?" Jim asked, while fantasizing about smashing the television.

"Ha!" Pearl answered with a sarcastic laugh. "He ain't got no job but mooching offa Marilyn."

Jim walked across the room and stood between Pearl and the TV, "Where'd he come from? What's his story?" he asked.

"Why you so interested in that bum?" Pearl asked, looking up at her brother's tightly drawn face.

"'Cause I don't like the way he's treating that family, Pearl. We need to do something about it."

Pearl saw that Jim's face was flushing. She pushed the button that shut off the television.

"I can't keep up with all of 'em, Jim. I done told Marilyn she needs to throw his ass out and I done told him he needs to get a job. I reckon she's just lonely." She paused, then shook her head and continued. "I don't know exactly where he come from. I think he used to live in Danville, with his dope buddies. I figured Everett would have run him off by now, like he did that other boy. But he don't come around enough anymore to even do that."

Jim crossed his arms, biting his bottom lip. After a few moments he spoke, "Glenn Earl is a cop, ain't he?"

"He's a guard at the jail. I don't know if that makes him a cop or not," she answered.

"Don't they live on this road?" Jim asked.

"Yep. In a double-wide about a mile down on the left."

"I know the place. Thanks, Pearl," Jim said, turning to leave as Pearl took a swig from her beer and turned the TV back on.

~~~

"It ain't no business of mine, Uncle Jim."

Glenn Earl Rowlett, like his grandmother, had been watching television when Jim arrived. Unlike her, Glenn Earl didn't mute it or turn it off, even though Jim had to shout to be heard.

Jim looked back at him, dumbfounded. "She's your sister," he said flatly.

"She's a grown woman," Glenn Earl answered.

What the hell are we coming to, Jim thought.

"Can't you at least have somebody check him out? See if he's got a record? See if he's wanted for anything?"

Glenn Earl just laughed. "That ain't my department. Marilyn can go fill out the paperwork if she wants to swear out a warrant for anything. Far as I can tell, she likes dudes like him. And I ain't seen no big problems."

Disgusted, Jim shook his head and left. Opening the door to his truck, he stopped and banged his boots against the front tire. Looking into Buck's welcoming but puzzled face, Jim said, "I'm shaking the dust off, Buck. Shaking the dust off."

~~~

On Saturday afternoon Jim drove Bobby back home. "You did good work this week, Bobby. I'll be back to get you Monday morning."

"Thanks, Uncle Jim," the boy answered, exiting the truck.

About an hour later, Jim dialed the number. After one ring, he heard, "Yo!"

"Who's speaking?" Jim said evenly.

"This is Tony, who's this?" a jolly voice replied.

"This is Jim Wrenn. I'm calling..."

"Uncle Jim! What's up? You calling for Bobby?"

After a pause, "I'm not your uncle."

"Right! I think he mighta gone outside, but I can check," Tony answered.

"No need. Bobby left his pay here and I'm calling to see if he wants to come back over here and get it," Jim said.

"I'll tell him. Thanks, Uncle Jim!" Tony said as he hung up.

Jim ground his teeth and shook his head.

Just as he had expected, it was only a few minutes later when Marilyn's battered old car turned into his drive, Tony at the wheel.

Jim was standing in the drive as Tony got out of the car and walked toward him. "Hey, Uncle Jim! Bobby sent me over to get his money for him," he said with a nearly toothless grin.

"OK," Jim answered. Looking across the road as if distracted, Jim said, "Wait right here a second, Tony." Then, as Tony stood there waiting, Jim walked over to the car, reached in through the window, pulled the keys from the ignition and dropped them into his pocket.

"What the…? What'd you do that for, Uncle Jim?" Tony said, his smile gone.

Jim took a few steps forward, until he and Tony were a little more than an arms' length apart, then he spoke. "I've got some advice for you Tony, and I'm only giving it to you for Marilyn's sake. You've got three warrants out for you and your dope dealer is ready to turn state's evidence on you. I'm gonna call you in, but I'm giving you a twelve-hour head start. For her sake."

"What the fuck are you talking about?" Tony's cheerful front was gone now, his eyes squinting. Jim didn't know if there were warrants and a dope dealer or not, but he could see from the fierce worry on Tony's face that there was enough truth in the claims to serve their point.

"I'm talking about you hitting the road and not coming back. If I catch you at Marilyn's place again, I'll make sure you're locked up. You're looking at twenty years if I do," Jim said with conviction.

"Look here old man…" Tony said menacingly, stepping forward. As he did, Buck took a step toward him, snarling with bared teeth. Tony froze.

"Yep, I'm an old man. But I can still whip your ass. Course, if I don't, Buck will," Jim said, as calmly as before.

With the hair rising on the back of its neck, the dog crouched lower, growled and took another step forward, causing Tony to retreat a step.

"Jesus Christ! Crazy fucking old man!" Tony said, his frightened eyes locked on the dog.

"Hit the road, Tony. You got twelve hours, and you got a long walk ahead of you."

"Shit, man. Give me back my car keys," Tony said, continuing to edge backward as the dog slowly advanced on him.

"They're not your keys, Tony. They're Marilyn's. You're gonna have to walk. It'll be good exercise."

"You old son-of-a-bitch. You ain't heard the last from me," Tony said as he continued to back pedal.

"Twelve hours. Best make good use of it," Jim said, just as Buck sprang forward, sending Tony into a panicked sprint toward the road.

"Buck, stop!" Jim said firmly. Obediently the dog returned, turning once to look back as Tony ran down the drive.

"Good boy," Jim said, petting the old dog's graying head.

~~~

Jim drove the car to Marilyn's trailer, where he found Bobby in the front yard. With a puzzled look, the boy said, "Why are you driving Mama's car?"

"Just bringing it home," Jim said. "Is your mama here?"

"She's still sleeping. She's got the late shift tonight," Bobby answered, still confused.

"All right, good. Get in, Bobby. I'll drive back to my place, then you can drop me off and bring the car back."

"I don't have a driver's license," Bobby answered, in his confusion.

"You don't need one for this. Come on. Let's go," Jim said.

Bobby was pulling away as J.B. arrived at the Wrenn place, carrying his usual Saturday evening brown paper bag.

He pulled out a can, put the bag into the refrigerator, and sat down in his usual rocker. After popping the top and taking a sip he said, "I think that was Marilyn Hendricks' friend Tony I just saw hitchhiking up the road."

Jim grunted and took a sip of blackberry wine, Buck resting contentedly at his feet.

~~~

Tony caught a ride to town. Dropped off near his old neighborhood, he had the misfortune to encounter a creditor who had taken offense at Tony's longstanding delinquency. Said creditor, believing that Tony's willful default was sufficient grounds to do so, was in the process of beating him senseless when a police cruiser intervened, the occupants thereof cuffing Tony and his assailant and hauling them both off to jail, whereupon Tony was required to answer for both the two outstanding warrants for his arrest, as well as for the narcotics in his possession. Their expertise being in law enforcement, not emergency medicine, the arresting officers had failed to appreciate the severity of Tony's injuries, the consequence of which was a midnight grand mal seizure, undetected until cell check at dawn. Thereupon Tony was transferred to a hospital, wherein he regained consciousness a couple of days later and was subsequently permitted to substitute pudding from a straw for his prior intravenous diet. In due course his public defender persuaded him to accept the prosecutor's invitation to spend the next five years in prison, rather than risk twenty-five.

Marilyn woke one Saturday night to find him gone. She just assumed he had grown tired of her.

~~~

"I ain't never felt right using a tractor for something a horse could do," Jim said as he hitched the disk to the tractor. "I didn't even own one until 1970. But I finally got me one and I have to say she's been a good one. A tractor is like everything else on a farm—you take care of it, and it will take care of you."

"When you got your tractor, what did you do with your horses?" Bobby asked.

"I didn't have but one left by then. Good old Buck. He was too old to work anymore. After I got the tractor he just lived in the pasture a few more years. I'd hitch him up once a year to plow up the potatoes, but otherwise he had an easy retirement. He died in 1972."

In fact, that Buck was the fifth Clydesdale named Buck to live on the Wrenn farm, going all the way back to the horse Caroline Wrenn's parents had given her as a wedding gift. And when there were no more work horses on the place, the name nevertheless lived on. Shortly after the final Clydesdale Buck died, a neighbor gave Jim a black lab puppy who inherited the name, eventually, in due course, passing it on to his son, the current Buck.

"Go on and disk up the south garden, Bobby. I'll bring up the slips," Jim said.

"Yes, sir," Bobby answered. But just as he was preparing to mount the tractor, he stopped, deciding to ask his uncle a question that had been on his mind that summer.

"Do you think about the past a lot, Uncle Jim? Were things better back then than they are now?"

"I don't know," Jim answered after a thoughtful pause. "Better in some ways, I reckon, but in other ways, definitely not. But to be honest, I'm not even sure there is a past. I think it all runs together somehow. Maybe yesterday won't be over until tomorrow…"

"And tomorrow began ten thousand years ago," Bobby said with a smile. "That's from Faulkner."

Jim grunted. "Faulkner?" he said. "Go on and get started on that field, Bobby."

~~~

Bobby had first started working for his uncle because he needed to earn money, not because of any attraction to farm labor. Any job would've done.

But what he had come to realize over time was that tending a farm, if done properly, wasn't a mere "job." It wasn't just a way to earn income. He had grown to admire the way Jim respected the farm, as if it was a living organism. He spoke respectfully of its places, honoring them with their stories, stories that he passed along to Bobby as if they were worthy of remembrance. The pond wasn't just a pond—it was the pond Henry Wrenn had dug, the pond where Jim had caught the fish he shared with neighbors during the Great Depression, the pond his wife Julia enjoyed swimming in, the pond where Morris and Gilmer Kilmon "liked to drowned" one summer. The old fence wasn't just a fence—it was the fence he and Bayliss Hardaway built in 1952 using wire from Bayliss' place, which Bayliss swapped for a half-hog, the fence that Curtis Rowlett ran into bare-chested when he was being chased by yellowjackets, the fence that Jim's best ram jumped so he could go fight with Pincie Simpson's ram. And at least once a week Jim took Bobby to the graveyard and told him stories of the three generations of Wrenns who lay there, waiting for Jim's turn to join them.

"If you love the land, it will love you back," he often told Bobby that summer. "Take care of it, and it will take care of you."

Bobby earned money that summer, dutifully saving it up as the time approached for him to leave. But in the years to come what he would value most from that summer was not what he had earned, but what he had learned. He learned the history of his family and of the farm, he learned how to grow food without harming the land, he learned how to raise animals with respect and compassion, he learned the peace of a good night's sleep after a day of good work. He learned stewardship. He learned to love the land. And he came to believe that it loved him back.

~~~

At first, Bobby didn't notice.

He and Jim were loading feed bags onto the truck, stacking them six deep. The previous summer Jim had tossed two of the 50-pound bags at a time into the truck bed, while Bobby struggled with one. Now, he realized, the tables were turned. He was hoisting two bags at a time, while his uncle seemed hard-pressed to manage one. Although still skinny, Bobby felt a little pride in realizing that he was now more fit than he'd ever been. He was about to make some teasing remark, then checked himself, in recognition of the fact that an 18-year-old should take no pride in outlifting an 86-year-old.

As he weighed the full implications of the reversal of circumstances, they saddened him. Uncle Jim was slowing down.

~~~

Jim and Bobby were taking a break, resting on the porch on a steamy hot afternoon, when Junior Lightfoot pulled onto the drive in his white

276

government-owned pickup. The county extension agent, Junior was the son of Allen Lightfoot, the agent who had preceded him. Jim could never see Junior, now 60 years old, without recalling him as the little boy who had accompanied his father on farm visits, dressed just like him and even carrying his own miniature clipboard. Not prone to envy, Jim had nonetheless envied Allen for the admiring son constantly at his side.

Like his father before him, Junior was a good-natured man, devoted to bringing the advantages of modern agricultural practices to the county's remaining farmers. And like his father before him, he had found Jim Wrenn a difficult nut to crack. Just a few years earlier, for example, with persistence and great effort he had finally been able to persuade Jim to attend a seminar he had presented at the county agricultural facility entitled "Modern Methods of Swine Production." Afterwards Jim, who had found the presentation ridiculous and offensive, had said only "It was interesting, Junior," and had gone on raising his pigs as he always had.

"Howdy, Mr. Wrenn," Junior said cheerfully as he mounted the steps to the porch.

"How do, Junior," Jim said, rising to shake his hand. "Do you know my nephew Bobby Hendricks?" he added, as Bobby rose and extended his hand.

Shaking Bobby's hand Junior said, "Your nephew?"

"He's my great uncle," Bobby said.

"Actually, I'm your great-great uncle," Jim replied.

"That's a lot of greats," said Junior.

"Yep. Maybe I ought to be called Jim the Great," Jim said with a smile.

"Wouldn't it be Jim the Great-Great?" Junior asked with a laugh.

As the men all sat down, Jim asked, "What brings you out this way, Junior."

"Well, Mr. Wrenn, I'm visiting pork producers to let them know about new enforcement procedures regarding retail meat sales." He had switched to government-speak. Junior had always seemed to have two voices—one for normal conversation and one for government business, an uncanny talent he had acquired from his father. When he switched voices, a person listening without seeing him might not have been able to tell that the speaker was the same person.

Jim nodded, knowing how seriously Junior took his job. He had grown accustomed to hearing Junior out politely, even though what he had to say was rarely of any interest to him.

"Retail sales of meat products are unlawful unless the animals were slaughtered at a USDA-inspected facility and the packages are appropriately labeled," Junior said. Jim just looked blankly at him.

Junior cleared his throat and continued. "Any retail sale of uninspected, inhumanely-slaughtered meat, including on-farm sales, may result in fines and jail sentences."

Jim waited a few moments, then said, calmly, "Pardon me Junior, but what the hell are you talking about?"

Junior switched voices and said sheepishly, "I'm telling you that you ain't allowed to sell sausage no more unless it's been processed and packaged at a USDA facility."

Jim stared into Junior's face for a few seconds, then spoke. "Are you serious, Junior?"

The official voice returned. "Pursuant to regulations promulgated in accordance with the Meat Inspection Act of 1906, uninspected meat products…"

"1906?" Jim interrupted him, incredulous. "I've been selling sausage to my neighbors and friends for almost 80 years. Hell, I've been selling it to your family for that long. You just bought some a couple of months ago."

"I know that, Mr. Wrenn." The other voice had returned. "The law has been on the books a long time, but now we've been told to crack down."

"What happened? Somebody get some bad meat?" Jim asked.

"Not that I know of," Junior answered, squirming in his chair. "I know you don't agree Mr. Wrenn, but this is progress. There are issues of traceability and food safety." After a pause he added, "You're still allowed to sell vegetables."

"I reckon I'm supposed to be grateful for that privilege," Jim replied.

"I must add, however, that vegetables may not be sold by weight unless the scales have been inspected and approved by the Office of Weights and Measures of the Virginia Department of Agriculture and Consumer Services," Junior said, in his official voice.

Jim sensed Junior's discomfort as clearly as Junior could see Jim's growing irritation. No point in shooting the messenger, he thought.

"You're right, Junior. I don't agree. But I don't see any point in arguing with you about it either. I understood everything you told me and I 'preciate you stopping by," Jim said, signaling an end to the discussion.

"Right. Well, good to see you Mr. Wrenn," Junior said as he stood up. "And nice to meet you young man," he said, turning to Bobby, shaking their hands before leaving.

As the truck pulled out of the drive Bobby spoke, "Does this mean you can't sell sausage anymore?"

Jim hesitated before answering. "I don't know. I'm probably too old to keep fooling with hogs anyway. But it's things like this that will end this way of life, for better or worse."

"Why would they make a law like that?" Bobby asked.

"City people make the laws. If you ask any city person if meat should have to be inspected by the government before being sold, nine out of ten will say yes. You ask a country person that same question, and nine out of ten will say no.

"The way I see it, they're taking away good honest work from people, treating us like young'uns, saying we can't be trusted to make our own decisions. But it ain't crap like that that worries me the most. It's the bigger picture. I'm not surprised that folks want the government to inspect their food. It's getting to be that way with everything. Ask someone nowadays who should help a neighbor in need and they will say 'the government.'

"Hell, it's hard for communities to survive when everything is for sale to the highest bidder. People will trade their homes and farms for money they don't even need, as if you can put a price on something as precious as a home. How can we hold on to something we don't care about no more? We're becoming people who know the price of everything and the value of nothing."

It was the closest he had ever heard his uncle come to ranting. Bobby thought for a second then said softly, "Not all homes are precious."

Jim grunted and sat silently for a few moments. "I reckon you're right about that, Bobby. I sound like an old man, don't I? Well, I reckon this old man has talked enough for today. Let's get on back to that field."

~~~

Bobby was already frying eggs when Jim entered the kitchen, just before dawn.

"None for me this morning," Jim said.

"No appetite again, Uncle Jim? Seems like you're never hungry anymore."

"It's too damn hot to eat. Besides, you been eating enough for the both of us."

Jim walked to the counter and turned on his ancient radio, tuned as always to the local AM station. Ever since he was a boy, it was the station that farmers had relied on for weather and market reports, country music filling the spaces between. Now it was unlistenable most of the day—hour upon hour of political whining and bloviating called "talk radio." But for the benefit of the few remaining farmers who tuned in, they still broadcast a weather forecast every half hour from five till nine in the morning. As he had done for the past few years, Jim listened to the 5:30 forecast, then shut it off.

"Just two more weeks, right?" he said, taking a seat at the table, where Bobby was eating from a plate piled high with bacon, eggs and biscuits.

"Yes, sir," the boy answered between bites.

"You've done good work here this summer, Bobby. I'm going to miss not having you around," Jim said.

The words took Bobby by surprise. He swallowed hard and looked up at his uncle. "This has been the best summer of my life."

Jim grunted. "Then I reckon I didn't work you hard enough," he said smiling. "I've been meaning to ask you, what are you planning to study?"

Bobby looked back down at his plate, shoveled in another mouthful, and mumbled, "Philosophy."

"Philosophy?" Jim answered, his voice rising.

Bobby braced himself for a lecture on the impracticality of his intended major.

"Fine choice," Jim said. "It'll be good to have a properly-trained philosopher in the family." Rising from the table, he continued, "You're going to be on your own today. After we get hitched up, I've got to run into town on some business."

Jim's trips to town were so infrequent that Bobby's curiosity was aroused. But recalling the last time he had asked his uncle where he was going ("If you're writing a book, leave that chapter out," the old man had replied), he knew it was best not to ask. "What do you want me to do while you're gone?" he said.

Jim answered quickly. "Just do what needs doing. You don't need me to tell you that anymore."

~~~

Bobby kept a journal that summer, reviving a practice he had been forced to abandon a few years earlier due to a lack of privacy at home. A simple three ring notebook he kept by his bed on the farm, initially he was only using it to keep track of his earnings. In time he began to jot down reminders of new things he'd learned, or interesting things his uncle had said or done. Within a few weeks he was writing several pages every night, hoping to capture and preserve what he was learning and experiencing—as well as he what he titled, "The Philosophy of Jim Wrenn."

As he grew to love his uncle, his fascination with the man increased daily. He came to appreciate that the old man could be both winsomely simple— "Don't worry about the mule going blind, just keep on loading the wagon," was a favorite saying—and deeply profound, remarking once "With meaning and purpose a hard life is bearable. Without them, a man might have an easy life, but it wouldn't be worth living."

Bobby had been so starved for mental stimulation that he had come to idealize intellectuals. His uncle Jim had been a good antidote for that. While not anti-intellectual ("Prideful ignorance is the worst kind," Jim had said), neither did he admire academic accomplishments for their own sake. "Book-learning is important, but it's not what makes a man," Jim told him that summer. "I've known plenty of good men in my life who weren't very smart. But I've never met a good man yet, no matter how smart he was, who was lazy." When Bobby wrote that down in his journal that night, he underlined it.

Once that summer they were repairing a barn, improvising with leftover materials from some earlier project. When they had finished, Jim looked it over, laughed and said, "Some future archeologist ain't gonna have no idea what we were doing here." Bobby delighted in sentences like that—his uncle had pronounced the word "archie-o-log-ist." The boy had come to realize that his uncle's vocabulary included words he'd never heard spoken before (and therefore didn't pronounce correctly), words he often sprinkled amid unorthodox grammar and double negatives.

One evening near the end of the summer Jim walked up as Bobby was reading a book, a collection of essays by Michel Foucault. "What you reading?" his uncle asked. Figuring he wouldn't understand and that it would be too difficult to try to explain, Bobby just handed him the book. Jim thumbed through it for a minute, grunted contemptuously, then handed it back, saying, "When a man speaks and writes that way, I take it that he does so because he doesn't aim to be understood. Being incomprehensible isn't the same thing as being profound. Sometimes if you can't make sense out what someone is saying, it's because they're not making sense. As for Mr. Foucault and his friends, you can be the judge of that. But that's the way this old man sees it." Bobby smiled, both in appreciation of his uncle's wisdom, and because he had pronounced the name "Foo-calt."

Perhaps the most important thing Bobby learned from his uncle that summer was the proper relationship between humanity and the natural world. "We're not separate from the plants and animals we raise here Bobby. It's all one big thing and we're just different pieces of it." When Jim summed up his agricultural philosophy, Bobby found it beautifully elegant. "All we do is harvest sunlight and rainwater. They grow the grass that feeds the animals who make the manure that fertilizes the gardens that feed us. It's a perfect and beautiful cycle designed by God and nature. There should be no waste and, as long as we don't get greedy, it will sustain us forever."

While his uncle could be irritable and grumpy, he never seemed to let himself be weighed down by negatives. "Sometimes you end up caught in a storm, Bobby," he once told the boy. "They usually blow over on their own, but sometimes you have to fight your way out of them. Either way, don't never lose sight of what's most important. Cultivate your garden."

~~~

"Oh good grief," Bobby said with frustration, pushing his chair back from the table, dropping the pen he'd been holding onto a small pile of paper before him.

Jim, standing at the kitchen sink cutting up a chicken, looked up at the boy. "Problem?" he asked.

"It's the forms I have to fill out for school. They obviously aren't intended for hicks like me," Bobby answered.

"Explain," Jim said, wiping his hands on a dish towel.

"Well, here's an example," Bobby said as he returned his attention to the papers. "'Father's occupation.' So what I am supposed to put? Unknown? None?"

"How about 'None of your damned business,'" Jim said.

"That's what I wanted to put, but I'd rather not draw attention to myself. So I put 'contractor.' I've heard Daddy sometimes cuts grass for beer money, so I reckon that qualifies."

Jim furrowed his brow, searching his mind for some wisdom or useful advice and finding none.

Bobby continued. "And here's another one: 'family physician.' I want to write, 'Sorry, but I'm a trailer park redneck and we don't go to the doctor.' I wonder if they're going to want to know who our stockbroker is too."

Jim stepped toward the table. "I don't know what to tell you, Bobby. That ain't my world neither. But my guess is that you're going to have to deal with that kind of stuff a lot from now on. I reckon you're just going to have to get used to it."

Bobby chuckled sarcastically. "I'm already used to it, Uncle Jim. This stuff ain't nothing new for me. But I still don't like it. It's like being constantly reminded that you really don't belong in their world."

"Well, it seems to me that you don't belong in the world you're living in now either." Jim sat down at the table, opposite his nephew. "You could just give up. But you're not lazy and you're not a quitter. You're not satisfied to just wallow in self-pity. You want out and you're going to have to fight your way out. I'm right sure you're going to end up doing just fine."

Bobby shook his head. "I'm not worried about the work. I'm honestly looking forward to that. But I am worried that I'm going to stick out like a bumpkin who doesn't belong there. I'm not looking forward to being constantly humiliated."

Having nothing to say, Jim got up, turned away and walked back toward the sink.

"So what do you think?" Bobby called after him, hoping he hadn't come across as too weak. "Am I making too big a deal out of this? Have you ever felt like you were in a place you didn't belong? Ever been ashamed of where you came from?"

Jim turned to face his nephew, who was looking at him expectantly. "Oh yeah. I've felt that way. Very painfully when I was a boy and it hurt bad." After a pause he added, "But I'm an old man now, just an uneducated dirt farmer, and folks don't expect much from me."

"But didn't you ever want to go somewhere else? Do something else?" Bobby asked.

"Not really. That's a blessing I guess. I like it here. I don't need much and I'm able to take care of myself," Jim said. Then, nodding toward Bobby's paperwork, he added, "And I don't have to answer questions like those."

Bobby sighed and scooted his chair back under the table. "I just want to learn. I want to be in a place where that doesn't make me weird. I reckon stuff like this is just a price I have to pay." He picked up the pen, and began writing on the form, saying aloud, "Family physician—Dr. Seuss."

~~~

"Are you all right, Uncle Jim?"

With the sun just beginning to peek over the horizon, Bobby returned from feeding the pigs to find his uncle bent forward with his hand planted against the barn wall, retching and dry-heaving. At the sound of the boy's voice the old man straightened his back, pulled a handkerchief from his pocket, and wiped his eyes.

"My stomach ain't working right today," he said hoarsely.

"Should you go to the doctor?" Bobby responded, worried.

Jim coughed, cleared his throat, put the handkerchief away and said firmly, "I reckon I been treating sick animals long enough to know when a doctor can help and when he can't. There ain't no need of me going to one." Seeing the concern in Bobby's eyes, Jim added, "I'm all right, Bobby. Something just ain't sitting well with me."

"How 'bout I go to the market without you today and you just stay home and rest," Bobby said.

"No, I don't want to do that. I feel all right now. Let's get the truck loaded," Jim said, his normal gruffness returning.

"I done loaded it already," Bobby replied, drawing a smile from his uncle.

~~~

Not long after J.B. had arrived as usual and settled into his customary rocker, a battered pick-up pulled onto the drive, coming to a stop next to J.B.'s car. Out of it emerged a tall middle-aged man with wiry black hair, wearing work boots, jeans, and an untucked western-style shirt. His bobbing walk made it appear as if he was trying to drive something into the ground with each step. "Evening, Mr. Wrenn," the man said as he reached the porch.

"Evening, Chicken Leg," Jim answered.

Jim had known Chicken Leg Mayhew since he was a boy. His father Chollie had been one of Jim's closest friends for decades. Both men having been fiercely independent and suspicious of hired labor, every year Chollie and Jim would kill hogs and bale hay together. Chollie had married Emma Kay Lewis, another childhood friend of Jim's, and they named their first son Charles Mayhew, Jr., in an effort to retroactively correct the spelling error of Chollie's parents. One year Emma Kay ended up with more fryers than she could sell, so she sent her son to school with fried chicken legs for lunch every day for a week, causing his classmates to attach to him a nickname that he had never been able to shake ("Thank God it wasn't boiled eggs," he liked to say.) Chicken Leg took over the farm after his parents' death, tending it for the past few decades like a captain refusing to abandon his slowly sinking ship. In the mid-80's he quit raising tobacco, unwilling to take on six-figure credit lines and imported labor in exchange for ever smaller profit margins, concentrating instead on raising beef cattle, hogs, and hay. Once a fixture at Jim's Saturday evening gatherings, for the past 15 years, in order to keep the bills paid, both Chicken Leg and his wife had full-time off-farm jobs in addition to their full-time farm duties, leaving no time for porch-sitting.

"Do you know J.B. Wainwright?" Jim asked, gesturing toward J.B., who had risen from his chair. "He's the Methodist preacher."

"Don't believe I do," Chicken Leg answered, shaking J.B.'s hand. "Charles Mayhew. But everybody calls me Chicken Leg."

"Chicken Leg?" J.B. said with a smile. "There must be a story behind that name."

"Yep, I reckon there is," Chicken Leg replied, laughing. Turning to Jim he said, "Mind if I help myself, Mr. Wrenn?"

"Please do," Jim replied, as Chicken Leg entered the house.

J.B. sat back down and Chicken Leg returned to the porch, carrying a mason jar half full of blackberry wine.

Just as Chicken Leg sat down, Bobby appeared from behind the house, carrying a notebook. This was his first Saturday evening on the farm. Normally Jim took him home on Saturday afternoons after market, returning to pick him up Monday morning. But this week Jim had asked him to stay till Sunday morning and Bobby had readily agreed. Already feeling homesick for the place, he had spent the last couple of hours walking around the farm, taking notes and recording memories. He had not expected to find visitors on the porch, and was particularly surprised to see the pastor there.

"Howdy, Bobby," J.B. said cheerfully.

"Hey, Mr. Wainwright," Bobby answered.

"Bring out another chair and join us Bobby. Pour yourself some wine if you want to. It's sitting on the counter," Jim said.

Puzzled, Bobby hesitated.

Chicken Leg stood up and extended his arm, "Charles Mayhew," he said as Bobby shook his hand firmly.

"This is my nephew Bobby Hendricks, Chicken Leg. Been helping me on the farm this summer. Leaving tomorrow for his first day of college," Jim said from the porch swing.

"Nice meeting you, Bobby. Always good to meet a young man that ain't afraid to do farm work," Chicken Leg answered.

Seeing Bobby's confusion, Jim spoke. "Sitting out here and watching the sun set on Saturdays is an old Maple Grove tradition. I been doing it as long as I can remember." He added with a laugh, "But it got to where I mostly did it alone."

Chicken Leg jumped in, "I been coming here since I was a boy. I remember when it seemed like half of Maple Grove was here every Saturday evening. Them was good days."

"Nice to meet you," Bobby said to him.

"Bring out a chair Bobby," his uncle repeated.

As Bobby returned with a chair from the kitchen table Chicken Leg spoke, "My boy went to college and now I hardly ever see him. He comes to visit every other Thanksgiving. His young'uns ain't never lived in the country and I reckon they never will."

"Where does he live?" J.B. asked.

"Chicago, Illinois," Chicken Leg answered.

"What does he do?" J.B. followed up.

"Hell if I know," Chicken Leg said. "It's got something to do with shuffling rich folks' money around."

"It's hard to keep the good ones here," Jim said. "Seems like Maple Grove don't have much to offer somebody with a college education."

"Can't hardly make a living out here," Chicken Leg replied. "And it costs a big pile of money to go to college. The only person I can think of who lives out here and went to college is Junior Lightfoot. 'Course he works for the government."

Turning to Jim, Chicken Leg continued, "Did Junior come by here yet and put you out of business, Mr. Wrenn?"

"I kinda feel sorry for him," Jim answered.

"A working man don't have much of a chance these days," Chicken Leg said. "The government only cares about the ones who don't have to work, and the ones who don't want to work."

As none of the other men wanted to encourage him, they remained silent.

"It's a damn shame when a man can't sell food to his neighbors without the government's permission," Chicken Leg added, looking at Jim, seeking affirmation.

"An unjust law is no law at all," Jim answered softly.

"Say what?" Chicken Leg said, as Bobby and J.B. exchanged glances.

J.B. took another sip of his beer, under Bobby's fascinated stare. "Are you allowed to do that?" Bobby asked, genuinely perplexed.

"Yeah, shameful isn't it? But I don't know how to make wine," J.B. answered.

"What I meant was…" Bobby began, hesitantly.

"I know what you meant Bobby. Just kidding. Yeah, it's OK," J.B. responded.

"Gladdens the heart, right preacher?" Jim said with a smile. J.B. nodded and tipped his beer.

"I've been drinking a little homemade wine on Saturdays at sunset for almost sixty years," Jim said. "I think of it as a way to celebrate the end of another work week."

"It's the sacrament with which you kick off your Sabbath," J.B. said.

Jim laughed. "I never thought of it that way preacher, but you might be on to something." Speaking directly to Bobby, he continued, "But it's all I drink—a little wine once a week. You have to be careful with it, or it can master you. Drinking has done a lot of harm to our family."

"I bring six with me every week, and take home five," J.B. added.

"Mr. Wrenn ain't never allowed no heavy drinking here," Chicken Leg said. Turning to Jim he continued, with a laugh, "I remember that time you run off Ernest Johnson for getting drunk and wanting to fight somebody. He picked the wrong place for that. But Reverend, with all due respect, what you're doing don't seem right to me," he said with a smile. "I'd be happy to take those poor unwanted cans off your hands. I sure hate to see 'em go to waste."

~~~

With the sky darkening and the whippoorwills beginning to sing, the gathering broke up. "I reckon I better go finish my sermon," J.B. said as he stood. "I'll be mentioning you in the service tomorrow, Bobby. I hope you don't mind. We're all real proud of you." Bobby answered with a nervous smile.

"Time for me to go too," Chicken Leg said, also rising. "I'm gonna try to come more regular, Mr. Wrenn. It was really good seeing you again, and nice to meet you fellas too."

As the two men walked to their cars, chatting, Bobby turned to his uncle and said, "I'll go shut the coops," noticing as he did that the jar Jim was holding still had all the wine he'd begun the evening with.

"All right," Jim said. "I might as well let you do my work for me one last time."

~~~

When Bobby returned to the house he found Jim sitting at the kitchen table, a stack of papers before him. "Have a seat, Bobby," he said to the boy.

Jim handed him an envelope across the table. "Here's your pay for your work this summer. I hate to see you go. You've done good work and I've enjoyed your company."

295

Before Bobby could speak, Jim continued. "This big envelope has a copy of my will in it. When it comes time for somebody to look at it, it's going to be in a box under my bed. The lawyer has the original.

"I wanted you to know about it because I'm leaving this place to you, Bobby. I've been hoping for a long time that one of us would turn out to be worth a damn and I'm satisfied that I got my wish. We've got deep roots here, Bobby. Take care of this place and it will take care of you. Love it, and it will love you back."

At first Bobby was too stunned and choked up to speak. Composing himself, he managed, "I don't even know what to say, Uncle Jim."

"I understand. But there ain't no need for you to say nothing. I still got plenty of talking to do," Jim said.

He pulled a folding knife from his pocket and laid it on the table. "My Pa gave me this knife and I've carried it every day since, for over 75 years now. I'm gonna tote it as long as I'm breathing, but when I'm gone it's yours. There's a note in the box that says so. Make sure you get it."

Deeply concerned, Bobby said with a cracking voice, "Are you all right, Uncle Jim?"

"Yeah I'm all right. As all right as I can be under the circumstances." He paused a bit more than normal, then continued. "My friend Lee Johnson died last year. They had to clear cut his land to pay for the nursing home. Then when the timber money was all gone, they sold his farm and house just so he could stay in that damn place one more year, with tubes stuck in him and him not able to get out of bed, not even knowing who his own family was. When I think of what happened to him, I feel sure that I'm all right. You're getting a medical power of attorney for me too, Bobby. I don't expect you'll have to use it, but if you do, remember what I said."

Tears welling in his eyes, Bobby nodded.

"There's something else I need to show you," Jim said as he stood up and began walking toward his bedroom. "Come on in here."

Jim opened the door and stepped into the room—the room Bobby thought of as "the forbidden place"—and Bobby followed him in. Reaching under the bed, Jim pulled out a box, sat it on the bed and removed the lid.

When Jim turned around, he saw Bobby standing open-mouthed and wide-eyed, looking around the room in amazement.

"Oh, yeah," Jim said, "I didn't tell you about the books."

The room was crowded with hundreds of books. Bookshelves filled with books lined the walls. There were books stacked in piles on the floor, shoulder-high. There were books four deep on the end tables. There were so many books in the room that they left little space for anything else. Bobby was astonished as he scanned the titles—literature, history, theology, philosophy, science.

"Uncle Jim," he said, his voice ringing with wonder, "Have you read these books?"

"Every one of them," the old man answered. "A lot of them more than once.

"These books have meant a lot to me over the years. Mama and Pa were strict about not working on Sundays. So out of respect for them I never worked on that day, even though at first I wanted to. Instead, I read books—every Sunday since 1942." Jim walked over to a shelf and pulled down a book, looking at it as he continued, "This is the first book I ever bought. *The Outline of Man's Knowledge*, by Clement Wood. I paid 85 cents for it, out of the Sears catalog. I learned a lot from this book. Got this one next," he said, replacing the book and pulling down a large red-covered volume, "*The Complete Works of William Shakespeare*. Boy, this one worked me hard. See, I ain't never had a days' schooling in my life Bobby. I learned to read out of a church hymnal and off of funeral home fans." Jim chuckled. "Paid 85 cents for this one too. That was right smart money in them days." After a few moments, he sighed and returned the book to the shelf. "I ordered books from Sears for a long time. Then I started joining the book clubs that would send you catalogs. I never ran out of books to read. I reckon even now there's still a little room in my brain that ain't full yet." He laughed again, and said, "Yep. These books have been good friends.

"But these books ain't what I came in here to show you Bobby." Returning to the bed, Jim reached into the box and brought out a large black-covered book, unmistakably a Bible. "All the books in this room have been important to me, but this is the one that really matters," Jim said, with weight in his voice.

"The Bible?" Bobby was a little surprised, having never considered his uncle a religious man.

"Not just any Bible, Bobby. My mama gave me this Bible in 1918, on the night she died. She called it our 'family Bible' and told me to keep it and to pass it on someday to my children." Opening it to the middle, Jim drew out an old yellow newspaper clipping. "Somebody stuck a newspaper under the door that night and this was in it. She didn't know I knew how to read." Jim stopped, his eyes gazing off unfocused into the distance of the past. "I can't even imagine the pain this must have caused my precious Mama," he said, his eyes clouding with an old man's tears. After a few moments of silence, he continued, "I kept that paper and later on I cut this part out and stuck it inside this book, right where the births of me and Pearl are recorded.

"My mama told me the stories of her life that night—the night she gave me this Bible." Jim paused, his chest tightening, the pain still there all those years later. He looked into Bobby's wonderstruck face. "I ain't never told nobody about that night, son. I ain't never passed along those stories.

"I reckon it's time I did."

Bobby listened, and Jim talked deep into the night.

The End

for Jim WREEN — Pearl

B off (R - 2g

Bluefield) → Danville

Fuller + Lillie
Snead   Mae
          Diggins
(Samuel & Rose)
        Scruggs)

Julian + "Gem Ariah"
X CLARK   Jim
d.
              Clara
              Pearl

Where is maple grove

93106771R00193

Made in the USA
Columbia, SC
04 April 2018